The Seventh Deadly Cruise

by

Craig Schultz

Lawrence Knipe;

God bless your read and your life journey

Craig Schultz

Ps 121:8

The Seventh Deadly Cruise
by Craig Schultz

Printed in the United States of America

ISBN 9781609573201

Unless otherwise indicated, Bible quotations are taken from The New International Version of the Bible. Copyright © 1973, 1978, 1984 by the International Bible Society.

www.xulonpress.com

To my wife, Martha, through whom by God's grace and guidance I have learned to discover the richness of love, commitment, sacrifice and faithfulness along our journey of two becoming one.

The Prologue

Professor and clinical psychotherapist Solomon Schimmel writes in his book entitled <u>The Seven Deadly Sins: Jewish, Christian, and Classical Reflections on Human Psychology</u>:

> Religious and philosophical moral reflection about sin, vice, and virtue, and the seven deadly sins in particular, has influenced the self-understanding and behavior of multitudes for centuries, and continues to do so for many today. But because it uses concepts foreign to the nonreligious it is necessary to translate its relevant teaching into an idiom that speaks to modern man while respecting his skepticism about religious dogma.
>
> Moral literature on pride, anger, envy, greed, gluttony, lust, and sloth does more than provide practical guidelines for controlling the vices. It is a fertile source of hypotheses about emotion and behavior that can be tested with the scientific methods of modern psychology. The seven sins directly relate to a host of problems addressed by clinical and social psychology. Low self-esteem, aggression, racial animosity, economic anxiety, executive stress, obesity, sexual dysfunction, depression, and suicide are among many problems directly related to the seven sins. Many

other contemporary ills relate to the sins indirectly. The Tree is a widely used medieval image for the seven deadly sins. The sins are its roots, trunk, or branches from which sprout innumerable evils and tragedies. The insidious effects of our vices extend far and wide. We may not at first recognize the connection between a deadly vice and its indirect effects but a deeper probing will often reveal it. Anomie, for example, the despair of finding meaning and purpose in life, is traceable in part to the materialism of greed, the spiritual apathy of sloth, and the narcissism of pride (p.10).

In the story that follows, I invite you to join me in a dual adventure. The story is first of all a recounting of my experience on a recent cruise to the Caribbean. Secondly, it is an observation on human behavior or as Professor Schimmel suggests, "a reflection about sin, vice and virtue as they are evident in people who resemble you and me." Deadly behavior is all around us although most of that behavior appears to be very innocent behavior until we either "probe a little deeper" (Schimmel) or allow time for the consequences or "indirect effects" (Schimmel) of the behavior to play themselves out.

As I returned home from my cruise and began reflecting on the many events from that week, I decided to write a story about those happenings. I also determined to organize my thoughts loosely, and I do stress loosely, around the traditional but I think still relevant and ever present seven deadly sins. While each major section of my story carries the heading of one of the deadlies, you will quickly discover that I have not so clearly and neatly segregated the seven vices. I have instead interwoven them as the story itself was knit together.

One final thought. If you have never been on a cruise ship then hopefully the experiences that I am about to share might encourage you to go cruising more than they might discourage such a venture. If you are a veteran of cruising then I trust you will relate to and even be moved to elaborate upon what I describe in the pages that follow.

I hope that you enjoy and maybe even profit from my tale.

Bon voyage,

Jonathon Copernicus Meyerhoff II

Bon Voyage

Lust

Envy

Anger

Sloth

Gluttony

Greed

Pride

Debarkation

One

As I stood alone on the deck watching the Miami skyline fade into the distance, I was unaware that this cruise, my seventh cruise, would be a deadly cruise. It would also be a cruise that would affect me in ways that I never imagined were possible.

Four of the people who would cross my path or touch my life during my hoped for seven day respite in the Caribbean would be killed and attempts would be made on the lives of two others. One of those lives would be my own. Yet, in spite of all that tragedy, I'm still not convinced that those deaths or near deaths were the worst of the week that was my seventh cruise, but fortunately for me, my first and hopefully my only, deadly cruise.

Two

The captain had pushed the *Caribbean Festival* away from the pier exactly on schedule. His departure maneuver occurred within seconds after the successful completion of the ship's mandatory muster drill. At least the drill was pronounced successful by the "all clear beeps" broadcast over the loudspeaker system.

The young crew in charge of my muster station seemed satisfied with the results of our dress rehearsal even though they appeared to be mostly indifferent to the procedure that was supposedly designed to save our lives. They reminded me of many flight attendants on airplanes who have repeated the safety protocols so often they could do it in their sleep. Safety devices on this ship included life vests, life boats and life rafts.

Perhaps their lack of enthusiasm was based on the worry that in the case of a real emergency very few of their charges would actually make it to the assigned rallying point. Perhaps they understood that should it be necessary to evacuate, only a handful of the bored throng now gathering before them would remember their life vests. Perhaps they sensed that even if the passengers did find their way to this assigned post, none of them would exhibit great calm, courtesy or control as they fought to occupy a premium seat on the emergency craft. Perhaps most of all they wondered what I wondered – would the launching mechanisms work, especially if the ship were damaged or tilting (listing?) badly?

Then in a moment of fantasy I pictured an ocean disaster. There I was rising to oversee the impending calamity. With strong, clear, commanding voice I championed, "women and children first" as I took charge over the clueless crew and floundering passengers. Once everyone was safe, I launched myself overboard to tread water for as long as it took the U.S. Navy to pluck me out of the briny mire. Such is a day in the mind of the wannabe-but-never-would-be super hero who can't even swim.

Those thoughts were interrupted by a mother who was in a losing battle with her small child over a green wristband. Every child was required to wear this bracelet identification as an added safety precaution for the duration of the cruise.

"I don't want this on my arm! Take it off, now!" The child screamed.

The defeated mother had run out of arguments and was shaking her head. My assessment of the situation was that this mother had been defeated in battle with this child many times before and would certainly be defeated many more times in the future. All indications were that this was going to be a long cruise for that poor woman. Chances were good that she would be ordering her first daiquiri within the hour.

Three

The Miami skyline viewed from the harbor is impressive. There are high rise buildings as far as the eye can see and on this bright and sunny afternoon a person could see far. Were it not for a brisk wind, the day would have been ideal for cruising or any other outdoor activity for that matter. The breeze was courtesy of a hurricane that had swept through the Western Caribbean. It had already gone ashore in the gulf. The storm registered only as a category two and was supposed to continue its track through Mississippi, Alabama, and Tennessee, the Carolinas, the Virginias and places north leaving a significant measure of moisture in its wake.

As you might imagine, hurricanes produce rain, wind and waves. While on a cruise ship, the rain is fairly easy to live with. The wind and waves however when they do happen along, require some intervention. We are talking interventions along the line of motion sickness countermeasures.

Some popular and effective treatments while bobbing and swaying on the water include patches containing scopolamine, medicines like Bonine® containing meclizine or Dramamine®. A few travelers prefer more natural remedies like ginger and wrist pressure bands. My wife had good results with the Puma® Method. These are a group of motion exercises developed by Dr. Sam Puma. According to his website, the good doctor is a USAF pilot physician, NASA flight surgeon and senior scientist at Northrop Grumman. You are probably familiar with the advertizing spiel – "in as little as 15 minutes a day, you too can . . . Consult your physician before beginning this exercise program." Give the program a try; it might be your drug free ticket to motion sickness relief.

As strange as this might sound, my wife was just beginning to think that watching and playing video games that involved racing cars on a large screen television was having a positive effect on her motion sickness. Unfortunately she ran out of time to fully test her theory.

Another way to help head off motion sickness is to stay away from spicy foods, alcohol and overeating. Good luck with that one on a cruise ship! When all else fails, distraught passengers can turn to the barf bags placed strategically around the ship by an ever diligent housekeeping crew. As the old saying goes – an ounce of prevention is better than a pound of mess for someone to clean up.

Hopefully, this cruise wouldn't need any of these fixes. Although it was still windy, the distant ocean didn't appear to reflect the windy conditions. Few whitecaps were visible. If the waves made the going rough I would be ready. If the ship encountered some serious wave action, not much of anything except dry land would help not only we passengers but many of the crew members too.

Four

The floating hotel effortlessly changed from its lateral movement away from the pier, courtesy of its side thrusters, and began its forward journey via the more traditional propellers. As the *Festival* inched its way through the harbor channel with an eye on the Atlantic Ocean, somewhere in the neighborhood of three thousand fun and sun seekers were settling in for a week full of adventures that would impress family and friends for years to come.

This was my first cruise since becoming a widower, my first cruise without my companion of many years, without any companion.

I had driven all night from North Carolina. I had paused at an I-95 rest area for a nap when I had hit the traveler's wall about 4:00 a.m. and my eyelids refused to comply with my brain's wishes to remain open. That brief respite sentenced me to time lost in the snarl of traffic that is every major city's morning nightmare.

Thanks to the reassuring voice of my GPS, I negotiated the congested route safely and surely. She did scream at me a couple of times for my inability or unwillingness to follow her crystal clear directions. Poor girl, through no fault of her own, she didn't realize that the route had changed. Her handler was too lazy to update the software and was too cheap to buy a unit that might keep current with present road conditions.

I was too tired to argue with the sometimes irritating voice so I turned her *off*. It's such a great feature I wondered why the creator hadn't included a similar *off* switch when he fashioned real people. It would come in handy especially on those individuals who seem to make a living criticizing and nagging! I chuckled to myself as a story buried in my mind surfaced:

An old hillbilly farmer was married to a woman who nagged him unmercifully. She was always complaining to him about something. The only time he got any relief was when he was out plowing with his old mule. He plowed a lot.

One day, when he was out plowing, his wife brought him lunch in the field. He drove the old mule into the shade, sat down on a stump, and began to eat his lunch. Immediately, his wife lit into him. All of a sudden, the old mule lashed out with both hind feet; caught her smack in the back of the head and killed her dead.

At the funeral the minister noticed that whenever a woman mourner approached the old farmer, he would listen and then nod his head in agreement; but when a man mourner approached him, he would listen and then shake his head in disagreement. This was so consistent, the minister decided to ask the farmer about it after the service.

"Why did you nod your head and agree with all the women, but always shake your head and disagree with all the men?" The farmer said, "Well, the women would come up and comment on how nice my wife looked so I'd nod my head in agreement. The men wanted to know if the mule was for sale."

I arrived at my destination, parked and advanced through the check-in protocols with time to spare before boarding commenced. I should add that check in was preceded by a successful search for a rest room. If you are closing in on sixty, already had strong coffee to arouse your neurons and had been sitting in a car for several hours, you can probably sympathize and empathize with such a search.

Now as I stood on the deck enjoying the warm air and breeze I not only was alone, I felt alone. Maybe I shouldn't have signed up for this cruise. Maybe I wasn't ready to do something alone that the two of us had done together. Already it wasn't the same without her. The emptiness (no, it was more like an acid attack that I was experiencing in my gut) indicated that being here was bothering me much more than I thought it would. As much as I wanted to, I could not blame the sensation in my stomach on the turkey Reuben already three hours into my digestive system.

I had booked this trip because I needed to get away. I had booked this trip because I thought it would help with some emotional healing that I still needed to accomplish. I had convinced myself that this was best done by doing what I really enjoyed doing. Cruising had always relaxed, refreshed and invigorated me. It had also been one of the best ways that Amy (short for Amelia) and I could somewhat escape the pressures of her illness.

The six cruises that we took together were wonderful, enjoyable, uplifting and yes, even healing experiences. Those six cruises were also uneventful, if you don't count occasional rough seas, cancelled shore excursions or itinerary changes due to flu outbreaks in Mexico as uneventful.

Five

A sudden blast of the ship's horn silenced both my thoughts and the enthusiastic chatter going on around me. Instinctively my senses shifted to alert mode. Someone hollered, "Look, over there!"

Sure enough there was something to see. It was a small boat heading straight at us. You will have to forgive me as I know almost nothing about boats. It looked to me like a type of charter fishing boat or perhaps a cabin cruiser or a vessel that a couple might use to wander up and down the inter-coastal waterway.

The captain of the *Minnow* or whatever it was christened must have been blind. He certainly was deaf. The *Festival's* horn blasted long and hard again but the fool kept coming. Maybe he was just liquored up. Maybe he enjoyed playing chicken. Maybe he was occupied below deck in some do not disturb mode. Maybe, heaven help us, he was a terrorist loaded to the hilt with fertilizer or C4! Where was that Coast Guard escort boat with the 5000mm machine gun/torpedo launcher mounted to its bow? Why weren't they protecting us? Why didn't they blow that idiot out of the water?

Why do I think of jokes at times like these? *It's a dark and foggy night on the sea. The captain of a large ship sees a light in his path. He signals, "Change your course 15 degrees to the North!" The light signals back, "Recommend that you change your course 15 degrees to the South." The ship signals again, "I am the captain of a warship. Change your course or suffer the consequences!" The light replies, "I am a lighthouse. Change your course."*

Somebody needed to change course and quickly. Unfortunately, the channel we were in didn't allow for much wiggle room. Even more unfortunately, my perch did not afford me the best view as the action prepared to culminate. A better word may be climax as I along with several hundred other curiosity seekers were about to discover.

A few moments passed and nothing more happened. I expected to hear a crunching noise followed by some wreckage floating by and was surprised when neither occurred. What I saw instead were some armed men in uniform staring down at a mostly naked man kneeling on the deck, humbled by the business end of a pistol. There was also a woman dressed in a robe under the watchful eye of another man in uniform. I doubted that either one of them had any clue of the trouble they were facing. Seeing his condition I was able to relax in the knowledge that our near disaster did not appear to be the result of terrorism but rather a mutual below-deck-longer-than-anticipated moment of lustful passion.

My limited boat knowledge was right on. It was a pleasure boat that was also being used by its captain to snag a trophy fish. What he was accomplishing below deck may have provided him with some momentary pleasure, but it was going to produce for him a lasting headache. It is no doubt because of situations like this that we are encouraged to pray, "Lead us not into temptation."

The skipper was fortunate that he wasn't dead and we were fortunate that we would not be delayed by an accident report or by having to complete our itinerary with the front third of our ship missing. Thank God for answering my terrorist prayer. Did I mention that I offered a prayer when I flirted with the terrorist/explosion idea?

The "incident," as passenger and crew would label it, summoned a few more bystanders than normal from the comfort of their cozy and I suspect rather expensive apartments that bordered the ocean and channel. They waved to us with obvious envy while we returned the gesture with an equally obvious sense of privilege. We were on vacation and they weren't.

Our cruise director from England, the ever exuberant Scooter Parker reminded us of this fact every time he opened his mouth. And he would open it a lot over the next seven days, exhorting the *Festival's* guests to "have fun!" That was his job. He was to make sure every guest had a great time by getting involved in the schedule of activities that he and his staff had planned. When he made an announcement, he would bark out his signature "whoop, whoop, whoop." When he made an appearance he would accompany the "whoop" by spinning in a circle, kind of like a dog chasing his tail. By the end of the week a good percentage of the passengers were imitating him. They called the move, Scootering. The man was happy and energetic and his enthusiasm was contagious. If I believed in reincarnation, which I don't, I would bet the farm that in a former life he had been a Golden Retriever, but to look at him he was every bit the mixed breed.

Six

Having cleared the channel buoys, Captain Timo Finelli turned us south, locked in our course for Key West, set our speed for 16.4 knots and probably retired below deck to do whatever cruise ship captains do (certainly not any fishing with passengers or crew!) I, on the other hand, had already started preparing for my second most favorite part of cruise life. That would be evening dinner. Number one on my list is no contest. It would be the twenty-four hour a day soft serve ice cream machine that the *Festival* made available.

Amy and I both loved the evening meal aboard a cruise ship. We rarely went out to eat at nice places in our "real life existence," so eating in luxurious, quiet surroundings with linen covered tables featuring immaculately presented place settings, more silverware than we knew what to do with, long stemmed water and wine glasses and folded napkins was a special treat. The experience was only made better by the smartly dressed waiters and wine stewards who respectfully and cheerfully attended to our every need.

We never hurried our meal. We sat and enjoyed the ambiance, the smells, tastes and presentations of the food, the respite, the service and the sights and sounds around us.

Because of all that the evening meal meant to us, we always requested a private table for dining. Our plea was not based on a dislike for people nor on an unwillingness to associate with others, mostly it was because we liked the company of each other better. We both worked in professions that required us to interact with and serve people all day long. Since so much of our time and life was spent with others we relished those moments that we could be together. We discovered that dining on a cruise ship was one of those unique times for us as a couple, especially when we considered that the price of entrees like lobster and prime rib are already included in the cost of the cruise.

I had hoped to continue our dining tradition and eat alone at a table on this cruise. Shortly after boarding I had talked with the maitre d' and was granted my request for a private table at the early dining time. I would give her a generous tip at cruise end for her kindness. In response to my good fortune, I found myself uttering a simple "thank you Lord for taking care of me in something that must seem rather petty."

Now is as good a time as any to give you an insight into my psyche. I'm an introvert by nature. So not only do I relish private time, I need private time to recharge. That means that at times I like to be alone and need to be alone.

While I enjoy talking to people and have met some wonderful folks on cruises, I would rather seek people out on my own terms than to be thrust arbitrarily into a group of strangers. When I am placed into a group of strangers I usually feel uncomfortable, sometimes even trapped and then I tend to withdraw into a non-verbal, observation mode. I know that there are many people who feel just the opposite. They love to meet new people regardless of the situation. I say, "More power to you!"

Being trapped by an eccentric someone for several hours on an airplane or tour bus, or by a half dozen similarly oriented people at a dinner table is not my idea of a relaxing time. If I can avoid such an occurrence I will. Some might call that being selfish or rude. Counselors would call that establishing healthy boundaries. I say it's called the freedom to politely choose who you want to befriend and when you want to befriend them.

Fortunately I would be sitting alone at dinner. If that arrangement could not have been made I would have gladly, not begrudgingly, sat with and interacted with a table full of people. Chances are good that most would have been pleasant and interesting dinner companions. Just because my natural tendency is toward withdrawal doesn't mean that I can't choose to cheerfully, politely and gregariously engage a table full of guests. Not to do so would be rude.

Should my dinner companions turn out to be a bunch of redneck rejects or worse, I could always excuse myself, put in another table request or eat at one of the ship's other dining venues. Trust me though when I say that the company would have to be very unbearable for me to leave my table. Because I do take such pleasure in the evening dining experience, I will not be easily driven from the dining room. Furthermore, I will not let a situation that doesn't go my way ruin my evening. Life is too short for that.

I see no purpose in taking offense when I don't get my way. I see no purpose in taking offense at anything for that matter. I realize that approach swims against the stream of what is popular in American culture these days. It's easier to blame others for our unhappiness than to own our unhappiness. It's easier to blame others for what goes wrong in our life than it is to face problems and correct them. While thin skin might be in vogue, thick skin makes for better neighbors, better friends, better relationships, a better family, and a better society.

In addition to trying not to take offense, I am also someone who tries hard not to give offense, although I realize that what I just finished saying was probably offensive to somebody. My advice to you, get some skin! Oops, there I go again, giving offense. I am sorry if I offended you. There, do you feel better? Are we good again?

Enough talk. It's time to dine.

A lovely, young Norwegian woman, Nora Swenson, according to her badge, introduced herself as my waitress. She handed me the menu and rattled off the featured items for this evening's meal before moving on to her other tables. It is a good thing I can read because I didn't completely understand her rendition of the evening's selections.

A member of the bartending staff was next to make an appearance. I politely sent him on his way with, "No thank you." I don't imbibe as a rule other than an occasional glass of wine or a beer after a long day working in the hot sun. I would probably have one drink at some point during the week. It would no doubt be a strawberry margarita. Amy and I normally shared one each cruise. We would sip our cocktail either at an evening show or on the sundeck after a go at the water slide. (Incidentally the slide comes in at number three on my list of favorite things to do on a cruise ship.) Truth be told, I would probably demand my money back if the ship had no water slide or if the slide was out of order. Hum, maybe I do get offended.

Nora's assistant, Randaldo, from Nicaragua, offered a choice of warm bread and rolls from a basket he bore. Carbohydrates and butter be damned! Only a fool would pass up those calories and I'm no fool. "I'll take that one and that one," I instructed as Randaldo placed both pieces on my bread plate. "Thank you very much, Randaldo and please don't come back with any more." I said that firmly but longingly.

The bread would be gone before I ordered. It would be half gone before I remembered my meal prayer.

Seven

Dinner was delicious as always, but it was lonely.

On the first night most passengers ate in the dining room. The waiters were busy getting to know their new clients' dining peculiarities and didn't have time to talk. Toward the end of the week they would be much freer in sharing their fascinating life stories.

I may work every day of the week by choice and am on call twenty-four/seven, but most employees on a cruise ship are away from home for seven or eight months at a time. An occasional phone call or email is the extent of their contact with family until their leave. Leave though amounts to several months at a shot.

Working on a cruise ship is a different life but a fairly profitable one, at least for non-USA citizens. Forty different countries speaking twenty different languages made up the melting pot of the nearly one thousand crew members assigned to the *Festival*. Those who were U.S. born and bred could be counted on one hand, maybe two.

Most of the crew seemed to understand and speak enough English to interact with the passengers. If they didn't understand what you were saying, they would politely smile, nod their heads and say "yes" to anything you said to them. Before an applicant is even considered by a U.S.-based cruise line, he or she is supposed to demonstrate a certain proficiency in English.

I ate in silence staring at the empty chair across the table from me. As I thought about the many special moments Amy and I had experienced at tables just like this, I could feel moisture gathering in my eyes. I tried closing my lids briefly and then opening them in the dim hope that she would magically appear, but alas, it didn't work. Instead of her beautiful, smiling face and large brown eyes staring back at me, there was only emptiness. Instead of her long arms and soft hands reaching across the table to hold my hands, there was only emptiness. This healing thing continued to be harder than the books said it would be.

I left the *Festival's Mardi Gras* dining room and killed time walking the decks until the stage show started. It was still windy. The big ship was cutting through the waves but it was obvious that the vessel's stabilizers and size were not winning every battle with nature.

My thoughts turned to the dancers. They might be challenged tonight on some of their moves. It's a good thing we don't have a juggler who uses knives or axes in his act or it might be his swan song. I used to make comments like those out loud. "Thoughts like those are much more effective when someone is there to hear them," I said to no one in particular wishing that someone in particular was there.

The show was typical of others that I'd seen. That's probably because they are mostly developed by the same bevy of writers. The dancers did a great job, displaying youthful enthusiasm. Like so many of the presentations though I couldn't figure out what the authors were trying to communicate or what their plan was for expressing the theme. It was billed as a historical perspective of the music from Hollywood's great films. The show seemed to me to simply be a collage of disconnected dancing and singing.

Granted some of my criticism may have been rooted in my mood. I was a bit angry with myself for leaving my earplugs at home. I have lived through nearly six decades. In that time I have come to understand quite a bit about life and human behavior. One of several truths that I still have not been able to wrap my head around is our contemporary culture's fixation with loud.

Why does everything have to be *fff*? Why can't some live music be *pp* or even *mp*? (For those of you who are musically uninformed, *fff* = fortississimo = very, very loud and *pp* = pianissimo = very soft and *mp* = mezzo piano = medium soft. If you already know musical shorthand then you just wasted 10 seconds reading this explanation.)

I'm not a financial consultant nor do I have money to invest, but if I were and if I did, I would consider putting money into hearing device research and futures. All this prolonged exposure to noise has got to be causing long term damage to people's tympanic membranes and other parts of the ear integral to hearing. That damage will most certainly require some means to augment diminished hearing in the future. We are talking big bucks for smart investors.

Before leaving the subject of hearing, allow me to encourage researchers who are studying solutions to hearing loss to also investigate the possible cure for an even greater malady that effects communication between people. This particular disease of the ears has led to more breakdowns as well as breakups in relationships than perhaps any other illness known to man. It is most often referred to as the deafness related disorder called selective hearing or listening disorder (SHD).

It is an amazing illness to observe. Two people can be in close proximity to each other and in an environment where there is no ambient noise. Yet when the party of the first part relates some piece of information or extends some instruction of a task to be accomplished to the party of the second part, the party of the second part while often acknowledging the message will later recall little or none of the original conversation. Of course the party of the second part never does complete what the party of the first part requested to be done in the first place because the party of the second part never remembers hearing it.

Does the solution to a problem like SHD lie in better hearing technology or in the more time honored smack upside the head with a two by four before launching into a request? One wouldn't think that either solution would be necessary since our heads are designed with two ears and one mouth. Shouldn't that mean that we automatically listen twice as much and hard as we speak?

A man comes home from the office and tells his wife he had a frustrating day at work. "Ahhhhh, tell me all about your day honey," his wife says. The husband looks at her and says, "Well. I just did."

Eight

Even before the show had ended I was feeling the effects of only a couple of hours of sleep in the last two days. I decided to return to my room and prepare for bed. It was obvious the waves and the ship hadn't yet settled their differences.

I am not prone to motion sickness but I decided to take a pill of prevention along with my other routine meds before falling asleep. Medication is one of the necessary evils of passing through middle age and into the golden years.

I opened the curtains on the window of my ocean view stateroom as wide as possible so that I could see the stars or possibly the moon should I awaken during the night. Housekeeping had left a cute elephant towel animal on my bed. I carefully placed it on the window sill so it could keep watch over me. Then I secreted my complimentary pillow chocolate into a drawer for later consumption.

I turned off the light, said prayers and went to sleep at a time when I suspect that ninety-nine percent or more of my shipmates were just getting their parties started. That was fine by me. Go ahead and party all night and into the wee hours of the morning. I didn't care. I'm an early to bed, early to rise guy and the result is that I am fairly healthy, not at all wealthy in the monetary sense, and about to discover that I'm not nearly as wise as a man my age and with my life experience should be wise.

Bon Voyage

Lust

Envy

Anger

Sloth

Gluttony

Greed

Pride

Debarkation

Nine

Even after a shortage of sleep the previous night, I woke up from a somewhat restless night at about 5:30 a.m. That happens to be the time I awaken every morning. We were scheduled to dock in Key West at 8:00 a.m., so I had a lot of time to roam around the ship.

I rolled out of bed. It always amazes me how comfortable these beds are considering all the use they get. My room had a single bed and a sofa that could double as a bed. Most rooms had two single beds. Often they were pushed together to make one king-size bed. The combining of the two singles left the occupants with a "hump" in the middle.

I often wondered if the king size beds in the suites of the high end rooms were different from those on the lower decks where the commoners sleep. By commoners I mean those of us who only consider discounted fares or last minute specials and are housed one deck above the crew quarters. Do the upper level kings also have the hump?

I am also amazed at the resiliency of the mattresses given the size of some of the passengers. I'm talking weight here not height. Why some of these mattresses haven't cried "uncle" long ago and developed some serious permanent sag is probably a testimony to their initial quality or routine replacement.

My fourth favorite thing to do on a cruise ship is to wander around the decks early in the morning with coffee cup in hand. I like the peace and quiet. I like to watch for the sunrise. I like to watch as we approach and dock at a port. I like to meditate. I like the fresh, often crisp ocean air. And I like to see who else is out and about and perhaps strike up a conversation or two. I find that some of the most interesting and friendly people are early risers like myself.

You may be thinking, I am already a full day into the life of this guy and I know virtually nothing about him. I don't even know his name much less what he looks like.

If that knowledge is important to you then I'll help you out. Picture Clint Eastwood at age fifty-six. Picture Matt Damon at fifty-six. Picture Shaquille O'Neal at fifty-six. No wait that won't work. I am nowhere near that big. Picture Robert Redford at fifty-six. Picture Kevin Costner at fifty-six. Picture Brad Pitt at fifty-six. That should help you form a good visual of me.

If those images don't work for you, picture a six foot male, weighing in at one hundred and eighty-five pounds with thinning and graying hair, no noticeable scars, limps or other distinguishing features. Picture someone who is rapidly closing in on the ability to claim his long accrued Social Security and Medicare benefits while at the same time battling to maintain some semi-balance of his memory.

Now what was I talking about? Oh yeah, what I look like. Picture Steve Martin at fifty-six. No wait that won't work. I am nowhere near that crazy.

You can call me Cooper. My friends call me Coop or Coops. My enemies call me Oops. I have other handles that I'll get to. But truth be told I don't care what I'm called as long as people call me "in time for dinner."

Ole came home from work expecting supper to be on the table, but no supper and no Lena. The house was empty. He was about ready to go out looking for her when the door opened and in walked Lena. "Where have you been?" Ole demanded. "I have been at the hospital with my sister. She just had her baby. That is why I am late." Lena informed him. "Well good for her. What did she have?" Ole asked. "She had a baby boy. That makes their fifth child." Ole holds up his five fingers. "Wow," he says, "Five children. That's a handful. What did they name him?" Lena answered, "They named him Chang." "Chang?" Ole questioned. "Why did they name him Chang?" "Well," Lena explained, "Sven told my sister that he heard on the news that every fifth child born today is Chinese."

Ten

This particular morning there was no one around to call me anything. Other than the crew getting the ship shaped for the new day I could have been Tom Hanks without even his friend "Wilson" to talk with. There was nobody on the stairwells, nobody out walking the decks, nobody at the coffee machines.

I did spot two people face down on a table laying in something that had more than likely already partially cycled through their digestive systems and decided to come up for air, and another person wrapped up in a blanket sleeping soundly on a lounge chair – was he in the doghouse after only one day of cruising or was this his bed of choice? America wants to know.

As I sipped my third cup of coffee I made my way to the serenity deck and spotted my first living passenger of the morning. She was wearing one of those semi-luxurious robes that are provided for guests. Those robes hold fifth place on my list of favorite things on a cruise ship, although that position became tenuous when she sensed my presence and turned to face me.

In that brief moment that she stood against the railing framed by the eastern horizon which was just beginning to produce a background of pink tint in the clouds and a shimmer off the water, I decided that the robe just might have bumped soft serve out of its most favored position. Of course it wasn't the robe itself, but rather the robe's occupant that was calling for the sudden realignment of my cruise top ten list.

Her warm, friendly "good morning" only confirmed that a realignment was necessary. This was definitely one lovely woman. The bit of glum that had settled over me during the last thirty minutes of fruitless searching for someone with whom to chat vanished in a breath.

"Good morning," I returned. "It looks like we're in for a beautiful day."

"Yes it does."

There was then an awkward and uncomfortable pause on my part as I struggled for the right words, for any words to say.

"You are up early. In fact, I have been all over the ship and you are the first person other than crew that I have seen, at least awake."

"I just got here a few minutes ago. Please forgive the way I look. I had a rough night. I needed some fresh air and some coffee."

You look great to me! "Motion sickness?"

"Not me, my niece. I was up with her all night. She finally went to sleep about an hour ago." The woman looked and pointed toward the eastern horizon. "Is that where the sun will be coming up?"

"Yes, and it should be a nice sunrise too. I hope your niece will be okay and able to enjoy the day in Key West."

"Thank you. I'm sure she will."

I was still struggling for even basic conversation.

"How old is she?"

"She's ten. Her name is Susana. She's really my great niece. Her mother, my actual niece, and my sister, Susana's grandmother, are also on the cruise. We decided to take this trip together to celebrate our birthdays. Believe it or not all four of us have birthdays this month."

How old are you? You don't look forty. But with a great niece you must be older than you look. That's a good thing. Are you old enough for me to consider? What am I thinking about? I just met her. You can't flat out ask a woman her age. Didn't your mother teach you anything!

"All in the same month? That is unusual."

More silence ensued between us. We both sipped our coffee. I finally thought of something to say. "So you drew the short straw as Susana's nurse while her mom and grandma did some bar hopping and dancing up and down the Promenade deck?"

"You got it," she laughed.

"Is this your first cruise?"

"No, I took one a number of years ago to Alaska. How about you?"

"This is number seven for me and I haven't been to Alaska."

The white robed woman turned to once again face the ocean. Part of me wanted to keep the conversation going. Part of me kept insisting that I needed to say good-bye, head to the breakfast bar and grab a Danish and some Raisin Bran, go back to my room and forget this whole encounter. The rest of me seemed to be in a wait and see mode. I made my decision. I walked up to the rail next to her.

"Have you ever been to Key West?"

"No."

"Were you planning on going ashore and looking around?"

"Yes. We haven't signed up for any of the excursions. We thought we'd just walk around and see what develops."

"Key West is a great spot. I've been here a couple of times. Ah , , , *(come on Coop you've got nothing to lose)* . . . ah . . .

I'd be happy to show you guys around or at least recommend some things to do."

"Well that's very kind of you ah . . . ah . . ."

I sensed that she was uncomfortable with my offer. "I'm sorry that was terribly forward of me. I didn't mean to put you on the spot. Let me just give you a suggestion or two of something to do and leave it at that."

"Okay, I can live with that. . . . How about if discuss your suggestions over breakfast?"

Excuse me while I reattach my jaw to my face. "Breakfast, I can do breakfast."

"Good. Give me about an hour to get cleaned up and make myself somewhat presentable before security decides to throw me overboard. I'll talk things over with my sister and niece and we'll see what's what."

"That sounds great. Shall we meet right here?"

"It's as good a place as any." The white robed angel extended her hand. I took it and we shook and she walked away.

"Wait," I called, "I don't know your name."

"Call me Beth," she answered looking back over her shoulder while continuing to walk and keeping her smile.

"You can call me 'in time for breakfast,'" I muttered after she was out of range, a smile breaking out on my face as well.

Eleven

I brushed my teeth, shaved, showered and then stood facing my closet ready to curse. Cursing is something I do less often than drinking.

One day a minister was riding down the street on his bicycle. He saw a lawnmower for sale and a small boy playing in the yard behind it. "Is that your mower that's for sale," he called out. "Yes," the boy replied. The minister asked, "I need a mower. How much do you want for it?" The boy was eyeing the preacher's bike. "Would you trade your bike for it?" The minister thought for a moment and agreed that he would. "Let me see how it runs," he said. "It runs great," the boy assured him, "but you have to cuss at it before it will start." The preacher declared, "Young man, I am a man of God and I don't cuss." The boy responded, "You will if you try to start it!"

My situation was probably not a classic cussable occasion but it was close enough to at least prompt me to pound on the closet door. I had not packed with the intention of meeting anyone that I hoped to impress on this trip. My wardrobe choices included blue jeans, t-shirts, swimming trunks and my attire for formal night.

I decided on jeans, a t-shirt and a cap, a sort of Jimmy Buffett look. For those of you unfamiliar with Jimmy Buffett and his ties to Key West, Google Jimmy Buffett and Margaritaville. I didn't have the resources for an Ernest Hemingway look, besides where do you get a six toed cat on such short notice. For those of you unfamiliar with Ernest Hemmingway and his ties to Key West you can Google that also. Beth would have to take me just as I am. My bigger concern at the moment, would she even show? Then I flashed back to her over the shoulder smile. Yes, she would show. But would she go? That one I wasn't as certain about. I wasn't even certain I should show or go.

Twelve

Less than thirty minutes after setting the appointment, I closed the door on my room and worked my way up the stairs to the appointment. I believe in being on time for appointments. To be on time really means being early. Besides, I wanted to stand on the deck and see the approach to Key West and then watch the docking maneuver.

Key West is a lovely port with a fascinating story. At one point in time it was the richest per capita locale in the United States and at another point in time it was the poorest. Key West is also the capital city of the Conch Republic.

The Conch Republic was established at noon on April 23, 1982 in response to a U.S. Border Patrol's blockade set up at Florida City just north of the Keys on Highway 1. Key West's Mayor, Dennis Wardlow, led a protest to the blockade. The protest included a declaration of the Keys as a sovereign republic independent from the United States. A civil rebellion followed.

The rebellion began and ended with the breaking of a loaf of stale Cuban bread over the head of a man dressed in a U.S. Navy uniform. After one minute of rebellion, the self promoted Prime Minister Wardlow, turned to the Admiral in charge of the Naval Base at Key West and surrendered. He demanded one billion dollars in foreign aid and war relief to rebuild the nation. Today citizens of the Keys may hold both U.S. and Conch Republic citizenships. There is obviously much more to this story.

Another of Key West's dubious claims to fame rests in the person of Dr. Samuel Mudd. He was convicted as a conspirator with John Wilkes Booth during the assassination of Abraham Lincoln. His imprisonment was at Fort Jefferson located on the Dry Tortugas, seventy miles west of Key West. He was pardoned by President Johnson after serving a four year sentence.

It appears that Mudd's conspiring included the repairing of Booth's leg which he broke while escaping from Ford's Theater after killing Lincoln. Although Dr. Sam was granted a reprieve for his actions, his name was never really cleared of wrongdoing and so he, along with his reputation and name remains to this day, Mudd.

Key West is also home to America's first international air flight. In 1913 Augusta Parla flew the ninety miles to Havana. Pan American Airlines began service in 1928. Key West's notoriety runs from sponges to margaritas to Hemingway to presidents. When you think about it all four go together quite nicely. Some people, especially presidents, are like sponges when it comes to margaritas and they often get written up over their imbibing.

If you want an informative and entertaining tour of the island then book a ride on the Conch Train. Since Beth was a Key West novice my plan was to convince her and her band of relatives to accompany me on that excursion. If she decided after breakfast that I was a liability, then I would still recommend that she and hers take the train tour. The train only looks something like a train. It travels around town on rubber tires.

In lieu of the Conch Train, a slow walk on Duval Street is also a great way to spend several hours. Duval takes you essentially from the Gulf of Mexico to the Caribbean Sea. It's about a mile and a half trip. There are plenty of shops, restaurants, bars and tourist attractions along the route.

If you suffer from walking fatigue you can rent bikes, scooters and electric cars to come to your aid. On you trek, you could well stumble across the southernmost point in the continental United States and also find the beginning or end, depending on whether you are coming or going, of Highway 1. The highway runs for two thousand three hundred and seventy-six miles from Key West, Florida to Fort Kent, Maine at the Canadian border and is the easternmost highway in the

United States. If Beth didn't opt for the Train then we or they could choose the walk.

Thirteen

I wasn't sure that the woman walking toward me was Beth. It was the correct time for her to arrive, but in my mind a woman can change something as simple as her hairstyle and I wouldn't recognize her. I'm sure that I was somewhat unrecognizable too. I hoped I looked better than I did an hour earlier having gotten rid of two days worth of facial stubble which was now working its way through the *Festival's* waste treatment facility. When the approaching woman smiled at me, I knew it was Beth.

"I hardly recognized you with clothes on." *That was pathetic.* I tried quickly to recover. "How is Susana?"

"She's up and getting ready to go. You know kids."

"Hard to live with, impossible to live without."

"That's the truth."

"So what's the verdict?" I asked as if I had known her all my life.

"My sister and niece will be up here shortly and then we'll be happy to have you show us around Key West."

"That's great. While we're waiting do you want to watch the ship dock?" She nodded and instinctively I reached out and placed my hand on her back in order to guide her over to the rail. "This is one of my favorite ports. I love to just stand and take it all in."

"It is lovely. What's that island over there?" She pointed toward the west and a small circle of land built up with many expensive looking houses.

"That's called Sunset Key. It looks fairly exclusive. And it's only accessible by boat." *Duh, how else do you get to an island?*

We stood in silence for a few moments taking in the atmosphere of Key West. Beth was fascinated by the sights of the multi-colored buildings, the yachts, the different blue hues of the water, the sail boats, the jet skis, the charter fishing boats, and people milling around the docks. I was mostly fascinated by the sight of Beth. She was one fine looking woman. I was about to comment on that fact when I heard a child's voice, "There she is. Hey, Aunt Beth."

I turned and a cute as a button dark haired girl came running up and grabbed Beth's hand. Without hesitation or fear she blurted out, "Is this the guy who is going to show us Key West?"

"Susana, mind your manners." The younger of the two women who had been trying to keep up with the girl had spoken. Both women were of above average height and build with medium length brown hair. They could have been mother and daughter.

"Forgive her. She gets a little excited," Beth apologized.

A family was sitting around the table enjoying Thanksgiving dinner when the little girl asked her grandpa to make a sound like a frog. The grandpa thought the request peculiar but played along any way. "Why do you want me to make a sound like a frog my dear?" She replied, "My daddy said that when you croak we would be rich."

"No problem. My granddaughters would do the same thing." I bent down and offered my hand to shake hers. "I am very pleased to meet you. You can call me Coop. What do you like to be called?"

"You can call me Susana. That's my name."

"Okay Susana. And who are these two lovely ladies with you?"

"That's my mom and my gramma."

"It's a pleasure to meet both of you. I hope you had an enjoyable first night on the ship?"

"Yes we did," the younger woman replied. "I am Genette and this is my mother, and Susana's grandmother, Anne."

I extended my hand to each of them. They received it without hesitation. First impression – nice folks. "I am Cooper

Meyerhoff. I answer to that or simply Coop." I noted that Anne could have almost passed for Beth's twin.

"I'm hungry," Susana announced and promptly headed to the breakfast bar. Her keepers obediently and with effort followed her.

I hung back and noticed that Beth did too. "Cooper? I wouldn't have guessed in a million years that was your name. I'm thinking there's more to your name that you're letting on."

I produced a half smile. "Funny, I was thinking the same about you, that there was more to your name than just Beth." I saw a flash of uncertainty sweep across her face. There was something she didn't want to reveal about herself. I can't say that I blamed her at this point. We were still very much strangers. I was thinking, even hoping, that stranger status was soon going to change.

Fourteen

The second evening aboard the *Festival* is formal night. That means passengers are encouraged to dress up in their Sunday best or even better if they brought along such best or better. If they didn't bring best or better, they are encouraged to dress up in the finest that they did bring with them or possibly rent some finery from the ship's store.

Captain Timo Finelli and other important ship officers would be on hand in the lounge to greet whoever wanted to greet them before dinner was served. Certain adult drinks were offered at a discounted rate.

I could care less about the Captain's reception. I was looking forward to dinner with Beth. She had agreed to join me and I was thrice blessed. I was once blessed because she agreed to dine with me. I was doubly blessed because I had been able to secure that private table for two. And I was finally blessed because I wouldn't have to inflict any more damage on my fist or closet. I had indeed brought my formal dining garb even though I left home planning on dining alone.

I'll admit that I looked good and felt good as I climbed the steps of the *Festival's* atrium to the deck where we had scheduled our rendezvous. Dark slacks, black shoes, white jacket, lavender shirt and complementary tie. I was primed for a great evening.

Our day on Key West had been absolutely wonderful. I saw little of the sights. I heard little of the Conch Train travelogue. My lack of interest in those things was not because I had already taken the tour and seen the sights. No, my lack of interest in Key West was exclusively because of my greater interest in Beth. I wanted to find out more about her. Unfortunately that didn't happen due to her ever present travel companions. Tonight though was going to be different.

At precisely 5:45 the elevator doors opened and time went into slow motion. I thought I looked good. The woman gliding toward me made me look like the doorman at a two star hotel. The sight of her took me back to happier days.

"You look lovely," I exhaled as I felt my loins already stirring. This was going to be a long, intense night.

"Thank you. You are quite handsome yourself."

"What do you say we capture the two us on film before we change back into pumpkins? There are photo stations set up all over this deck. We'll find a background we like and snap off a few memories."

"Sounds wonderful to me."

We settled on a sunset. The photographer had no clue that we were still strangers and put us in some poses that while not bordering on the embarrassingly uncomfortably, were certainly pushing the envelope. Her skin was soft, smooth and warm. She wore just a hint of perfume. All that put a big smile on my face and kept luring me away from the camera lens. If the picture poser managed even one good likeness of us, there was no way I leaving this ship without a finished print in my possession. I may be cheap and at times stupid, but I'm not a fool.

Fifteen

Marta stopped at our table while we were enjoying our appetizer. She bore two stripes on the sleeve of her maitre d' jacket. That meant she was fairly high up on the maitre d' ladder. Her Austrian accent was evident. "Good evening Mr. Meyerhoff. Is everything satisfactory?"

"Just perfect, Marta. Thank you again for arranging this private table for me."

"It was my pleasure. It was my understanding that you would be dining alone?" She had trouble concealing her suspicious smile.

"It was mine too until I met this lovely lady this morning. I so enjoyed her company and she so didn't enjoy who she was dining with that I asked her to join me at my table. I hope that is okay."

"Of course, I will see that Nora provides you with everything you require for a perfect dinner."

"Thank you. You have been most kind."

"My pleasure. Have a wonderful dinner and evening." Was that a wink that I detected from Marta?

We talked about many things as Beth feasted on lobster and I on prime rib. Our conversation became comfortable as we exchanged names, biographical information and other innocuous details about our life journeys. I was surprised and pleased to discover how parallel a path our lives had traveled to this point.

She was christened Mary Elizabeth. My handle was Jonathan Copernicus II. Since my father preferred to be called Jon, I became known as Junior. That moniker stuck until high school when JC became more fashionable. When I went off to college, my friends decided that I should be Cooper and that's what stayed with me or at least some configuration of my abbreviated middle name.

Beth's story was similar. She started out as Mary then morphed to Elizabeth then to Liz and finally to Beth. She was a Catholic girl and a product of Catholic schools – grade school and high school. I was Lutheran and a product of Lutheran schools – grade school, high school and college. I suspected that as long as we stayed away from discussing topics like the Council of Trent or praying to saints or the Bodily Assumption of the Blessed Virgin or transubstantiation or indulgences, we would probably be fine.

I grew up in rural upstate New York learning the art of farming. She grew up on mostly urban Long Island learning the art of survival.

She had a daughter and two sons and I had a son and two daughters. I had three grandchildren. She was still waiting for her first.

She had been living in Charleston, South Carolina for the past eight years. Before that she spent most of her time on Hilton Head Island. That made us both transplanted Yankees as I have been rooted near Charlotte for nearly a dozen years. In spite of our many years in the South, neither of us were a fan of grits or liver mush for that matter.

We had both been married once and both our spouses had died. My Amelia had passed less than a year ago from cancer and her Tony ten years ago from an accident. The way she dropped her eyes and face as she related his demise told me that there was more to that story. And I wasn't quite buying "accident." Like Paul Harvey I wanted to know the rest of that story, all of that story. Or did I? A person should really be careful what they desire. Curiosity doesn't just kill cats; it can and would leave a poor unsuspecting schmuck like myself in a world of hurt.

Sixteen

Dinner was progressing much better than I dreamed it would. Through my brilliant questioning and dialoging skills, I was learning vital information about Beth and was coming closer to determining her age. For some reason figuring that out was important to me. I suspect the reason probably goes back to my mother's influence. *You shouldn't be involved with anyone who is not close to your own age, son. It is not a proper thing for a Meyerhoff to do. People will talk.* I had to find out her age and soon.

One day at the rest home, an old man and woman were talking. Out of nowhere the woman says, "I bet your dessert that I can guess your age." The man doesn't believe she can, but he agrees to the bet and tells her to go ahead and try. "Pull down your pants," she says. He doesn't understand why but does it anyway. She inspects his privates for a few minutes and then says, "You're eighty-four years old." "That's amazing," the man says. "How did you know?" "Simple," she said, "You told me yesterday."

I decided that life is too short to waste any more time trying to guess her age. I could ask questions like what was your favorite TV show or song on the radio when you were six and then extrapolate a birth date from there, but that was too much mental exercise. I wasn't going to try the pants or skirt trick because I didn't know how it worked. Instead I opted for do or die.

"Forgive me Beth. I know it's not polite to ask a woman this but in lieu of devising some sneaky way to learn your age . . . how old are you?"

From out of nowhere Beth cooed and fanned in her best Scarlet O'Hare imitation. "Why Copernicus Meyerhoff, ah am shocked. Is that anythin' to be askin' a lady?"

If I had been sipping from my water glass at that moment I would have sprayed liquid everywhere. I laughed, we laughed, until my sides hurt.

Sometime during that outburst I had reached across the table and grasped both of her hands.

"Where did that come from?" I asked.

"You know, I'm not sure. I can't remember the last time I've done something so silly. I can't ever remember doing something like that."

"It was great."

I found myself looking intently into her eyes. She was returning the favor. Those eyes were comfortingly similar to the beautiful brown ones that I was so accustomed to, yet they were lovely in their own right. They were dancing. They were sparkling. They were inviting. There was "yes, yes" in those eyes.

"I'll be forty-eight this month," she said in a matter of fact tone.

"Forty-eight," I repeated softly not as a question but as a statement. I was still gazing, my conscious mind processing her words and sending them to wherever my mother hung out in the dark recesses of my sub-conscious. I was receiving back a nod of approval. I don't think it would have mattered either way.

"Would you like to see the dessert menu?" Nora offered not once but twice or maybe it was three times. I don't really know. I heard her but I wasn't really listening. Maybe I was too hasty in trying to rid the world of selective hearing. Maybe there is a time and a place for it after all.

Seventeen

After the stage show Beth and I walked around decks. Tonight's show had been a juggler followed by a comedienne. The juggler was actually pretty good. The *Festival* had left Key West for our next port of call and was enjoying calm sailing so out came the axes. We were both going to suggest to the comedienne however that he insert some kind of knife routine at a relatively early point in his act. We would pray for rough seas and then the audience could hope for the best.

The ocean breeze was cool as it passed over the ship so I offered Beth my jacket. It was the gentlemanly thing to do and I try to be a gentleman.

I struggled mightily with the decision to provide that service because the portion of her gown covering her upper torso was quite generous in revealing and emphasizing this woman's most excellent features. Of course the gown's full length bottom half with a slit rising to the knee and form fitting style did an equally admirable job displaying the fine features of this woman's lower extremities.

She chose to move her body close to mine as we stopped by the rail to gaze at the star filled heavens. I circled my arm around her shoulder to draw her closer. Beth broke a prolonged, peaceful silence.

"I had a wonderful day. Thank you."

"No, thank you. It was my pleasure, believe me."

"I could stand here all night."

"It is beautiful. It's an absolutely perfect night on the ocean." I was back to struggling for words again. "You know, I have been both dreading and anticipating this particular day and moment."

"I know what you mean," she said quietly.

"This is my first attempt to spend any time with a woman other than Amy. I have been afraid to do so up until now. I didn't want to betray her, betray us. I have missed her so much. I have missed holding her. I have missed talking with her and laughing with her. I have missed a thousand other little and big things that we did together. Yet deep inside there has been something else going on for quite some time, a different kind of loneliness that has been pushing me to let go all of that missing and to begin reaching out for something new. Am I making any sense?"

"You're making perfect sense. You have to understand that you are new to being alone Coop. I've been a widow for ten years and I still miss that companionship I had for over twenty years. I didn't have a great marriage but still we built a life together and he is alive in my children. I've made a couple of attempts at romance over the years but nothing came of them. I don't know why. I certainly wanted them to work. So over the years I've mostly occupied myself with work and my family."

"I'm glad you took some time off from and are giving me a shot at getting to know you."

"I am too."

"Hey, how about some soft serve?"

"I think I'll opt for the hot chocolate if you don't mind." How did she know that hot chocolate was number seven on my list of favorite things found on a cruise ship?

Eighteen

"Do you want to come in?" Beth asked as she slid the key card into the lock on her stateroom door.

I hadn't pondered that question. I had a more important concern occupying my mind on our walk from the Lido deck's ice cream and hot chocolate stations to Beth's upper deck stateroom. The question mulling around in my mind was: *Do I kiss her good night? Does she or does she not expect a good night kiss? Where is a daisy when you need to pluck its petals to help a person decide?*

We had already come very close to a first kiss about 30 minutes earlier under the moonlight, but I had chickened out. Once I arrived back in my own room, I would engage in a relentless point/counterpoint debate the remainder of the night, replaying the videos of that failed move from every angle. I would no doubt decide that I had blown the call. *So, kiss her good night you fool. Don't ask her. Don't think about. Just do it.*

"Ah, yeah, sure, I'd love to come in but just for a couple of minutes. I've always been curious what the high end staterooms look like."

They didn't look much different. She did have a balcony. That was sweet. After a quick look around I thanked her for a wonderful evening, backed to the door, opened it and let myself out.

"Tomorrow morning at the breakfast bar?" I asked hopefully, standing in the doorway.

"Yeah, fine."

"Eight o'clock alright with you?"

"Ah, yeah."

"See you then. Good night." And I closed the door on a face filled with surprise and disappointment.

Nineteen

I went to hang up my dinner jacket when I discovered that I didn't have it. I had been so pre-occupied with dating protocols, personal fears and clumsiness that I forgot all about it. On top of that I had been whipping myself unmercifully all the way back to my room over my inexcusable behavior. I could wait until morning to retrieve my coat or I could hustle back up the stairs and secure it now and hopefully rescue our relationship. *The way you treated her when you left her room, don't be surprised if she never wants to see you again and hasn't already started shredding your coat to pay you back, you loser.*

It took two sets of knocks before Beth answered her door. She was already in her robe.

"I'm sorry that I treated you so rudely and left so abruptly," I said using my best blood hound look. I fully expected her to thrown my coat in my face and tell me to travel some place where air conditioning doesn't have a prayer. When she didn't say or do anything, I offered, "May I come in?"

Beth hesitated. "Okay."

While still entering the room I began. "I don't know what got in to me. I don't know why I treated you so coldly. I know that it was the wrong way to end a perfect evening. I must have been afraid or something. I know that I felt bad all the way back to my room. And the worst of it is I probably wouldn't have come back to tell you any of this if I hadn't left my jacket here and that I was worried sick that you would probably tear it to shreds and feed it down the toilet and then get yourself into all kinds of trouble for violating the "do not flush foreign objects" rules posted on every commode."

She tried to look upset with me but suddenly broke out in laughter. "You . . ." punching my chest with her fist, "you . . . I should be mad at you but you're so weird at times."

"You've found me out. I don't always operate with all my oars in the water. I don't even know where my oars are most of the time."

We sat down on the sofa facing each other. I took her hand and held it in both of mine, looking at it as I rubbed it gently. Without looking up I said, "I am truly sorry for walking out the way that I did. I have no excuse for doing what I did. My mind was giving me so many messages of what I should do and what you might be expecting me to do and what was the right thing to do that I decided just to run away from the pressure. I'd like to say that's not the real me but I can't, because I did what I did."

Beth sat in silence.

I released my top hand from her hand and moved it to her face, caressing first one side with the back of my fingers and then the other side. Such soft skin. She closed her eyes. Her breathe paused. I studied her intently. My hand moved to a place under her chin. She moved toward me and I toward her until our lips touched. *There may not have been joy in Mudville the day mighty Casey struck out, but in Stateroom 1010 the fans went crazy.*

We broke from that brief first kiss both feeling a little flushed. Body core temps had probably jumped to 100.6 degrees or higher.

"I feel like a teenager on my first date," I offered.

"That was much better than any other first kiss I can ever remember, not that I've had a lot of them."

"I think now would be an excellent time for me to gather my coat and get going while the going's good and then stand in a very cold shower."

"You could take that shower here."

"I'm thinking that would defeat the purpose."

"Please stay."

"Believe me I want to stay, but this is all happening way too fast."

"It has to happen fast. We only have a few days and then we'll probably go our separate ways and never see each other again."

"Is that what you want, to never see each other again?"

"I don't know what I want. I only know that right now I want you."

"I want you too, but I want something else more."

"What's that?"

"I want to know whether or not what has started between the two of us can go some place good and some place wonderful or whether what's happening between us is simply going to be a flash in the pan, a here today, gone tomorrow kind of thing. That's what I think we need to try and figure out."

"How can we do that?"

"I know that we're not going to discover the answer by groping each other on the couch or lathering up together in the shower or romping around in your bed or mine as appealing and gratifying as each of those might sound." I began working my fingers between the front collar of my shirt and my neck. "Is it getting hot in here or is it just me?"

"It's not just you, Coop."

"The only way we're going to discover the answer to us and a possible future is through a process very similar to the one we plowed through today.

"So I have two suggestions. The first is that I go to my room and you stay in yours where we each retire to our respective showers and stand under the cold water for as long as necessary. We then try for a good night's sleep, meet each other for breakfast in the morning as we planned and spend the day in further discovery. When tomorrow ends we should know each other a little better and be in a more favorable position to evaluate where we want to go and how we want to get there.

"Second, you need to close the top of your robe. A man in my fragile condition should not be forced to choose between looking at your big, beautiful eyes and your big, beautiful . . ." I nodded toward her ample chest spilling into my space.

Beth secured her robe, stood up, retrieved my dinner jacket and reluctantly handed it to me. "I want to give this relationship a chance too. What you are saying makes good sense although I'd rather try my hands at some of that groping and lathering and romping stuff."

"I bet you would."

"Is there nothing I could say that would make you change your mind?"

"No."

"Do we need to shake on this agreement?"

"I don't think so. If you start shaking you will probably cause your entire robe to come undone and there's not enough cold water on the *Festival* to calm me down after an experience of that magnitude. Let's hug on it instead."

"I meant a handshake, but I like your idea better."

Twenty

I was aroused from a meditation on nothing while staring out over the pre-dawn Caribbean by a pair of arms reaching around my waist.

"Guess who?" Beth asked.

I turned slowly around in those arms so as not to break their grip, gently placed my arms around her and we enjoyed a morning kiss.

"Good morning. I didn't expect to see you out so early."

"I couldn't sleep any longer. I knew you would be some-where out on deck so I came looking for you."

"I'm glad you did. I knew I should have brushed my teeth before venturing out this morning."

"No problem. Let's just chalk it up to the discovery process." She pretended to write on a notepad. "Cooper Meyerhoff has dog breath first thing in the morning. Ignore him until at least noon."

"Come on. It's not that bad."

"Let me do a second test sample just to be sure." She kissed me again. This time it was a little longer.

"I was wrong," as she crossed off her imaginary note, "breath is satisfactory. You know this research and discovery stuff may not be half bad after all."

I held her closer. Beth pressed her pelvis tightly against mine only to make another early morning discovery.

"I thought you took a cold shower last night," she quipped while moving her hips slightly back and forth to make sure we both knew what we both knew.

"I did, but this is another day and it seems to me that I will need another one and soon."

"There are other ways to take care of that issue." Beth was suddenly sporting a sheepish grin. It was obvious she was enjoying this. It was obvious I wasn't.

"I am well aware of those other ways."

"But you are not ready to hear a motion for that kind of discovery yet."

"That's correct, at least not before my Raisin Bran and a Danish," as I pushed her away with a laugh and led the way to the breakfast bar.

Twenty-one

I thought Beth looked good in a robe. I thought she look good in Capri's and a short sleeve top. I thought she looked good in an evening gown. That was before I saw her in a swimsuit.

We spent the day at sea lounging around the ship. There is a lot to do on a cruise ship even if you don't like doing much.

Neither one of us were into the art auctions, bingo, the casino, mud treatments at the spa, lectures on how to whiten your teeth or cleansing your body of all things obnoxious, bingo, the hairy chest and belly flop contests along with a host of other activities that Scooter, the wonder director, paraded past his growing throng of vacationing admirers.

We set up on the serenity deck. This area is off limits to young children and offers recorded music that is maxed at *mp*. We divided our time between the chaise lounges, the water slide, the hot tub, the soft serve machine, the chaise lounges by the pool, the water slide, the dessert bar (which is tied for seventh place on my favorites' list with hot choco-late), reading, talking (a lot of that), did I say the water slide, slathering on sun screen (now that was a treat both as a slath-erer and a slatheree), walking, playing miniature golf, grazing on the lunch buffet, working out in the exercise room, turning down about a hundred requests from the roaming bar hops, scanning the horizon for passing ships or leaping whales (I'm not sure there are any in the Caribbean) and simply enjoying the good life.

Discovery didn't include learning any more about Beth's husband or his "accident." We ran into Anne and Genette a couple of times. It seemed to me that they had made friends with one or more of the bar hops. When I mentioned that observation to Beth she just shrugged her shoulders.

Susana was being supervised by the ship's child care per-sonnel. It's a great service and it's included in the price. She seemed to be having a great time when we ran into her group at lunch. I think I saw the kid from the muster drill duct taped to one of the yard arms.

Before we knew it the dinner hour was upon us. I show-ered with hot water first, to scrub the sun screen and other remnants of the day off my body and then with cold, both out of habit by now as well as necessity. Then I slipped into my dress slacks, a long sleeve shirt and dress shoes.

Beth met me in a long sleeve, dressy blouse, dark slacks and flat shoes. She stood about 5'10". Perfect.

"What's on the menu tonight?" she asked as we waited to be let into the *Mardi Gras* room.

If I had known what was really on tonight's menu, I would have avoided the entire evening at all cost.

Bon Voyage

Lust

Envy/Jealousy

Anger

Sloth

Gluttony

Greed

Pride

Debarkation

Twenty-two

Marta came by our table once again to greet us. It was beginning to become obvious that she wasn't just plying for a tip. She was good at her job. She was driven to have the best dining room staff in the fleet. She had Nora and Randaldo working together like a finely tuned Swiss watch. They attended religiously to our every need.

They swapped out clean plates for dirty ones, full plates for empties. They watched over and refilled our beverages. They quickly whisked away the unnecessary silverware and replaced it with the proper utensils for the upcoming course. Bread crumbs disappeared from the table cloth almost before they had a chance to cool. Every exchange was accompanied by "ma'am" or "sir" or "Beth" or "Cooper" or "Ms." or "Mr." That wonderful service is one reason why evening dinner holds the number two spot on my favorite's list.

Dinner lost out in its bid to claim the top spot because the wait staff insists on singing "happy birthday" to the guests. Tonight it was Beth's turn to be so honored or embarrassed whichever the case may be. When a handful of waiters have the opportunity to perform, they assemble at their quarry's table and sing the traditional birthday song.

Through no fault of their own they sound laughably pathetic. Most "no speakay de gooda anglish an no singa eet eeder." That doesn't stop their enthusiasm. The birthday song chorus concluded: "Hoppay birtday deer Be-eht. Hoppay birtday to eeyew!"

We applauded their courage and thanked them.

The show that was scheduled in the *Crystal* Lounge didn't appeal to either of us so I asked Beth if she wanted to go dancing. She brightened at the idea.

The *Festival* has several music bars, clubs, lounges or whatever you call them. Each one features a different theme with different music. Each one caters to a different age group. We passed a couple that were blasting noise. We entered one featuring karaoke. We listened awhile. A couple of the acts that performed were ok. None of them would get a try out on *America's Got Talent* or *American Idol*.

The mic stayed empty for a period of time undoubtedly due to the last couple of acts which had driven the few remaining stalwarts scurrying for other venues. I looked at Beth and she looked at me. We discussed the possibility, decided on Sonny and Cher's "I've Got You, Babe" and headed to the stage.

There wouldn't be a record contract forthcoming but we made some pretty sweet music together.

Eventually we found our way to a room featuring some big band tunes. Now that's some serious dancing music, you know like the Waltz, the Swing, the Foxtrot, the Cha-cha, and maybe even some Tango. Amy and I had spent a fortune on lessons over the years. We didn't dance much though. That was my fault. I was always too busy and real dancing seemed like a frivolous use of time.

As I watched Beth warm up her motor I regretted that previous attitude of mine and those wasted opportunities. I learned about forty years too late that there is a time for work and there is a time for play. I learned that there is a time to take one's responsibilities seriously and there is a time to have fun. I learned that you can't turn back the clock on your mistakes so you better learn quickly from those mistakes or you will repeat them and regret them. And I learned that the truly wise are those who listen to those who have already learned life's lessons and are willing to teach you the very lessons they have learned.

Twenty-three

I looked at my watch. It was after midnight. We had danced the night away. "I'm ready to leave whenever you are."

"Then let's go," Beth replied.

I took her by the hand and led her out to the hallway. "How about if we go top side for a few minutes and get some air."

"I'd rather go back to my room. How about if we relax for a while on my balcony?"

"Sounds good to me."

Once in stateroom 1010 we both took off our shoes and I my socks and we went out on the balcony to savor the moonlight.

"Man that feels good," I said as I worked my toes and feet and breathed in the fresh, salt air. *It doesn't feel near as good as some of those slow close dances felt! Not by a long shot!*

"So, Coop, have we discovered enough about each other yet to get naked and make mad passionate love the rest of the night?"

"You really do have a one track mind, girl."

"*I* have a one track mind?" She glanced at a hidden member of my body located just below my belt which was relaxed for the first time in several hours.

"That's not my doing, ma'am. That is merely nature's way of responding to the company of a beautiful and stimulating woman."

"Excuses, excuses, that's all you give me is excuses. How about some action?"

"Why is sex so important to you?"

That question seemed to have caught her off guard.

"It's what people, it's what two consenting adults do when they want to express the feelings they have for each other. It's . . . it's just . . . natural, it's what you do to have fun, to get close to each other, to, ah, you know, express desires, release tension and the like."

"Is that what you were taught back in Catholic school?"

"Of course not."

"What were you taught?"

"You known, no sex before marriage, wait for the right one; be a virgin like Mary, no sex outside of marriage, no sex after marriage, no sex at all except to make a baby or when your husband demands it."

"You were really taught that?"

"Yeah pretty much, if and when they talked about it at all. That's what I remember any way. Sex was dirty. It was not something to be enjoyed. It was for procreation, I think that's the correct word. Good little girls didn't think about having intercourse with guys. You could be damned to hell for that. We were supposed to think only about someday becoming mothers and raising large, happy families."

"Interesting," I mused.

"No, not interesting!" I had hit a bit of a nerve. "Restricting, frustrating, psychologically damaging, but definitely not interesting."

"It sounds to me like I've ventured into a sensitive topic for you."

"Yes, you could say that."

"And . . ." I urged her to continue, using my hands to coax her on.

"And what? Why has this conversation suddenly shifted to my sexuality?"

"We are in the discovery phase, my dear, remember? And it was you who raised the topic."

"Alright, if that's the way you want it. I had some serious hang ups about sex and my own sexuality growing up. It was maybe the main reason that I got married young, right out of high school. My parents demanded that I wait but I knew better than they did. I was tired of being the good the little girl. I was tired of being sheltered from everything. I knew nothing about the real world. Along came Tony, Antonio, and he knew all about the world. He swept me off my feet and began teaching me all kinds of things about life including the forbidden pleasures of sex. Everything seemed so right, so good. He asked me to marry him. I said 'yes.' We had a beautiful Church wedding just like I had always dreamed about having except . . . my parents didn't attend."

"That must have hurt," I sympathized.

"It didn't so much at the time because I was angry with them and I didn't believe that they were interested in my happiness. The only thing that was important to me then was this man who said he loved me more than anything in the world.

"I truly believed that he would do anything for me. He was my knight in shining armor. He was my ticket to freedom and the good life. He was my dream come true."

I cut in. "But that's not the way he felt about you, was it."

"No," she said, surprised by my observation. "In fact, he saw me as a prize, as a trophy he could display, as another puzzle piece he could manipulate at his pleasure. I was nothing more than his mistress. I was expected to do his bidding. I was merely someone he could drape on his arm in order to convince others what a wonderful family man he was, what a good husband, father and provider he was.

"He never abused me physically. He gave me everything I wanted and more. He was polite, but he was demanding. My life had to be consistent with his.

"I reconciled myself to being his obedient wife and I bore his children. I know that it sounds cold, but believe me when I say that I loved those children. I was, I am a good loving mother to them.

"I put on the appearance that everything about our relationship was harmonious, but deep down I resented him and I continued to resent most everything else I had been taught in Catholic schools and by the Church." She paused to gather her thoughts. Her voice grew quieter and her words became slower as she continued.

"I eventually resolved some of the conflict with my parents. They welcomed me back into their lives and gave me a lot of much needed support as I struggled to stay in the marriage.

"Truth be known, I was glad when he was killed. I cried only for the sake of the children. They loved their father. I made sure of that. He was good to them. But the day he died was the day I started coming alive."

Another pause, longer this time. Her tone was becoming more serious, her words more deliberate, but less convincing. She was no longer speaking directly to me. She was staring out toward the water.

"I found a good therapist. He helped get my thinking straightened out. I've made total peace with my parents. I've gotten my degree. I'm running a successful business. I've left the Church behind. I have a great relationship with my children. And I've just met a wonderful man while on a cruise ship in the Caribbean Sea." She paused before continuing. "Life is good." Then silence.

Beth sat with her hands on her lap. She was continuing to stare out toward the ocean at nothing in particular. When I could endure the quiet no longer, I spoke.

"There's something still missing in your life isn't there?"

"You can tell?"

"Yeah."

"What is it? What's missing? Why do I have all this going for me and yet feel so empty and alone?"

"You'll get it figured out."

"Yeah, right," Beth snickered. "Let me guess, I will figure it out through the process of discovery."

"That's the path. It won't be an easy path. Just be open and be patient. The answer will come. Look what you've discovered already tonight! You at least know what hasn't worked to fill that emptiness."

"And what's that?"

"Sex. Other than producing your wonderful children it has only served to confuse, frustrate and mislead you your whole life."

She gave me a quizzical look but didn't say anything. After a moment she returned her gaze toward the ocean. Beth was in deep thought. This time she broke the silence.

"You know, Coop, I'm suddenly very tired. It's been a long day."

"I was thinking the same thing; a long day, but a great day."

I took her hand and gently kissed it. She smiled.

"Good night Beth."

"Good night."

I left her on the balcony and walked slowly out the door of her stateroom and even more slowly down the halls and down the stairs to my room. There was way too much discovery to process.

Twenty-four

I was deep in thought myself as I slipped into my room, yet I noticed that there was no light to greet me. Hadn't housekeeping been here? They always leave a light burning. Oh, bummer, there wouldn't be a cute towel animal on my bed either. I reached for the wall switch but nothing happened. That's not quite accurate. No electric current flowed from the switch to a working bulb. Something else though did happen.

One huge powerful arm wrapped itself around my body from behind me pinning my arms. At the same time a second equally huge and powerful arm covered my face and mouth. I couldn't move or talk and could barely breathe. Since I had never been trained in the art of self-defense I possessed no repertoire of moves to free myself or disable my attacker.

He forced me into the room and kicked the door closed behind him.

I don't ever remember being this afraid in my life. What was happening? Why was this happening? Was I about to die? *Lord, remember me . . .*

A voice, very Italian, from out of the darkness spoke from across the room.

"Are you Meyerhoff?"

It wasn't a question as much as it was a demand. Of course I wasn't able to speak in order to answer the question. Worse, I wasn't smart enough to think through all the ramifications of how to gain my freedom. Which course of action was better for me? Would a lie give me a better chance at freedom or would telling the truth? I didn't know. When in doubt tell the truth. I struggled to nod a "yes."

Apparently I communicated my answer effectively. The voice spoke once again. "My associate is going to remove his arms from restraining you. He will do so under one condition. That condition is that you remain still, that you do not do any-thing stupid, that you answer my questions correctly and that you take to heart what I say. If you do not live up to this condi-tion, my friend will re-engage himself with consequences to your physical well being. Do we have an understanding?"

I had at least two issues that needed clarifying in my mind. For one, I counted four conditions not one. Second, I am not in the habit of making promises to people before I know what it is I'm promising. However given the situation that I was in, which was eerily similar to a scene straight out of *The Godfather*, I waived all rights to finding clarity and nodded vehemently.

"Wise decision my friend."

I decided in my mind to call the muscle, Vito, and the voice, Vinnie. Vito carefully let go of me while Vinnie clicked on a reading light by the bed. He stood facing the window with his back to me. Both men were wearing suits. Vinnie was as small as Vito was huge. I don't know how I let a guy that bulky sneak up on me. Of course what would I have done even if I had seen or heard him coming anyway?

"Now, Father, it pains me to talk to a man of God in this way. So please forgive me. But like you have your duty to do, I have my duty to do also."

Father? I'm not a priest. What is going on here? Maybe this is simply a case of mistaken identity. I should interrupt and set the record straight and put an end to this nightmare. No, maybe I should hear him out at least a little longer. Interrupting may be hazardous to my health.

"I have it on good authority that you are being intimate with the widow Gambolini. This is not behavior becoming for a priest of God."

Twenty-five

*T*he widow Gambolini? And there's that priest reference again. This is getting more bizarre by the minute. I decided it was time to intervene. I would raise my hand like we did back in grade school when we had a question, but do it very slowly and carefully. Maybe Vito would understand the gesture and would grant me permission to speak and not reapply his death grip.

"Ex . . . ex . . cuse me, sir?" I braced for a whap upside the head.

"You have something to say to me?"

"Yes, I do. May I speak, sir?" I thought being polite and showing respect might help my cause.

"Speak." He still had not turned to face me.

"I mean no disrespect sir, but first excuse my ignorance, who is the widow Gambolini? Second, the only person I have ever been intimate with is my wife. And third I am not a priest and have never taken a vow of celibacy or chastity for that matter. Now I am sure that you have done your research well, but could it be possible that we have a case of mistaken identity here?"

"There is no mistaken identity here, sir. My associate and I have been watching you and Ms. Gambolini for the past two days. You spent a portion of last night in her room and a good portion of tonight as well. She is a good looking woman and you are no doubt a man with needs. Shall I convince you of our position by playing some of the recordings we have of your conversations or perhaps you would like to see several of the pictures we have taken of the two of you."

Ms. Gambolini. Mrs. Antonio Gambolini. Mary Elizabeth Gambolini. So that's her married name. She never told me her married name. I never asked for her married name, not that it would have mattered to me.

"You are referring to Mary Elizabeth," I said.

"That is very wise of you to admit."

"I admit that I have been seeing Mary Elizabeth. I admit that she is a beautiful woman. I admit that I enjoy being with her. But I will not admit to doing anything inappropriate with her. And I would challenge you to show me a picture where I have."

My comment drew that whap alongside the head from Vito. I grunted.

"Watch your mouth," he warned, then added, "No offense, Father."

Vinnie spoke up again.

"This is what's gonna happen. I work for someone who is very concerned about Ms. Gambolini's welfare. He would consider it a favor if you were to break off this relationship with her immediately. I think that your parishioners would also benefit greatly if you respected his wishes. Am I making myself clear?"

"Yes, sir, you are making yourself perfectly clear."

"Very good, I am glad that you are a reasonable man. God bless you Father. I hope we don't have to meet again and if we do may it be under better circumstances. And Father, please forgive in advance one last act on my part. I trust that you will understand that I have no choice but to leave you with a reminder of the seriousness of this agreement."

A fist that could have been a sledge hammer blasted my kidney from behind and stars began to circle my head. A second hammer caved in my stomach and emptied my lungs as I doubled over in anguish. The moon and a dozen planets joined the swirling constellation. *Please no more.*

Three friends were together on a desert isle. One of them died. The second said, "I'm pretty sure he was Catholic. We should give him a Catholic burial but I don't know how to do it." The third friend offered, "I've attended several Catholic funerals. I think I know what to do." They dug a grave and placed the body next to it. The third friend stood over the body and said, "I bury you into the name of the Father and into the name of the Son and (giving the body a push) into the hole he goes."

The third hammer came crashing down over the back of my neck and down I went into the black hole of a deep sleep.

Twenty-six

I was in heaven. I opened my eyes and there was an angel. She was beautiful. Yet something wasn't right. I had thought that heaven was a place of no more pain and I hurt like I was in hell. Yet I couldn't be in hell because hell had no beauty and I was looking at beauty.

Slowly my memory started returning to me. This was my stateroom. A picture that included Vinnie and Vito returned to my mind. I recalled the words of their warning.

I was lying on my back. I was on my bed. *How did I get here? The boys must have done it. They apparently couldn't bear to leave me bunched up on the floor? What a couple of class guys.* I tried to sit up but pain shot through my upper body like knives were stabbing me.

"Cooper . . . Cooper, what happened? Are you alright? I've been worried sick."

It was the angel. It was Beth. Who was the other guy with her? My eyes wouldn't focus on his badge.

"Help me up," I rasped.

Beth and her companion got me to a sitting position. The stars returned along with some nausea.

"What happened?"

"Let me collect my balance first. Who is with you?"

"He is from ship security. When you didn't show up in your usual spot and when you didn't answer your phone and when I couldn't find you anywhere I called security and had them come and check your room. Are you all right?"

"Not anything some extra strength pain killers won't help. There's some ibuprofen in my shaving bag in the bathroom. Would you bring me four please?" Beth headed to the bathroom.

For the first time the security man spoke. His badge said, Sashi Squatchma, Malaysia.

"Is there something that I can do?"

"No. I'll be okay. I ah . . . I came in last night and the . . . ah . . . the ah . . . lights didn't turn on. I must have tripped over something and hit my head and knocked myself out."

"I see. I will contact maintenance and have them check your lights immediately sir."

I couldn't tell if he bought my story or not. "Yes, that would be a good idea. Thank you. Yeah, thank for your concern and help. I really appreciate it."

"I will also contact housekeeping." He nodded toward the sticky and wet mess around me.

"Yes, that would also be good." I had just noticed the obvious odor of body fluids that had escaped during my forced siesta.

Sashi bowed slightly, turned and left Beth and I alone in my room. She handed me the pills and a glass of water.

"What really happened, Coop?"

"You don't want to know."

Twenty-seven

Coffee and breakfast following a hot shower and the pain pills were working their magic. Beth was livid after I told her what had happened. She now understood why her previous love interests had bailed on her.

"That man won't leave me alone even from the grave!"

"Did you know that Tony was involved with the mob?"

"Yeah, but I chose to ignore it. He never wanted to talk about his work and I didn't much care about him or what he did so I quit asking. He had his life and I had mine."

"Who is left in the family that would be so jealous of you? Who doesn't want anyone else," I shifted to my best Marlon Brando as Don Corleone impersonation, "Fondling the merchandise so to speak?"

"That would probably be his brother, Frankie."

"The question is why? Is he in love you?"

"Frankie? No, Frankie is in love with Frankie. He never paid me any attention. He barely even talked to me."

"Okay, then do you still have a piece of the family money or information that is worth money?"

"No, Tony left me a generous life insurance policy and an adequate trust for the children, but nothing else was in my name. The family gave me the house on Hilton Head so that I would have a place to live and also I suppose as a gesture of good will. I sold it and bought the place in Charleston. Like I told you before I knew nothing about his affairs."

"Was there something about the house?"

"I don't think so. I told them that I didn't want it. They insisted I take it. I told them that I was going to sell it and they said 'do whatever you want with the place, we don't want it. It has too many memories.'"

"Did they believe you had something to do with his murder?"

"No, it was business related. Tony double crossed the wrong guy."

"Are your boys involved in the family business?"

She shook her head. I pressed on.

"Do you think that Frankie's afraid you are trying to keep his nephews from their rightful place in the clan? His excessive interest in your affairs is possibly his way of maintaining leverage over them through you."

"If that's his game, he's a sicker bastard than I thought."

"You don't have to convince me of that."

"So what are we going to do Coop? I don't see any way out of this mess. I don't want to lose you, but if we break things off I lose you and if we keep seeing each other I lose you."

She looked like she wanted to cry.

"I feel the same way Beth." I took a cleansing breath. "You know back on the farm we had a saying that if the bull won't go to the cow, then bring the cow to the bull. I'm thinking that the only way to scratch out a win in this situation is by going directly to the bull. You wouldn't happen to have a phone number for Frankie would you?"

"You're not going to try to call him, are you?" Her look suggested that only someone with a death wish would make a phone call like that.

Twenty-eight

Beth didn't have Frankie's personal number but she did have one that rang to the family manse or whatever a mafia's base of operations is called.

"Hello," a thick Italian male voice answered, "what do you want?"

"Good morning," I said cheerfully, "May I speak with Frankie Gambolini please."

"He ain't available."

"I'm sorry to hear that. Would you be so kind as to inform him when he is available that Father Meyerhoff from over at the rectory called and needs to speak to him at his earliest convenience?"

Beth's eyes grew wide. She pointed a finger at me while whispering, "You're a priest!" I quickly shook my head, put my index finger to my mouth and then pointed and waved it at her as a signal to "Be quiet."

"Yes Father, I will certainly do that. In fact why don't you hang on for a moment while I see if Mr. Gambolini is still indisposed or otherwise unavailable."

"Thank you. You are most kind." I waited, contemplating my next move, but not for too long.

"Father, Mr. Gambolini will be right with you."

"Thank you. God bless you sir."

"God bless you too, Father."

You are not really lying or deceiving here Coop. After all Mr. G really believes you are a priest, so he has the problem and not you. Then why am I feeling so sick to my stomach?

"Father, this is Frankie Gambolini. I am sorry to keep you waiting. How can I help you?" This was now the third representative of the family I had talked too and they all sounded like a cross between Sylvester Stallone, Al Pacino and Danny Devito.

"I appreciate you taking time out of your busy and important schedule for me. I am calling in reference to a visit that I had earlier this morning from two of your associates. I regret I don't know their names. The calling card they left was too smudged to decipher. They were very polite and respectful; however they had other business to attend to and left before I could converse adequately with them."

"I'm sorry but ah, I don't know that of which you are referring."

"I am referring to a woman that I have met. Her name is Mary Elizabeth."

"I know several Mary Elizabeth's."

"The Mary Elizabeth that I am alluding to was referred to by your associates as your brother's widow. God rest his soul. Now that I know this fact and now that your associates have made it clear to me how you feel about Mary Elizabeth seeing someone like me, I thought that the Christian thing and perhaps more importantly the respectful thing for me to do would be to talk directly to you about this situation."

Silence; he hadn't hung up. I could hear breathing. So far so good.

"Please indulge me sir. I do owe you an apology for behavior that I am ashamed of. I admit that I deceived you so that I might be able to have this conversation with you. For some reason you believe that I am a priest and I used that belief to my advantage.

"I am not a priest. I am not even Catholic. Some of my best friends are Catholic. I like Catholics. I can understand the confusion. I am an ordained clergyman. I am a Reverend. I am the pastor of a parish. However, I am of the Lutheran persuasion.

"As I'm sure that you know one of the differences between a Catholic priest and a Lutheran minister is that while your clergy may only be married to the Church, someone like myself may choose to be married to a woman."

"What you are telling me is all very interesting, but what does it have to do with me?"

"Please be patient with me for just a moment more. You should know that I am a widower. You should know that I do not believe in sexual intercourse outside of marriage. You should know that I would never violate a woman and that includes Mary Elizabeth. I respect God too much. I respect her too much. And I respect her first marriage and her children too much to do that."

"So I ask again, what does all this have to do with me?"

"I would like to continue seeing Mary Elizabeth and she would like to continue seeing me. Neither one of us knows where this relationship will lead. Right now we're only interested in learning about each other. I don't want to do anything that would hurt her and I certainly don't want to bring any disrespect on the Gambolini family. I have heard that you are a fair man, a wise man and someone who can be trusted.

"Therefore I am asking for your permission to continue seeing Mary Elizabeth. However, if at any time you feel that my presence in her life is detrimental to her or her children or your family, I will walk away. I only ask that you respect me by informing me of that decision face to face. I promise to respect you by keeping you informed from time to time concerning the status of our relationship."

There was more silence on the other end of the line. Had I pushed too far? Had he hung up?

"This is going to take some thought on my part. I will get back to you with my decision. Good day, Mr. Meyerhoff."

"Thank you again sir for your time and please inform your associates how much I appreciated their courtesy and the polite, efficient way that they handled a most delicate situation."

"Sure." Click.

Twenty-nine

"I have never heard so much BS coming from one person's mouth since I listened to Tony's wedding vows!"

"It may have sounded like BS to you but it was a carefully crafted attempt to KU the unsuspecting Mr. Frankie Gambolini."

"What do you mean KU?"

"Kiss Up. My hope was to soften Frankie up, to convince him that I wasn't any kind of threat, that I really liked him and respected him more than anyone else in the world, yada, yada, yada."

"So what do you think? Did it work? Is there hope for us?"

"I'll tell you as soon as I start breathing again and my heart returns to its normal fifty seven beats a minute."

"Come on, don't keep me in suspense."

I laughed to relieve some of my tension and then relayed that part of the phone conversation that Beth couldn't hear along with my impressions of the chat. There wasn't much to relay.

"Your guess whether or not I helped our cause is as good as mine, Beth. It's a first step. Hopefully I've created an environment of good will. That's all I can do. Hopefully he won't see me as a threat. At best he'll want to keep me around because he likes people stroking his ego. The key to this still lies in the question, why is he so jealous of you? If it's not about money and it's not about love and it's not about family business or secrets, then it must be about his pride."

"You said secrets?"

"Yeah, secrets. Maybe Frankie believes you know something about him or Tony or someone else in the family but he's made a pact with his brother never to hurt you. I've heard that among certain families these kinds of promises are more sacred than baptismal or marriage vows."

"So rather than bump me off, he is just picking one way to make my life miserable?"

"It's one scenario that makes sense."

"But I don't know any secrets."

"Well, at this point we're only speculating. My gut tells me it's just his jealous pride – if his brother can't have you then nobody can have you. If that's the case then I'm dreading the next visit from Mutt and Jeff."

"Mutt and Jeff?"

"Yeah," I replied with irritation in my voice, "my new found friends, Vinnie and Vito, Curly and Moe, Big Bird and Kermit,

Beavis and Butthead, Bugs and the Tasmanian Devil, whatever their names are."

"Oh, no, what have I gotten you into? Let's walk away from this!"

"No. I can't do that. I'm not going to do that. 'Even though I walk through the valley of the shadow of death I will fear no evil.'"

"I recognize those words."

"They are among the most familiar and oft quoted words from the Bible. They are part of the twenty-third Psalm."

"Why did you think of those words?"

"Because they're appropriate for the moment. They were presumably authored by Israel's greatest king, David, after God had delivered him from some calamity in his life."

"What calamity was that?" Beth inquired.

"No one knows for sure but his trial may have been an assassination attempt or a coup or an enemy attack or maybe a severe illness or possibly even temptations to commit sins that would cause him to betray either personal oaths or his oath of office. Whatever the reason, the Psalm celebrates deliverance and it became a staple in the worship life of Israel and a favorite among troubled Christians to this day.

"The Psalm presents the shepherding nature of God. God provides. He brings peace. He restores. He guides. He protects with his presence. He surrounds his people with goodness and mercy all their living days. And he promises a forever dwelling in his heavenly home.

"I am not alone in drawing great comfort and strength from these words. With the Lord as my shepherd, what can mere man do to me?"

Beth wasn't convinced. "Yeah, but I seem to remember something about we're not suppose to tempt God. Wouldn't riling up a mafia boss be tempting God?"

"Good point. The answer to that lies in trying to find the balance between standing up against evil on the one hand and not forcing God's hand to act as you want him to on the other. Do you remember the story of Jesus' temptations?"

"Was that when he was in the wilderness for like the forty days of Lent or something?"

"Yeah, something like that. The devil tried to defeat Jesus or at least derail his mission. Satan took Jesus to the Holy City and had him stand on the highest point of the temple. He said, 'If you are the Son of God throw yourself down because God's angels will protect you.'

"Jesus rejected Satan's offer for two reasons. One reason was because of the mission he was on. Part of that mission was to confront and defeat the powers evil, death and hell. God, his father was behind him and with him in that battle. Therefore he approached his task with confidence and purpose. He knew that it would mean suffering and ultimately a horrible death but he also trusted that he would be vindicated and that people like me and you would benefit from his sacrifice.

"Satan didn't want this fight. He didn't want to be exposed. To this day evil doesn't like being exposed. You can always tell when people are involved in evil activity. They fight back, they try to cover it up, try to shift blame, try to overcome their opponents with anger, give insincere apologies, refuse to talk, lawyer up or use some other method to obfuscate their situation.

"Jesus was not going to back down from his mission against evil because he knew that God was with him.

"The second reason Jesus rejected Satan's offer was because he understood that no one tempts God. We do not force God to do what we want him to do. God promises to protect his people in all their normal ways and in all the ways he calls them to live and serve. It is simply not normal behavior to jump off of buildings, hence Jesus told Satan 'do not tempt or test the Lord, your God.'

"It might be stupid to stand up to Frankie but it's not out of the normal. In fact it would be wrong not to stand up against the evil he represents. This fight isn't just about us. This is about evil. This is about jealousy or pride or anger or something else trying to rule the day. I cannot give in to the temptation to let that go on. Hence I will walk this valley trusting in the rod and staff of God to be with me. I trust too that if I am wrong about this, a gracious God will steer me in the right direction. To say I am not scared about the potential consequences at the hands of Vinnie and Vito would be a lie. In the meantime, I must walk by faith and not by sight. And I must proceed carefully, as sheep among wolves being as wise as a serpent but as harmless as a dove."

"Do I know how to pick 'em or what," Beth mused. "It's bad enough I latch on to a preacher but then I go and fall for one who thinks he's Rambo."

"Not Rambo," I assured her, "More like Wylie Coyote."

Thirty

I was in no condition to go ashore in Cozumel. I had visited this port once before and was looking forward to this return trip along with the opportunity to explore the island paradise. The shore excursion that Amy and I had booked when we had previously visited the island was cancelled due to windy conditions.

On that visit we had found pleasure in watching two other excursions attempt to embark in the wind and the rough waves. Neither of those outings had appealed to our tastes even on a calm day.

One of the tours was a speed boat adventure that explored much of the island and stopped at various points of interest. The guides outfitted their guests first with life vests and then strapped them into seats similar to those found on corkscrew roller coaster rides at theme parks.

The other tour was a catamaran party boat with loud music and booze. They were scheduled to motor off to a hot or cool, depending on your perspective, spot or two, weigh anchor and savor the island's delights along with whatever other delights were on the boat or in your possession. Swim suits were recommended as I recall from the write up along with a designated guide to return you to the cruise ship if needed.

We laughed as the crews attempted to steady their vessels enough to board their passengers. Amy became motion sick just watching them. The fun seekers though would not be deterred from their appointed destinies.

Eventually the spaces on the boats were filled, the ropes were released and the crafts ventured off for a three hour or longer tour. Except, that is, for one of the speed boats. It was having trouble cranking its engine. Its partner got tired of waiting and bounded off alone. The catamaran bounded off too, just not quite as Tigger like.

Speed boat II finally solved its mechanical problem after being tossed around the harbor by the relentless chop. The pilot pushed the throttles to the stops and off it slammed after its friend. Our fun was over. We went back to walking and revisiting the many shops that were located near the pier.

Thirty-one

Beth elected to stay with me on the *Festival*. Her sister and niece had already left for a shore excursion without her. I seemed to recall that they were going snorkeling. Susana preferred to remain in the company of the ship's care givers.

It wasn't time for more pain pills but I decided another dose would hurt me far less than the pain that was reintroducing itself in an increasingly unpleasant way.

Relaxing in the warm Cozumel sun on the serenity deck only a few paces from the soft serve machine in Beth's company may not have been what a doctor would order, but it was a prescription that suited me just fine.

Here's a bit of wisdom from Copernicus Meyerhoff that you can put right up there with the best of the old timey remedies – nothing helps a body mend faster than ice cream.

The day passed without incident. I slept through much of it. That is rare for me. Beth, out of respect for me, I assume, didn't venture near the water slide. She brought me a cheese burger for lunch along with a slice of chocolate cheese cake and lemonade to drink.

Instead of the juice of the lemon, I probably should have invited the juice of Johnny Walker or Jim Beam or George Dickel or even Anheuser Busch as my guest to calm the irritated parts of my nervous system.

Better than any of those would have been some of that fine clear liquid occasionally still being processed by a couple of good old boys from my in-some-ways-backwoods North Carolina congregation. Of course their product is for medicinal purposes only and to kick up the Christmas eggnog a notch or two.

A young boy was hauled in front of the local magistrate. He was being charged with making and selling illegal whiskey. The judge being a Bible-believing man himself and seeing the age of the youth in front of him decided to show his merciful side. Politely he asked, "Young man what is your name?" The boy replied, "Joshua, sir," The judge, attempting to show off his Bible knowledge continued, "Are you the Joshua who made the sun stand still?" The boy answered, "No, your honor. I'm the Joshua what made the moonshine."

"Do you feel up to dinner, Coop?"

"Is it that time already?"

"It will be once I shower, wash and dry my hair and get ready."

So we have two hours. "Yeah, I'm up for dinner. I'll walk you to your room."

"No, I think that I'll walk you to yours. Wait here. I'll be right back."

Thirty-two

Dinner was as always a splendid experience. The crowd was thin. I expected a low turnout since the *Festival* was not scheduled to leave port until 10:00 p.m. Many of the passengers would be eating authentic Mexican onshore. Not me and not because of "don't drink the water." My reason was purely economic. I didn't want to pay twice for something. I had already paid for dinner on the ship so why throw that money away and pay for dinner in a restaurant to boot.

Beth had already arranged before we left the serenity deck that we would be met at my stateroom door by security. It was Sashi again. He went in first and cleared the space. He said that he would return at 5:45 and accompany me to Beth's room. Beth glared unspoken but crystal clear words at me, "Don't leave your room without him or you are dead meat!"

Most women believe that they are experts at non-verbal communication. Most men get into serious trouble because they either don't receive those communiqués with equal clarity or they chose to ignore them. I have learned the hard way over the years to sharpen my receptors and not to dismiss such messages that are meant for my obvious well being.

At precisely 5:45 Sashi appeared as directed at my door. He and I had a friendly and uneventful stroll from my place to Beth's. The security man left us to find our own way to the *Mardi Gras* room.

Marta showed up and asked about our day. I didn't get in to any of the events of the previous eighteen hours. And since my back was to her I didn't have to explain the bruising showing up on my neck.

Bread time was interrupted by a visit from the barman. He had been pushing a cart before he stopped by our table. I was about to once again say "No, thank you" when he took a bottle from a bucket of ice and presented it to me. It was some kind of champagne.

"This is a gift to both of you from a friend of yours. He asked me give you this message."

Micahkos from Greece set the bottle down, pulled a note from his jacket pocket and began reading.

"Please accept my most sincerest apology for this most terrible of misunderstandings that has happened between us. I hope this heartfelt gift will be a suitable peace offering between us and that there will be no lasting hard feelings."

I looked at Beth and she at me. We smiled and together breathed a sigh of relief.

"Thank you very much Micahkos. Did the gentleman leave you his name?"

"No sir, he said that you would know who he was."

"Do you know what he looked like?"

"He was a small man, well dressed."

"Is he in the dining room now?"

"I do not know. I did not remember seeing him before in my areas of responsibility."

"If you should see him again, would you be so kind as to thank him for me, to thank him for both of us?"

"Of course, sir. Shall I open this for you to enjoy now?"

I looked at Beth. She nodded slightly.

"Yes, that would be fine."

Micahkos followed his training to a tee. With great care he set out the glasses, handled, and then opened the bottle, pouring enough for me to sample. I told him it was good. What was I to know about fine wine? I won't pay more than seven dollars a bottle for Asti Spumante at Christmas.

Beth was more of a woman of the world than I would ever be a man of the world. After Micahkos made his way to other customers she commented on the quality and cost of the bottle. I've never had car payments in that range. Beth spoke first.

"Does this mean that you are off the death watch list and we are free to continue with our discovery phase?"

"I would say that's what this means," offering up my glass in a toast. "Frankie has made a decision much quicker than I expected."

"You underestimate your Meyerhoff charm."

"That may be, but I'm still at a loss about what his game is."

"Well let's not worry about that any more right now. Let's savor the victory. What are we going to discover tonight?"

"How about after dinner let's grab our ship key cards and take a walk."

Thirty-three

I wanted Beth to see Cozumel at night. We recorded our departure from the ship by sliding our card into the security checkpoint at the gangplank. We had about two hours before the runway would be hauled back into the ship and anyone not on board would have to find their own way to the next port or back home.

It's a fairly long walk from where the ship is moored to a security gate that guests must pass through. Beyond that point a small village was created to greet, fleece and entertain visitors to the island.

Cozumel lies eleven and one-half miles from the mainland. A forty-five minute ferry ride will take you to what is known as the Mayan Riviera. After the ferry you can hop a bus for a one-hour ride south to the Mayan ruins of Tulum, travel north to Cancun or you can venture to other places of your own choosing.

Cozumel is billed in the travel brochures as Mexico's largest island. It possesses astounding natural beauty and is famous for its superb scuba diving and snorkeling.

The island has gorgeous beaches, coral reefs, sub tropical forests and sea turtles. If you desire you can explore Mayan ruins and associated artifacts dating from 300 CE, (which is still A.D. to my way of thinking) or visit the earliest modern settlement dating from 1847.

We would get to do none of that on this trip. What I wanted Beth to experience was the sight of the *Festival* all lit up against the night sky. I'm not sure which is the more impressive sight, seeing one of these floating marvels in the daytime or as we now observed it, all aglow at night. A second ship from another line appeared to be casting off. "I wonder where it's going." My question was mostly a verbalized thought.

"I hope it's not someplace better than where we are headed."

The wind had died down. The sky was clear. Music flowed from the bars and restaurants. People were having a good time. There was dancing, drinking, eating and plenty of laughing among people who a few short hours earlier were mostly complete strangers. Inhibition did not as a rule seem to be in folk's vocabulary. In fact several girls whether they realized it or not were receiving tips while dancing on tables having bared most everything accept their feet. Maybe this was the real reason why they said, "Don't drink the water?" I quickly escorted Beth toward the shops and away from the revelry. She already had enough of her own mating ideas. I didn't need to be pumping any more fuel into her tank.

The atmosphere gradually grew quiet and certainly less crowded as we moved away from the bars and began checking out the many merchants still open for business. Thankfully there was little hawking for our dollars. That was no doubt because it was the end of a long, and hopefully for them, profitable day.

We settled on some inexpensive souvenir and continued our slow, hand in hand walk. It was warm. It was quiet. It was peaceful. It was the calm before the storm.

Bon Voyage
Lust
Envy
Anger
Sloth
Gluttony
Greed
Pride
Debarkation

Thirty-four

Beth dropped me off at my room. She made sure that I took my pills before she tucked me into my bed.

I was not exactly sure why I was feeling so much better. I could attribute it to the champagne, the walk or the meds. My money however was riding on the ice cream. Dinner ended with a scoop of vanilla atop my apple pie. I swallowed my allotment of ibuprofen just the same. I devoured them more as a sleeping aid than anything else.

Beth didn't raise the getting into bed together issue or the would you like a back rub or any other kind of rub issue for that matter. It was fine by me. My powers of resistance were slightly suspect considering the bubbly and the medication. I was also thankful that there was no heavy machinery around that I was required to operate.

We didn't discover anything earth shattering about each other after the armistice was called by the Gambolinis. Or then again maybe we did. Maybe we learned that we could endure trial. Maybe we learned that together we were more resilient than we were alone. Maybe we learned that we didn't simply dwell on our troubles or try to overanalyze ways to resolve our dilemma but instead we were proactive in trying to overcome them. Maybe we learned that we couldn't simply dismiss the whole affair as just a bad dream or wish that it would go away but that we had to face our troubles as real. Maybe best of all we learned that we didn't have a desire to announce to the world: "Hey, everybody you need to watch *Oprah* or *Sixty Minutes* and see what happened to us!"

We also learned that we we're pretty good at taking care of each other. Beth was useful in a nurse sort of way and in a protecting sort of way. I guess I was pretty impressive at rising to her defense and standing up for her honor.

She leaned over me and kissed on the forehead.

"Good night," she purred.

"In case you had forgotten," I said, "It is my neck that hurts, as do my kidney and my guts. My lips are fine."

She smiled. I loved that smile. It was so natural. I gently grasped her face and pulled her toward me until our lips met. We both agreed that was a much better way to say, "Good night."

"I would lay down with you, fully dressed of course, but there isn't much room in your single bed."

"No there's not. So I guess that I'll see you in the morning then. Usual spot, usual time?"

"I'll be there."

"I hope I'll be."

Beth drew herself up and turned to leave. As she did an image passed through my head.

"Oh, Beth."

"Yes." She turned to face me.

"My room is designed for a single. I have this bed and a sofa. I seem to remember your room has a sofa and two single beds. Is that right?"

"Yes, I'm sharing the room with my sister. I know you'd never know it. She's only been there a couple of hours the whole trip. She likes to party and doesn't like to sleep alone if you know what I mean. She's not especially particular who she spends her time with and since her bed has been untouched, I suspect she has found somebody to spend her time with."

"Okay."

"Why do you ask?"

"No reason. Like I said, it was just a random thought that came into my mind."

It was one random thought that I was soon glad I had.

Thirty-five

The first day that I was on the ship I had signed up for a behind the scenes tour of the *Festival.* Captain Finelli graciously opens his ship to one such tour each cruise. It was limited to a dozen people, first come, first served.

It surprised me how easy it was to book the tour. Guest services took my money and insisted only that I dress properly. That meant having the right kind of shoes. Cameras and recording devices were prohibited.

If I were running a tour that included showing my guests sensitive areas on the ship, I would have insisted on finger prints, a DNA sample and an FBI background check. None of this appeared to have happened. But maybe somewhere in a deep, dark basement of company headquarters it did.

I will not bore you now with a slew of facts and figures that I learned on this fascinating tour. That delight will be saved for a more appropriate time.

Our guide did steer us everywhere from the bridge to the engine room. We were privy to the tiny crew quarters and to the massive storage rooms. The *Festival* and all of its sisters and cousins are more than floating hotels. They are small cities.

I wouldn't have guessed that the ship had built in sewage treatment and water purification facilities. I was under the false assumption that waste products were stored and then off loaded at various ports. Human waste along with food scraps are actually processed then chopped into tiny pieces and deposited in the water as fish food. United States as well as United Nation maritime regulations permit the dumping of biodegradable wastes into the ocean as long as the ship is so many miles from shore.

I also incorrectly assumed that drinkable water was pumped onto the ship while in port and then stored for use. That is partially true, but an average size cruise ship uses about a quarter million gallons of water a day so it is constantly refilling its storage tanks through a desalination process.

My assumptions were right on about the food. Enough provisions are stockpiled for the cruise's duration plus a few extra emergency days, four days is about normal. The edibles are stashed and inventoried throughout a number of holds, pantries, refrigerators and freezers. Care is taken to keep various meats segregated from each other.

In the bowels of the ship runs one long corridor wide and tall enough for forklifts to move freely and quickly from almost one end of the ship to the other. Along this corridor are located several bays to off load and on load pallets full of supplies as well as bins full of passengers' luggage. Goods are moved by crew members from the holds to the various places they are needed through the ship via a number of elevators, lifts and stairways in order to service the passengers above.

Even as the passengers are housed in differing levels of comfort and in different sized rooms, some with no views, some with ocean views, some with balconies and some as suites, so too the workers are treated to different grades of housing and service. The high ranking officers have their own mess and are served their meals. They also have private quarters. The lowest level of workers have their own mess and must gather their food from a buffet line. They usually cram four together in a tiny cabin; however there are rarely four in the room at the same time as their work schedule usually rotates between twelve hours on and twelve hours off, seven days a week.

There are several levels of cabin size and food service in between those two extremes for junior officers and ship staff and other workers. It is in these messes that waiters in training as well as cooks in training gain valuable experience before they are turned loose on passengers.

The *Festival* provided a recreation area for the crew. It amounted to a medium sized flat screen TV with some lounge chairs, a pool table and a Jacuzzi with no water in it.

The crew was allowed to go ashore when the *Festival* docked, provided they were not scheduled to be working. Most of those able to go ashore did so to take advantage of free Wi-Fi in order to contact family. The Festival did not provide that service to its workers or to its guests for that matter. People on a budget didn't use cell phones outside of the U.S. especially after they looked at their first bill following such a cell phone call or text message.

Each new door we passed through opened up new surprises. The electronics that operate the ship's engines and generators and that navigated the ship would have indeed put both Columbus and Magellan over the edge.

Driving, steering, guiding or whatever the Captain does to one of these monsters is in some ways easier than operating a car. He has a lofty perch that extends from one side of the ship to the other. From there he can supervise the docking depending on whether he docks port or starboard. The Captain doesn't normally steer the ship or set its course. He calls out the order to his Quartermaster who in turn plots the course or enters the command to move the ship forward, backward, sideways or in a circle. I'm sure there are nautical terms for each of those movements, but I don't remember them. If you really need to know them, you can Google a dictionary of nautical terms.

The Captain or his next-in-command is always on the bridge. When the ship is moving, in addition to other electronics experts watching over the progress, there is an officer scanning the water through binoculars or with his naked eyes. He/she is on the lookout for obstacles that are undetectable to the ship's radar.

What is really amazing is how these up to two hundred and twenty thousand ton behemoths can turn on a dime! Something to do with side thrusters. *More power to the thrusters, Scotty! . . . I'm given them all I got Captain!* In case you are interested, the world's largest aircraft carriers on the drawing board will displace less than half the weight of the largest cruise ships. The oil carrying super tankers however have the cruisers outweighed by over two times.

Thirty-six

The tour eventually found its way to security central. I immediately recognized the supervisor on duty. It was Sashi. I gave him a friendly nudge while our guide rambled on. Most of what she said was in recognizable English.

Sashi smiled. "Good morning, sir. It is good to see you again. Are you feeling well?"

"I'm feeling much better, thank you for asking Sashi. What are you doing here?"

"Today I have duty in this room. I am supervising all of the cameras around the ship. We can keep an eye on most everything that happens on the *Festival*. If we see something out of the ordinary, we immediately dispatch someone to address the situation."

There were dozens of monitors. Several crew members were scanning them according to some pre-established pattern. The screens showed stateroom hallways, dining areas, sun decks, the spa, the casino, the engine room, the kitchen, the children's areas, the pools, some crew areas, you name it;

a camera was likely on it. Every minute or so a monitor would flip to a different scene.

Sashi continued. "Everything is recorded and not just what you see on the screens. The recordings are kept for a period of time and if there are no issues the recordings are eventually erased."

"It seems like a very tedious job sitting here and watching this."

"Yes, it is for sure. But we are on a rotating schedule. I am here for a full shift once a week but the crew who actually watches the screens are here for a much shorter time. They leave for a while and do other jobs. Then they come back and observe some more."

"What kind of incidents do you see on the screens?"

"I am not at liberty to talk about such things. I am sorry."

"I understand. I shouldn't have asked." I studied the monitors before continuing with another question.

"Those are really good pictures for security cameras. Are they high definition?"

"I am not sure if they are high definition. They are just very good definition. We recently were given an upgrade to our security system. I think it is maybe a trial or pilot program in the fleet. The upgrade included state of the art cameras and recording equipment."

"How expensive was the upgrade?"

"I don't know anything about the cost."

I noticed that my tour group was preparing to move on to its next point of interest. I found myself staring at a monitor down a particular hallway that was captioned *Panorama stateroom/bow/port/57*.

I noticed the head of a man sticking out of one of the stateroom doors. He glanced up and down the hall as if looking for someone. He then came out of the room. He shut the door behind him. He took off a pair of what looked like latex gloves and stuffed them in his pants pocket. Then he straightened his tie and coat. What was he doing wearing a tie and coat on a cruise ship at eleven a.m.? He took one last look at the door and walked briskly down the hall right toward the camera.

There was no look of satisfaction on his face. It was all business. While he walked he kept turning his head in quick back and forth motions as if looking for someone or was afraid someone might be watching him. Before reaching the camera he turned around one time to check behind him. He appeared to be a fairly big man, maybe the size of my pal, Vito.

I looked to see if one of the monitor specialists had noticed what I noticed but if they had they didn't let on. It was business as usual.

"Excuse me Sashi, what staterooms do that camera on monitor twelve record?"

Sashi studied the monitor only briefly. "That would be Panorama Deck, the lower ten hundreds. I would have to check the deck plan for the exact room numbers."

That bit of research would not be necessary. The door that man came out of, the second door on the left side of Panorama Deck was Stateroom 1010. I needed to leave the tour immediately and find out what was going on. My memory was clear on this – Beth had told me she was probably going to spend the morning in her room.

Thirty-eight

It took me a while to convince the guide that I had to abort the remainder of the tour.

"This is highly irregular. There is no one to escort you out of the secure areas and back to the main lobby. Surely whatever you have to do can wait thirty more minutes."

Surely it couldn't. Fortunately Sashi was one of the sharper knives in the drawer and carried some authority. His previous experience with Beth and me put him immediately in my corner. It only helped my case when I told him about the suspicious looking man I saw coming out of her room.

"I will see to it that," Sashi took a quick glance at my temporary security and tour badge; "Mr. Meyerhoff is escorted safely from here back to his room."

That seemed to partially satisfy Dafne Panagakos. Her look told me that I had single handedly destroyed her perfect record of never having lost a member of a tour group. Any chance for her being named tour guide of the year had just been flushed down the toilet. I wanted to reassure her that it was not personal and that I would still give her all fives on her evaluation card, but I was in a hurry.

As soon as Sashi made arrangements for a substitute supervisor and we replayed the security recording for his benefit, we made a beeline for Panorama Deck 1010.

No one answered either our pounding on the door or our yelling.

Sashi inserted his master key. Part of me wanted to crash past him but the other part was afraid to move. Fear won this round.

Sashi went into the room as I hung in the doorway holding the door open. I could barely see past him but I could see just enough. There was a clothed someone sprawled on the bed, on top of the covers.

Sashi turned to me, pointed his finger and said, "Please, sir, wait right where you are."

"What is it? Is it Beth? Is she . . ."

"Please, just wait right there." He emphasized every word.

I turned away. I couldn't look. Tears filled my eyes. I leaned my head on my forearm against the door and prayed.

I heard Sashi speaking on his radio. He was calling for help. I didn't understand the codes he was using to describe the situation but they didn't sound like good codes. I heard no "Ten-four, good buddies."

When he clicked off he came over to where I was still standing. He looked grim. "I don't know how to say this. I can find no pulse. I can find no sign of life in her body."

He said her. It is Beth. Beth is dead. "What happened?" I rasped.

"That I do not know. I have not been trained in those things. I do not see any wounds. I do know that we must not touch anything. We must go out into the hallway and wait for the proper authorities."

"Is it Beth?"

"I do not know. It is a woman. She has dark hair. She is lying face down on the bed. There appears to have been some struggle that took place. That is all I know."

I was searching for the courage to do what I was about to ask.

"May I go in and at least see if it is her?"

"Please do not ask me for such a favor. If it were in my power to grant such a favor I would certainly do so, but I cannot allow it. I am sorry."

I wanted to argue. At least I think I wanted to argue. But it was a mute point as I looked up the hallway and saw that several men were walking quickly our way. The big guns had showed up and were taking over the crime scene.

One of higher caliber of the bunch looked very official and very US of A. He was wearing a dark blue suit.

Thirty-eight

I waited outside Beth's closed door for about a half an hour. Blue suit came out with Sashi. He introduced himself as Agent Lewis Bender, FBI. I was impressed. I had never met an FBI man this up close and personal before. He was about my size. I guessed him to be about ten to fifteen years younger than me. He was still a kid.

He looked at his notes, then at me and then at the tour badge that I was still wearing. "You are Jonathan Meyerhoff?"

"Yes."

"We obviously have a situation here. I understand that you were first on the scene."

"I arrived here with Sashi." I pointed with my head at the security man. "He went into the room. I never ventured past the doorway."

"Uh-huh. And what was your interest in coming to this room?"

"I suspected that something had happened here and I convinced Sashi to come with me and have a look."

"How do you know the possible victim?"

I swallowed hard, victim? Is that all she was, a victim? "I met her the first morning of the cruise."

"Would you say that you know the victim fairly well?"

"Yes. We have seen each other almost non-stop since we met."

Agent Bender was working his jaw slightly. "I hesitate to ask you this, Mr. Meyerhoff. It would help speed the investigation along if you would be able to positively identify the body for us. Do you think you could do that?"

I now knew the purpose of his introductory salvo. He might have been simply confirming Sashi's story. More than likely though he was searching for answers to two questions – Was I qualified enough to make the ID and did I have guts enough to make the ID? I wasn't sure that I could pass muster for either, but like Agent Bender I had to know who it was, I had to know whether or not it was Beth.

Bender, Sashi and I walked into the room together. The FBI man chased the others out. We stood over the body. It was still on the bed. It was now covered with a sheet.

Bender spoke softly. "I know this is hard. Take your time. Do the best you can. That's all I ask."

I took a deep breath and released it, then nodded my approval.

"I am going to pull the sheet back. Take your time."

It looked like Beth and yet it didn't look like Beth. Death changes a person's appearance. It drains their natural color. It also drains their glow, if they had a glow about them before death took it away. Beth was one who glowed. Death drains other things too but that's a more metaphysical type discussion for another time, another place.

I have seen many dead bodies over the course of my life. I have watched many people die. I have watched members of my own family die. I have watched virtual strangers die. I have watched beloved people from my congregations die. I have watched people die quickly. I have watched them die slowly. I have watched them die after suffering long and hard. I have watched them die easily after living long and full lives. I am familiar with death, but that doesn't mean that I am comfortable with death or that I like death.

Death is the worst enemy we humans face. It smashes dreams. It interrupts plans. It puts an end to everything we value. Yes, it does resolve the issue of pain and suffering for the one it claims, but that's not much of a blessing in the greater picture that death paints.

Death strikes suddenly and unexpectedly. It can strike any organ in your body or any system of the body. It strikes in the womb. It strikes the newborn. It strikes the young. It strikes those with potential. It strikes those with great responsibility. It strikes the productive. It strikes those past their prime. It strikes the rich and the poor. It strikes the healthy and the unhealthy. It strikes the strong and the weak. It strikes the high and low. It strikes the famous and the infamous.

It strikes mostly when we don't expect it to strike. Even when we think we are prepared for its arrival, it still sneaks up on us. Sometimes it strikes violently. Sometimes it strikes silently. Sometimes it strikes because of stupidity. Sometimes it strikes when we're doing the right thing. Sometimes it strikes when all we are is the innocent bystander. But however it strikes and whenever it strikes, it leaves behind sadness, loneliness, emptiness, regret, despair and usually anger. And when it's done with its victim, death laughs at its triumph and at every tear that is shed by those who mourn!

I have been very fortunate in my encounters with death. I have never witnessed someone dying violently. I can't imagine and I don't want to imagine the horror of dying by drowning or dying at the hands of a rapist or a torturer. Yet lying before me was someone who did die in that way. This body was treated violently. Maybe my trouble identifying this woman was due in part to my refusal to believe that Beth could have died so horribly.

Most people that I have seen in those first moments after death are at peace. In most cases, I would have had the opportunity in the preceding days or moments to pray with them or read a comforting scripture to them or sing a familiar hymn for them or perhaps even converse with them about dying and about the hope that they believed someone named Jesus brings to the death bed.

As I would look into their eyes I would see a calm, a peace, an end to suffering and an end to the battle to try and stay alive. For them there were no more good-byes to be said. There was no more need to exchange an "I love you." It was time to depart in peace. It was time to leave this veil of tears.

This was not the case for the body in front of me. This corpse was not at peace. To me it wasn't Beth. It wasn't any-body. It was just a shell.

Yet it was somebody. It was somebody who had died violently. It was somebody who had died prematurely at the hands of an evil person. Why had she died? Was it because of lust, envy, jealousy, pride, greed, anger, power, vengeance? Which of those had done this to her? Who had done this to her? That was Lewis Bender's domain. I hoped he was good at his job.

Laying there was somebody and because she lay there, another somebody needed to pay for ending this somebody's life. It was up to me to identify who this dead somebody was and help jump start the process for nailing that other angry, criminal somebody.

Thirty-nine

"I'm not sure it's Beth." I muttered as apologetically as I could mutter. "I'm not sure it isn't Beth either. It looks kind of like her, but not exactly. Her clothes are throwing me off too. This is not what she was wearing when I left her this morning. I'm sorry."

"That's okay. A lot of people have trouble with this sort of thing. Bodies sometimes look different after . . . you know."

I nodded in agreement.

"How about any distinguishing marks that you might have noticed. Tattoos, scars from surgeries, piercings, things like that."

"No, nothing that was obvious on Beth or on this body."

There was silence in the room. Agent Bender was thinking about his next course of action. That's when I noticed the other bed.

"Beth had a roommate," I said, a glimmer of hope in my voice.

Bender looked up from his notepad. "What? A roommate?" He looked as Sashi who shrugged and punched in some numbers on his communicator.

"Yes. This is Sashi Squatchma with security. I need for you to check the guest registry. Panorama 1010, please. I will hold."

We all waited in silence.

"Thank you." He belted his device. "There are two guests registered in this room. Mary, who is our Beth, and an Anne Malone."

"Who is Anne Malone?" Bender asked.

I jumped in. "She is Beth's sister. I met her a couple of times. They look a lot alike. That could be why I'm confused on the ID. This could be her." *I hope it is her and not Beth. No, no, what am I saying, I don't. It might be better for me but it will be far worse for Genette and Susana.*

I continued. "Maybe we could page Beth. If she's alive then she can identify her sister."

"All right," Bender said. "That might be worth a try. What's her full name?"

"Mary Elizabeth, ah, I'm not sure."

"You're not sure of much are you Mr. Meyerhoff."

"Well, let me explain. She's a widow but I don't know if she's still using her married name, Gambolini, or if she has gone back to her maiden name."

"Did you say Gambolini?"

"Yes sir."

"She wouldn't happen to be part of the infamous Gambolini family?"

"Yes. She was married to Tony Gambolini who was killed about ten years ago."

"Mary Elizabeth Gambolini? My, oh, my, isn't this getting more interesting by the moment." He paused and wiped his lower face with his hand. "If she goes by that name, I don't think we should try to page her."

"Why not?"

"Trust me on this one."

"But if that's her sister, wouldn't it be the smart thing to have her identify the body?"

"Mr. Meyerhoff. I'm not as dumb as I might appear."

A customer was about to leave the barbershop when the owner spotted a kid walking by the open door, "Hey kid, come here." He turned to the customer. "Watch this. You are about to see the dumbest kid in the neighborhood." The barber put fifty cents in one hand and a dollar bill in the other. He closed both hands and told the boy to pick the one he wanted. The kid chose the one with the fifty cents. Then he took the money and left the shop. "Didn't I tell you he was dumb?" The barber laughed. The customer left the shop and spotted the boy in another store buying candy. He walked up to him and said,

"Why did you take the fifty cents and not the dollar?" The kid replied, "If I would have taken the dollar, the game would be over."

"Sir, I did not mean to imply that you were dumb. I'm sorry. Do you know Ms. Gambolini?"

"No, I don't. I probably shouldn't tell you this but it is fairly common knowledge. The Gambolini family has been under federal investigation for years. Every once in a while I get assigned to some aspect of the case." He turned to Sashi. "We need to find out Beth's traveling name. Could you check into that for me?"

"No need sir. It is also Malone."

I said. "Beth Malone could be an innocent enough name to page."

Bender replied, "Yes, provided Anne Malone was the target. However if they offed the wrong Ms. Malone then that puts your Ms. Malone potentially still on their hit list."

My head and my heart were swimming in circles. Why would anyone want to hurt Beth? Then again why had they wanted to hurt me for being with her?

Forty

We still needed to find Beth or Anne. I had another of those random thoughts flash through my mind. "The security camera! Wouldn't the camera outside this room tell us who came and went all morning?" I looked at Sashi. He looked at Bender. Sashi spoke.

"If you want we can review the recordings right now. One of my people is already studying the record and noting the times there was some activity outside this room."

Special Agent Bender passed out assignments then turned and headed for security central.

"Can I come along?" I asked.

"I don't think that would be a good idea."

"I would be able to identify the living Beth and Anne or any other family members that might have gone into the room."

Special Agent Bender moved his jaw. He would not be a good poker player. Uncertainty was all over his face as he hunted a decision.

"All, right. Let's go." He turned to the man standing guard at the door. "Call me immediately if anyone shows up."

Forty-one

The camera recorded Beth entering the room at 9:03 a.m. My heart doubled its beat and not for the usual reason when I saw her. Housekeeping knocked at 9:40 a.m. She let them in. Beth left at 9:42 a.m. My heart returned to normal. Housekeeping was in and out of the room several times and left for good at 10:17 a.m.

At 10:46 a.m., Anne entered. At 10:51 a.m., a large man appeared in the hallway. He was wearing a suit. He looked around several times, pulled two latex gloves out of his jacket pocket and slipped them on. He knocked on the door continuing to look back up the hallway. A brief moment later he rushed into the room hands first.

"Do you know who he is?" I asked.

The fed said nothing. I stared with him at the screen as we watched what surely was the killer exit the room. It was the same scene that I had viewed live nearly two hours earlier. The next to appear on the screen were Sashi and me.

"I think it's time we had a talk," I said.

162

Special Agent Bender listened intently to the story of my encounter with Vinnie, Vito and Frankie. Occasionally he would work his jaw and purse his lips. He was trying to get two and two to add up to four, but it didn't seem to be working out for him.

Sashi interrupted our conversation by handing Bender two pictures and a couple of pages of printouts. "We have been searching through the record of every passenger as they boarded and checked onto the ship. So far we have located these two men. They checked in together. I hope you do not mind that I took the liberty of authorizing this procedure." Sashi was not looking for praise. He was only doing his job. He continued. "As you can see the one in this picture closely resembles the man who was in Room1010."

The agent glanced at the print from the hallway camera outside Stateroom 1010 and compared it to the one Sashi had just handed him from the atrium camera.

Sashi continued. "His name is Emilio Raggali. The information that we have on him including his stateroom number is on this paper. The man who checked in with him is Lorenza Fiorenzo."

"Excellent work, Sashi, but would you keep searching for anyone else who might match the description of the man we're looking for?"

"That is my intention. I will bring you any more matches that I find as soon as we are finished with our search." Sashi turned and left us alone.

"You don't think that this Emeril guy is the one who did it, do you?" I asked.

"It's Emilio, and no I don't."

"Why not," I questioned studying both pictures. "They look almost identical to me. Same size, same build, same suit, same ugly mug."

"The bum in this photo, the one who roughed you up, he's Italian. The slime in this one, the one who offed Ms. Malone, is Russian."

"How can you be so sure?"

"That's why they pay me the big bucks." Bender smiled for the first time. It almost made him likeable.

Forty-two

Sashi produced the pictures and documents that verified Bender's claim. Two Russians boarded together, an Alexi Cherenkov and a Svetlana Zabbarova. Bender jawed and pursed, pursed and jawed as he scanned the papers, until I heard a just barely audible, "Alexi, Alexi what have you done?"

I decided it was time to address something that had been bothering me. "You knew who that guy was the first time you saw him on the recording, didn't you?" This was not a question as much as it was an accusation.

Lou looked up from the documents that he was still studying intently. "Huh? What did you say?"

"You heard me. You knew that it was Boris Badenov in that hallway all along."

"Yeah, I did."

That answer got someone who didn't usually get riled, a bit riled. "My goodness man, if you knew . . ."

"Wait. It's not what you're thinking." His whole face was working. Bender took a deep breath and let it out slowly. "I know that you are a reverend. You are bound by a confidentiality code of conduct, correct?"

I nodded, but very subtly.

"What I tell you in confidence you can't repeat or God will send you to hell or something like that, right?"

"Or even worse," I semi-joked.

"All right, here's the short version. My partner and I followed the Russians onto the ship. We had it on good authority that they were going to meet up with a drug cartel while in one of the ports that the ship is visiting. Apparently one of their brighter bulbs concluded that this low profile approach to the drug business would go undetected by our surveillance."

"So how does Beth or Anne tie into that?"

"I don't know. This murder comes totally out of left field. I can't see how it's related to my case, but now I have to treat it as if it does. Neither woman was a person of interest to us. Neither was a person-of-interest to the Russians as far as we know. If there is a link then it's probably tied to the family drug business somehow. The Gambolinis are into drug trafficking and so are the Russians. I don't know enough about both cases to say anything for certain, but I am saying that if both families are serving some of the same clientele, and I think they are, then we have the potential for some less than neighborly behavior."

"You're saying Beth is some big wheel in the family drug business and that the Russians are trying to eliminate her so they can take over the Gambolini territory?"

"It sounds crazy I know."

"You're wrong about Beth."

"I hope so, but at this point understand that I'm throwing every possible theory at the wall and seeing what sticks. Unless this murder is just some arbitrary act of violence, then there is likely a Gambolini link. In my thinking Beth is the more likely tie-in because Anne has no connection to the family at all that we are aware of. And if Beth is involved, then Alexi mistakenly targeted the wrong woman. If he meant to kill Beth then obviously she is still in danger. I admit this is all weak speculation unless of course your Ms. Gambolini or this Anne Malone are very different people than they appear to be."

I really didn't want to hear any of this. No, that's not quite true. I didn't want to hear Bender defaming Beth in this way. I consider myself a fairly good judge of character and she did not strike me as being a disingenuous person. Speaking of Beth, where was she? I had another thought, a different direction in which to steer Bender.

"Beth told me that her sister liked to pick up men and that she wasn't all that particular about the type of men that she reeled in. I'm thinking she snagged this guy, Alexi. He got a little too rough for her or he couldn't perform for her and so she dumped him for a better model. His pride couldn't handle the rejection and being the violent, angry sort and being somebody who always got his way, he got too rough with her and killed her." I sat back in my chair having planted a look of satisfaction on my face.

Bender studied the glob I had thrown at his wall. "You could be right. It could be that simple. Criminals usually see things that way, very simply, very black and white. They deal in the universe of good and bad. It's a different universe than yours and mine. Ours is governed by some absolutes and by some principles that consider the well-being of others and the common good. The criminal thinks purely from selfishness. He believes that if something is good for him, then it's right and if it's bad for him, then it's wrong. If the criminal mind decides that it needs money then it's not wrong for him to steal it. If the criminal mind thinks that someone is an obstacle to what he needs to do then it is not wrong for him to remove the obstacle. Life is very simple.

"Law enforcement on the other hand is complex. We have to build a case to put the criminal away – piece by piece by piece. We need motive. We need opportunity. We need evidence. We need to follow all sorts of protocols and hope we don't violate any rights along the way."

I chimed in. "Is that why you let Sashi continue his searching through the recordings even though you knew who did it all along?"

"Yep, build the case piece by piece. Gather the evidence."

"Speaking of evidence, something else has been bothering me since I saw Alexi leave that room. He had to know that there were security cameras watching him, yet he made no effort to shield himself."

"My guess is he didn't know that there was a camera on him or he would have mugged for it. He is one arrogant SOB. He believes that he's above the law. Even worse he believes that even if he's caught he won't be convicted. He knows that all we'll have on him will be circumstantial evidence. We won't be able to produce a witness or fingerprints or a weapon. Even the recording is useless. A good lawyer would contend that it was prejudicially doctored. He knows that even if his defense attorney had an IQ of seventy, his handlers would get to the jury and insure that it was hung."

A defendant in a lawsuit involving large sums of money was talking to his lawyer. "If I lose this case, I'll be ruined."

"It's in the judge's hands now," said the lawyer.

"Would it help if I sent the judge a box of cigars?" the defendant suggested.

"Oh no! This judge is a stickler on ethical behavior. A stunt like that would prejudice him against you. He might even hold

you in contempt of court. In fact, you shouldn't even smile at the judge."

Within the course of time, the judge rendered a decision in favor of the defendant. As the defendant left the courthouse, he said to his lawyer, "Thanks for the tip about the cigars. It worked!"

His lawyer responded. "I'm sure we would have lost the case if you'd sent them."

"But I did send them." the man said.

"What? You did?" his lawyer replied.

"Yes. That's how we won the case."

"I don't understand," said the lawyer.

"It's easy. I sent the cigars to the judge, but enclosed the plaintiff's business card."

Bender's communicator buzzed. He listened, shut it down and turned to me. "Beth showed up."

Forty-three

Beth was madder than a wet hen after an April thunderstorm. That picture may not do much for you unless you've encountered such a bird. Maybe fit to be tied is a description more to your liking. Beth was in a fit, but no one was brave enough to apply the ropes. The woman renewed her scorn as she saw Bender and I approach her stateroom.

"What is going on here? Why won't this moron let me into my room? And where have you been, I've been looking all over for you?" She looked at Agent Bender. "And who are you?" This was a whole new side to the woman. I was discovering that she had some spunk to her.

I reached out to hug her and perhaps bring her some calm but she wasn't interested in calm. Her interest resided in answers.

Bender introduced himself and his partner, Michael Andrews. Andrews was ready for a trip to the soft serve station, or maybe an upgrade to a gin and tonic, hold the tonic. Lou calmly began filling her in on the day's developments.

I stood near Beth. I was readying myself for that moment when her own strength would fail her and she would need someone else to lean on. Right on schedule she collapsed against me in tears.

The first wave of grief didn't last long.

"You're not absolutely sure that it is Anne, are you?"

"No, not yet," I answered for the agent, but it was not an answer filled with much hope.

Lou spoke up. On our walk from security central we had decided to go more informal with our names. "If you are up to it ma'am, we would like you to try and identify the body. We want to be sure."

"Okay."

Beth did what I was unable to do and then bravely volunteered to break the bad news to Genette and Susana. She was behaving like I observe many women behave in times like these. She had told herself and was communicating to anyone with eyes, "Mary Elizabeth, you need to be strong because others need you to be strong right now. You will have time later to weep and mourn."

"I'll go with you when you tell Genette and Susana," I offered.

"That's not necessary."

"I know it's not, but I'd like to, just the same, if you want me to."

"Okay."

We left to find Genette. Lou, Mike and the *Festival* medical personnel stayed behind. They were responsible for cleanup and transporting the body to the ship's morgue. I wondered how they would move the body without attracting the attention of passengers. Maybe they would wait and move it during the wee hours of the morning.

Cruise lines don't like negative publicity. Airlines don't either. Neither do hotels. Come to think of it, no business does. How would they keep this quiet? What spin would they put on it? Certainly a story had already been devised to placate those who had begun wondering and speculating about all the attention being shown to the room down the hall from their staterooms.

Beth's and my problem was as formidable as the *Festival's*. We had to find Genette and tell her that Susana no longer had a grandmother.

Forty-four

Genette reacted in a way very similar to the way the majority of women react when death intersects with their lives. She went berserk and ballistic. She screamed. She pounded. She wept. She stomped around the room. She blamed everyone she could think of including God and herself. Eventually she ran out of rant when her anger was temporarily diffused. She sat down with her head in her hands crying softly. "What am I going to do?"

"You have to tell Susana." Good for you Beth. Give her responsibility, but be gentle.

"I can't. It will kill her. She loved her gramma."

"She'll be okay, Genette. She's a strong girl. I'll go with you."

"I can't do it."

"Yes you can. You have to. She has to be told."

"Then you do it," Genette bristled.

"You are her mother," Beth countered with more bristle.

"Genette." I stepped in and put the brakes on a conversation that was quickly escalating out of control. "I know you don't feel like talking to her right now. That's okay. You don't have to go right this minute. You have just received a terrible shock. You need to take some time. You need to collect your thoughts. There's no hurry."

Genette nodded, her face still in her hands.

When her heavy sobs and breaths mostly subsided, I continued with a question that I had been debating in my mind for several minutes. Lou might not be happy with me, but he'd have to get over it. "I need to ask you something very important, Genette. Was your mother seeing anyone in particular on this ship in the last day or two?"

Genette didn't look up. I couldn't tell if she heard me or if she was thinking about my question. Beth did look up at me. Her wide open eyes indicated that she could do the math.

"Not that I know of. She had hooked up with a couple of different men, I guess, but none that she talked about with me."

"Were there any that she said she had any kind of trouble with?"

"No. My mother isn't like that. She likes to have fun but she's always very careful." That's what they all say and believe.

"Did she come on board the ship with anyone or has she had a bad breakup with someone recently?"

"No."

I wished that I had Alexi's photo to show her, but I was confident that she would see it eventually. It would be sooner, rather than later.

Forty-five

Paging, Mr. Jonathon Meyerhoff. Please pick up the nearest courtesy phone and dial 7777. Oh, no, this better not be what I think it is?

I found a phone and followed the instructions. "Meyerhoff, speaking."

"I am sorry to bother you sir, but could you please come immediately to guest services. There is someone from the medical staff who needs to speak with you."

I excused myself and left Genette in Beth's capable hands. We discussed a couple of scenarios for meeting after I had taken care of this piece of ship's business. There's a saying that crises always happen in three's. There was my attack, Anne's death and now whatever this page was about.

A female nurse from Sumatra whose name I couldn't pronounce met me at guest services. She led me down several decks to the infirmary. I was now officially off vacation. Sorry Scooter.

As a clergyman I had on previous cruises offered my services as a kind of chaplain in residence, should individuals request someone of my skill set. Thinking that I would have plenty of available time on this cruise I made my availability to help with certain spiritual crises known to the purser after I boarded the *Festival.*

By crisis I don't mean two people who suddenly fall in love and want to get married. By crisis I don't mean conducting some burial at sea. By crisis I usually mean two people that have fallen out of favor with each other for various reasons or who have injured their relationship and can't stop the bleeding but want some immediate help in trying. The hurts are mostly caused by alcohol, gambling, flirting or some unresolved issue that the cruise was suppose to miraculously or magically fix.

This crisis lay on a bed in the infirmary. As I approached her I guessed that her age was in the mid-thirties. She probably was attractive except that she had been through the proverbial mill. She looked tired and worn. Some of her skin was covered with bandages and contusions that were beginning to color up. Chances were good that she was a faithful church going-woman of some denominational persuasion or she would not have sent for a preacher.

I introduced myself and began innocently. "How are you feeling?"

Abuse laws in the United States are rather specific. On the high seas and in various international waters they are a bit more nebulous. Laws or no laws the strong feel compelled to take advantage of the weak. Those with muscle like to bully and bruise those they believe have lesser muscle.

I haven't been everywhere in the world, but I've studied a lot of history. I've studied most every culture. I stay somewhat current with the behavioral and social sciences and I watch some local, national and world news. I would conclude from that potpourri of educational experience, that pretty much every where a person travels in this world he will observe people expressing anger in inappropriately violent ways toward others. Much, perhaps most of that violence, is directed toward family and those sharing "close" relationships.

Anger in itself isn't evil. Much good has been accomplished because anger has motivated people to fight for just and noble causes, to throw off oppression and tyranny, to correct abuses, and to change what would be considered deplorable life situations. The Bible does says, "In your anger do not sin: Do not let the sun go down while you are still angry" (Ephesians 4:26). Simply let me suggest that this means in part that we are not to use anger in a self-serving way and we are not to let it fester or accumulate inside of us.

Perhaps the easiest way to tell if anger is being expressed inappropriately or as we would say from a theological perspective, in a sinful way, is if it hurts or harms someone or something.

Anger can be directed inwardly or outwardly. When people direct anger inwardly they will either beat themselves up, i.e. self-flagellation or self-deprecation, or they will beat themselves down, i.e. depression or guilt. When people direct anger outwardly they will beat each other up or down with words, looks, fists, sticks, stones and all manner of blunt and sharp instruments.

Again, it can be said that anger has spurred many people to correct all manner of abuses that they believe exist around them, but when you abuse someone in an attempt to correct what you consider to be an abuse, have you really gained anything of value?

The woman before me was more than likely someone whom someone else felt needed some improvements made to her life. And rather than coach her or encourage her or take her by the hand and show her how to improve, he decided to correct her through brute force.

Figuring out why he and so many other people have a need for such violence may be a helpful exercise in ultimately rewiring that troubled person's psyche, but that lengthy process wasn't going to help this poor woman right now.

Unfortunately, in the time it took me to reach the infirmary, the woman had a change in heart. She decided that it would be better for her not to rat out the weasel. I could get nowhere with her. She would not talk about the obvious truth of what had happened to her. This woman was in a bad way. She had convinced herself that what had happened to her was all her fault. If she would only treat her man better then he would behave better. If he didn't have such a hard life, if only he'd get a break, then everything would be better. She just needed to pray harder and everything would work itself out.

I shook my head in disgust at her warped view of marriage and her even more warped view of God and prayer. I have asked myself often where people get some of their ideas about God and why they pray prayers something like – *Dear God; give me the grace to ignore whatever evil comes my way. Turn me into a limp noodle and whipping post and help me live long enough until all my problems go away. Amen.* That's not the God I know and serve. He rather says something like – "Stand in my strength, my grace and my love against the powers and darkness of this evil age, using not the weapons of the world but put on my armor and use the weapons of my kingdom and my spirit."

I wasn't very compassionate with her. Her life was based mostly on lies that she believed about herself and her role as a wife and mother. I challenged every one of them as gently but as convincingly as I could. But once a person constructs a pile of manure to live on they become accustomed to the smell and do not easily want to abandon the soft warmth that it provides.

When I learned that she had a young son and daughter, I wanted to scream, but instead spoke calmly. "Do you know what you are doing to them? Someday your daughter will marry a man just like your husband. And someday your son will treat his wife just like your husband treats you. In fact, I bet your father, if he's still alive, treated your mother the same way you are being treated." Her refusal to look me in the eye told me I was right.

I felt horrible for being so blunt with her and I apologized to her. I had challenged her in this way for two main reasons. One was that I would probably never see her again, so I wanted to do everything I could to reach her in the time that I had. Secondly, there is simply too much of this behavior going on in homes and families today and it has to stop. I don't know if it's any worse now than it was in generations past or if it just seems that way. All I know is that with each new case I become more and more angry, both at the behavior I observe and my own inability to try and change the behavior.

Why do people bring children into this world and then abuse them, yell at them, ignore them, demean them, mislead them and even abandon them? Why do women seek out and cling to worthless, domineering and abusive men? Why do men seek out clingy, helpless, susceptible women?

Unfortunately, I know the answer. It's what gives a guy like me job security. But in all honestly, I would rather be unemployed.

I offered the woman what comfort I could. I prayed for her and her situation and told her that I could be reached twenty-four/seven for the duration of the cruise. I encouraged her to talk to her pastor and social services when she returned home. I had my fill of anger for one day. I looked at my watch, almost time for dinner. A hot shower wouldn't begin to scrub off the filth that now enveloped my body and soul.

Bon Voyage
Lust
Envy/Jealousy
Anger
Sloth
Gluttony
Greed
Pride
Debarkation

Forty-six

I didn't expect Beth to be much of a dinner companion and she wasn't. It had taken most of my best arguments to convince her to join me. Often my most effective mode of persuasion involves guilt. This is no doubt a method used by the majority of people to win over the dubious. While effective, it is the lazy way to argue. I admit that while I use guilt, I endeavor to avoid it except as a last resort. I fortunately did not have to apply that deceptive reasoning on her. Beth bought the suggestion that we could both use a quiet evening alone.

Before venturing up to the *Mardi Gras* room, we had both talked through the content of our afternoons. Susana had taken the news about her grandmother quite well. Beth said that she hung her head for a moment and blinked back a few tears before perking up and asking if it were okay to return to her friends.

"Did her reaction surprise you?" I asked.

"Well ye . . . no, not really. Susana is a free spirit. You've seen her enough to know that. I mean, she loves her mother and grandmother and they love her, but I don't think she really has a sense of family or is close to them. I can't say that I blame her. She's never had any consistent care other than nannies and over the years she has probably had a couple of dozen of them. Most of them have been young inexperienced students.

"So she isn't loved and doesn't know how to love," I offered.

Beth bristled. "Of course she is loved. She is given most everything she wants. She has a nice home. She's being sent to a good private school. Her mom does the best she can and my sister is . . . was there for her a lot and I . . . ah . . . I have done what I could for her."

"That's not love that you're describing Beth and you know it. Giving a child what she wants, doing the best you can, caring for a child only when it's convenient, that's not love, that's not parenting, that's not building a family, that's being lazy." I wanted to say negligent but that would have been cruel in this situation.

From the look on Beth's face I feared that I had blown our dinner date. Instead she hung her head and spoke.

"You're right. I'm only kidding myself. I gave my sister and niece a similar lecture many times before and they told me to mind my own business. So I pretty much have. That's not to say that my kids are perfect. I made mistakes with them. I just don't want to see others especially those in my own family make the same mistakes I did."

"Join the club. Parenting is the most important work anyone of us can do. It is also the most difficult work that we can do. Kids don't raise themselves, but too often we think they can and should. Yet it never ceases to amaze me how some children can survive the most horrible of situations and how others seem to become lost in spite of growing up in the most nurturing of environments. Parenting is not an exact science. I suppose the best any of us can do is to be lovingly consistent, not to become discouraged and to realize that our time with them will bring us the greatest of life's joys along with the greatest of life's heartaches."

Forty-seven

Marta stopped by our table within moments after we settled into our seats. She offered her condolences and any other help that she might be able to provide. As one of the ship's officers, she apparently was privy to whatever spin was in place. I asked her if our waiters were aware of the situation. She assured me that they had not been informed. I asked her to maintain that status.

I returned the conversation to Beth's niece. "How is Genette doing?"

"She is resting. The ship's doctor prescribed a sleeping aid."

"You said before that nannies have done most of the parenting for Susana. Is there no father around?"

"No. Susana was conceived during one of the more promiscuous times in Genette's life. She has never admitted who the father was. I'm not sure she knows and I'm not sure she even cares."

"Is there a father figure around now?"

"No. Genette has never been married. She's had a number of temporary live ins. None of them lasted very long. My sister has been married several times. Each of those relationships ended badly and none of those men took much of an interest in Genette or Susana when they were a part of the family. As far as I know they haven't come around since they moved on with their lives."

I was becoming sadder by the moment. Here was yet another product of child abuse. She was not being victimized by anger but by careless, clueless, lazy maybe even callous parents and adults. This abuse brought on by negligence and abandonment may not be worse than that fostered by anger but this lack of commitment to be responsible is just as deadly. "How does Genette support herself and a nanny?"

"I'm not sure. She's never worked. I don't think she receives any child support. Certainly government welfare wouldn't be paying that well. My guess is that Anne has been footing the bill."

"Okay, then where does Anne get that kind of money, not just for Genette's lifestyle but for her own?"

"I don't know that either. If I had to guess I would say from her divorce settlements. She's had three."

Ralph was driving home one evening and realized that it was his daughter's birthday and he hadn't bought her a present. He drove to the mall and ran to the toy store and he *asked the store manager, "How much is that new Barbie in the window?" The Manager replied, "Which one? We have Barbie goes to the gym for $19.95, Barbie goes to the Ball for $19.95, Barbie goes shopping for $19.95, Barbie goes to the beach for $19.95, Barbie goes to the Nightclub for $19.95, and Divorced Barbie for $375.00." "Why is the Divorced Barbie $375.00 when all the others are $19.95?!?" Ralph asked surprised. The Manager replied, "Well, Divorced Barbie comes with Ken's car, Ken's House, Ken's boat, Ken's dog, Ken's cat and Ken's furniture."*

Maybe there was enough money to support all of them comfortably. But this situation as Beth understood it caused me to think about another issue that I have trouble getting my head around – How do people who have no apparent source of income and who don't appear to come from wealth still manage to live higher on the hog than I do and people like me who work hard do? How come those of us who bust our butts and squeeze every nickel can barely make ends meet while others who seem to muddle along have giant screen televisions or drive brand new SUVs or go out to dinner several times a week?

"Can I join you?" It was Lou Bender. Beth sighed, gave me that "I told you we wouldn't be able to spend an evening alone" look and offered a barely discernable shake of her head "no."

"This would not be a good time, Lou," I mumbled.

"It's never a good time for loveable Lou Bender." He pulled up a chair and sat down. As he did the lights in the dining room blinked on and off several times. Lou noticed but didn't say anything. I smiled inside. I knew what was coming. I knew this conversation would be short.

Lou looked back and forth between us and then settled on Beth. "I haven't been able to locate your niece. Do either of you know where she might be?"

Beth spoke first. "The doctor gave her a sedative. She's asleep in her room." He worked his jaw.

"What do you need to know, Lou?" I asked.

"I've got some questions to ask her."

Oh, oh. I spoke cautiously. "Maybe I can save you the trouble." Lou studied me as I continued. "I may have over-stepped my bounds but I asked Genette if she was aware of anyone her mother was involved with on the ship. I also asked if she had come aboard with anyone or if she had recently had an unpleasant breakup with someone."

"You did." There was a hint of accusation in Lou's response.

"Yes."

"And . . ." Now there was more than a hint of impatience.

"And she said that to her knowledge her mom hadn't."

"And then I suppose you invited Alexi up to the room and gave him the opportunity to confess that he murdered her mother?"

"As a matter of fact, I did." I said, hoping to match his sarcasm. "His signed confession is on the commode in my room. Now if there's nothing else we're in the middle of dinner." My tone was polite and respectful.

"Thank you very much James Bond. It's a wonder I ever clear any cases with guys like you mucking up the works."

"I'm sorry Lou. It seemed like the right thing to do at the time."

Before he could respond the ceiling lights flickered on and off again followed by Marta's voice filling the room. I was momentarily rescued from a well deserved tongue lashing. Marta introduced her wait staff who then attempted to entertain their guests with an energetic and amusing but less than Emmy award winning rendition of *Amore.* About halfway through the song and dance number, Bender tapped my shoulder, stood up and said, "We need to talk later" and left.

Forty-eight

B eth decided to move in with her niece for the time being. Her own room remained a crime scene and she wasn't all that thrilled sleeping someplace where a murder had just taken place. Before dropping her there for the night, we decided to stroll about the star drenched decks. We walked until we found an isolated and quiet spot.

"You need to talk about your sister."

"I'm okay, really."

"Beth, your sister was killed today. You had to identify her body. No one admires your strength more than I do. But you've only shed a few tears since it happened."

She looked out toward the growing blackness of the sea, staring at nothing in particular. I decided to fill the silence.

"When I first saw that man leave your room this morning, I was scared. I was scared that I would find you in that room. I was more scared at that moment than I was when I thought that mafia thug was going to squeeze me to death. I knew deep down in my gut that you were dead. And when I saw that lifeless body on your bed, I cried. I cried for you, but mostly I cried for me. I cried selfish tears. I cried because I thought that I had lost you. I cried over someone I hardly even knew. But I had to cry. I had to let my pain and my fear out. I had to let go.

"And here you are having lost a sister, having lost someone you have shared life with for nearly fifty years. It's not only okay to cry, it's necessary to cry. You have to let go."

Beth turned to face me. Her eyes were misty. "I can't let go. I have to fix it. I have to make things better."

"Fix what? Make what better?"

Tears were now running down her cheeks. "You don't get it do you? Genette is worthless as a mother and Susana . . . poor, sweet Susana, she is so messed up. I didn't tell you what she really said. It was pathetic. 'Oh, gramma's dead? Couldn't you have waited to tell me until after kid's camp was over?' She was more upset over being taken away from her friends than over her own grandmother being gone! She could have cared less. And she got that attitude from her mother and I dare say from my sister. For both of them the world revolves around them. They use people and collect things. They won't work for anything. They expect the world to attend to their needs. I thought that I could keep Susana from that same kind of life and help her find a different path but so far I've failed. I've got to find a way to reach her, to help her, to change her before it's too late, if it's not already too late." She broke down in heavy sobs and fell into my arms. We stayed in that embrace for what seemed like hours, yet it was only a minute or two.

"It's going to be okay. You are going to be just fine," I assured her, stroking her hair.

Beth tipped her head back. I used my fingers and hands to wipe away tears from her red face and eyes.

"I'm sorry Coop."

"For what?"

"For losing control."

"Who says that you have to be in control?"

Beth thought for a moment before answering. "I guess I have always been the one to be responsible, the one to take charge. My father worked for the railroad and he would be gone for weeks at a time. My mother, well she was lazy. She did next to nothing around the house. I didn't realize until I became a teenager what my family was really like. My sister was the good daughter. She could do no wrong. I was Cinderella. I did the cleaning and the cooking while my mother and sister went shopping or visiting or played fantasy games. I resented all of them. I believed that I was responsible for maintaining order and peace in the home and that if mom or dad or sis weren't happy or if there was any conflict in the home, it was my fault."

"That's a heavy burden to bear. When did you figure that all out?"

"In therapy."

"Your marriage to Tony at a young age was just one part of your rebellion against your life at home."

"Of course, I married him to get away from my oppressing situation like I told you before, but also from my family. The irony was that I turned to someone just like my father. I married someone strong, domineering and absent. I became lazy like my mother but fortunately in only one way and that was in being Tony's wife. In every other way I remained a fixer. I remained someone who had to make sure everyone was happy and everything went smoothly.

"I know I interfered too much in my own kid's lives but I've managed to correct those mistakes and now we have good, healthy relationships. I feel like I've failed Susana though. I feel like I didn't step in when I should have and now I need to correct that mistake too."

"I know you feel that way Beth, but your relationship with Susana is entirely different than the one that you had with your own children. For one, you don't have the influence over her that you did with them, and you certainly don't have anywhere near the amount of power over her that you did with your own children. At best, all you can do is model, suggest, befriend, pray for, encourage and invite her to share moments of your life, but you cannot be her mother or fill in for her mother."

My comment produced a smile. "You sound like my therapist."

"Then it will be alright to bill you a hundred bucks for these last thirty minutes?" That generated a slight laugh. I took her by the shoulders, looked as empathetically as I could into her eyes and slowly closed the gap until our lips met. If my memory served me correctly that was our first kiss of a long and trying day, but a day that had been rich with discovery for both of us.

Forty-nine

Lewis Bender was standing outside of Genette's state-room as Beth and I approached. "Hey, you two, I almost gave up waiting for you."

I looked at Beth. "I told you we should have played one more bingo card but you said, No!"

Beth unlocked the door and addressed Lou. "Are you here to talk with my niece?"

"No, it's your boyfriend I need, if you can tear yourself away from him for a while."

"He's all yours. Maybe you can get further with him that I can." She tossed me some eyebrows and a smile. "Good night Coop. Thanks for everything."

"Good night Beth. Meet you for breakfast same time and place provided Lou is finished water boarding me by then?" She nodded.

Lou led me to a quiet table on the Lido deck but not before helping himself to a bowl of soft serve. "I need a machine like this at the office," he quipped as he spooned some of the treat into his ready and waiting mouth.

"What's on your mind, Lou?" I was tired and was trying not to allow my impatience and desire for rudeness to rule the moment.

The FBI agent proceeded to fill me in on his day. The day for him appeared to have included quite a bit of study time. The home office had sent him everything they had or wanted to on the families Gambolini and Milodanovich. That included resumes on Emilio, Lorenza, Alexi and Svetlana. He had not yet made contact with the Russians, although his partner Michael Andrews whom he referred to as Mike or Andrews was keeping a close watch on them.

He shared the results of his uneventful chat with Emilio and Lorenza. "They know a lot more than they are willing to talk about. Ostensibly they are taking a much needed vacation. They feigned surprise when I mentioned both Ms. Gambolini's presence on the ship and their late night visit to your room. I got a different kind of reaction when I mentioned Ms. Malone's death. I couldn't tell if they reacted because they already knew about the murder or they reacted because they knew her."

"Odds are good that they would have known Beth's sister."

"Perhaps, but that's been what, ten years ago? That's a lot of water to pass under the bridge." His jaw and lips were working hard.

"So why tell me this?"

"It helps me to talk about these things out loud and . . . I want your help with something." *Yeah right. First I'm condemned for being too James Bondish and now he needs an Inspector Clouseau.* I said nothing. I waited for him to continue. "I want you and Ms. Malone to go with me when I talk with Emilio and Lorenza again. I think your presence might go a long way in loosening their tongues."

I didn't know whether to be flattered or to flatten him. "Let me think about it and talk to Beth."

"Take all the time you want. I need an answer first thing in the morning."

Fifty

We met up with Lou in the atrium just down the hallway from Emilio and Lorenza's room. They apparently didn't venture out much for two men on a luxury vacation cruise. A security camera and watcher kept an eye on them twenty-four hours a day. They ordered mostly room service. Only one of them would leave of the room at a time.

Lou had talked with Genette while Beth and I ate breakfast. She had told the agent the same things she told me. The picture of Alexi did not register with her in any way. Lou did get a reaction with the two Italians, although Genette was vehement in her denial that she knew them or had ever seen them. "She's hiding something," was his last comment before discussing a strategy for handling Emilio and Lorenza.

We headed to the rendezvous with our Italian antagonists.

"Who's there?" An irritated voice responded to Lou Bender's knock.

"Agent Lou Bender, FBI."

"I gave at the office."

"I have a few more questions to ask you, Mr. Fiorenzo. May I come in?"

"I got nothing more to say to you."

"I don't think it would be in your best interest Mr. Fiorenzo for me to have to get a search warrant. Let's do this friendly like, okay?"

Silence. "All right, give us minute."

The door opened and I followed Lou into the room. It appeared to be a suite. Somebody either had some pull or some bucks or maybe, both.

"What's this? You got a new partner, Bender? The old one get sea sick or something?"

"I don't think Mr. Meyerhoff needs any introduction. It is my understanding that you boys have already greeted him up close and personal like."

Lorenza shrugged and turned to Emilio who was watching TV. "Do you know this bum that Agent Bender has with him?"

Emilio stopped shoveling whatever into his mouth and mumbled, "Nah, ain't never seen him before."

"Hey, where are your manners. Didn't your momma tell you never to speak to guests with your mouth full?"

Emilio took another bite. "Sorry Lorenza. It won't happen again."

Lorenza looked back at Bender. "I would invite you two to sit down, but I don't think you will be staying that long."

Lou ignored him and pulled out a desk chair for him while he motioned for me to sit down on the couch.

""Make yourself at home agent Bender. What can we do to help the US government today?"

"I need some better answers than I got yesterday."

"We told you all that we knew."

"No you didn't." Bender was firm. His glare could freeze fire.

"Hey Emilio, they come to play rough with us today. What's your plan, Bender? Break a few arms?"

"No I was thinking more like rearranging your manhood." Bender glanced at Lorenza's genital area.

"Yeah, right, you fibbies can't take a piss without permission."

"True enough in the states, but we're in international waters and I can do pretty much anything I want." Bender glanced at me and used his head to motion me toward the door. That was my signal to go and get Beth. She was supposed to be waiting outside the door for me to come and get her. Much to my surprise she was there. I ushered her into the room ahead of me.

Lorenza and Emilio might have preferred genital reconfiguration to seeing Mary Beth standing there. The fight seemed to go out of them.

"It's been a long time boys. You're both looking good." Beth said.

Fifty-one

"I told you yesterday that I'm investigating the murder of Beth's sister. I know that you didn't do it. I know who did it, but I can't prove a thing. I need some help. I need some information. I know that you are holding back on me. I need to know what you know. I want to nail those bastards who killed Ms. Malone and stop them from whatever else they are planning. I know that what they are planning to do will have some effect on the Gambolini family. Now, I don't care why you boys are on this ship. You can be stealing the chef's pizza recipe for all I care. But I need to know what you know. Talk to me about these Russians or any Russian. Why do you think they might have been after Ms. Malone or Ms. Gambolini? I swear anything you tell me will be off the record. Both Mary Beth and Mr. Meyerhoff will witness to that. Come on guys. Talk to me. Give me something."

Lorenza thought for a moment, then he looked at Emilio who didn't appear to move a muscle and then he looked back at Bender. "All right, but here's the deal. Some of what we know, all of what we know has nothing to do with Ms. Gambolini. She does not need to know any this. She never knew nothing about anything that went on in the family and she's not going to start now. She has to leave the room or we don't talk."

Beth wasn't happy with that deal. "Anne was my sister, Lorenza. I have right to be a part of this investigation. You can't . . ."

"Beth," I interrupted, "There is a lot more going on here than any of us realize. I know it's asking a lot, but you need to trust Lou and Lorenza to tell you what they think you need to know when you need to know it." I turned to both men. "I know that I'm an outsider in all this, but while you're in the let's-make-a -deal mode, will you do something for Beth? Will you keep her in the loop? Will you tell her as much as you can and when it's over, give her the answers she wants?"

The men looked at each other and then at Beth. They nodded simultaneously, albeit reluctantly. Beth didn't want the deal but she knew it was more important to solve the murder than it was to satisfy her own present curiosity. She got up and moved deliberately toward the door. Before she put her hand on the knob she turned and faced the Italians.

"Have you two been interfering with my life for the past ten years?"

Lorenza answered. "Interfering is a very derogatory word for the service we have been providing, Ms. Gambolini. For the last ten years and more we have been watching over you and ensuring your well being. Tony wanted to make sure that nothing bad happened to you or the kids, especially if anything would ever happen to him.

"Of course we never thought that anything would happen to Tony. We loved that man. He was good to us. He was good for the family. Emilio and me we still have nightmares from the day Tony was killed. We failed him. If only we would have been a little smarter or a little more alert maybe he would still be alive. We owe him for that failure, so maybe we get a little overprotective with you at times, but we're trying to do our best for you and for Tony."

"Does Frankie know that you are still watching over me?"

"Yes. He wants it done too. I'm not sure it's necessary anymore. We haven't had a threat on you or the kids in ten years, but we do check out pretty thoroughly anybody you or the kids might hook up with. We present them with certain facts and find out what they're made of."

"So you're okay with Mr. Meyerhoff?"

"For now."

Beth seemed satisfied. She squeezed my shoulder and left the room.

An old Italian Don is dying. He calls his grandson to his bedside. "Guido, I want you to listen to me. I want you to take my chrome plated .38 revolver so you will always remember me."

"But grandpa, I don't like guns. How about you leave me your Rolex watch instead?"

The grandpa said. "You listen to me, boy. Some day you are gonna have a business, a beautiful wife, lots of money, a big home and maybe some children. Someday you are gonna come home and find your wife in bed with another man. What are you gonna do then? Point to your watch and say, 'Time's up?'"

Fifty-two

We left our meeting with Lorenza and Emilio feeling like we had found some new but reluctant allies. We also felt that we didn't know much more than we did before our meeting. I waited for Lou to speak first.

"What was your impression of our chat?"

"I assume that the information they shared on the workings of the family especially as it related to the drug business and the Russians was accurate. You would have to be the judge of that. I thought it interesting how their tone and mannerisms changed whenever you brought up Beth or Anne or Genette. They were uncomfortable talking about those women. It could be either because women in general make them uncom- fortable or because they know more about these particular women than they're telling us."

Lou chimed in. "Oh, they're still hiding something, and you're right it involves one or maybe all of those women. But I'll find out what it is. I'll get to the truth."

Lou and I parted company. I looked up Beth and after a quick stop at my stateroom we headed for a much needed respite on the Serenity Deck.

We were docked in some port, but I didn't have a clue which one. I had lost tract of the ship's itinerary. I frankly didn't care either. I wanted a day to do nothing, a day to let my mind wind down, a day to process everything that had happened, a day to clear my thoughts and a day to enjoy more of Beth's company.

When we passed the main sun deck we observed that only a few people were occupying the pool and so we decided to set up there instead going to the serenity area. As we arranged our lounge chairs, Beth pointed out a young stud directly across the pool from us. There were three bikini clad babes with him. They were attracted either to him or the bucket of beer next to him. "That is the third or fourth time I've noticed him around the ship and I swear he's had a different set of girls with him each time I've seen him."

I had noticed him too. Not so much because of the ever changing bevy of beauties that surrounded him but for the man's ability to hold, not to mention pay for, that much beer.

That's one of the interesting phenomena about a cruise ship. Here you are with two, three or four thousand people occupying a limited space and you seem to keep running into the same handful of people over and over again both on and off the ship. There are no doubt some perfectly good reasons for that, but I'm at a loss to explain them.

Here's a case in point. While waiting in the terminal to board the *Festival*, I sat in a row of chairs between two couples. On one side of me were potato farmers from Saskatchewan, Canada. I didn't even know they grew potatoes way up there. It was a huge operation – several thousand acres. They had come to Florida to visit their daughter and they decided to take a cruise.

On the other side of me were relative newlyweds from Tennessee. They were taking a belated honeymoon. I had already met them earlier in the parking garage, but here we were an hour later after security and check-in next to each other in the boarding line. As coincidence or fate would have it, I had run into both couples numerous times while picking up food, at the hot tubs, at the water slide, in the gift shop and just walking the hallways. Someday I'll have to do a master's dissertation on this phenomenon. No, I don't think so.

Beth had postponed her interrogation for as long as she could. Her first question about my meeting with Lorenza and Emilio interrupted what was for me a most enjoyable time of mutual sun screen slathering.

I filled her in as completely as I could. There wasn't much to tell especially when I left out most of our unsubstantiated suspicions. The Russians had been moving into the Gambolini territory with their drug business for quite some time. There had been some minor skirmishes between the two families and the tension was growing. Lorenza and Emilio had been to some of the meetings between the family big shots but they said that they had never met Alexi and Svetlana. Lorenza hinted that he didn't have nearly as much confidence in Frankie running the family as he did Tony. In fact I got the impression that he didn't like Frankie much at all. His comment, "Frankie's brain is in his dick" contributed to that conclusion. Lastly Lorenza admitted that their vacation included keeping a loose eye on Beth.

"Are they still watching me?"

"They say that they aren't and Lou's surveillance of them would indicate that they are telling the truth."

"Don't they feel like I am still in any kind of danger?"

"Apparently not."

"So, Anne's death wasn't a case of mistaken identity. She was killed for a reason."

"It would appear so, but not for anything tied to the Gambolini and Milodanovich feud."

"At least not according to Lorenza."

"At least not according to Lorenza." I echoed.

"Do you believe him?"

"Yes." I tried to sound as convincing as someone who felt like he was lying could sound.

Fifty-three

We spent a mostly uninterrupted day. Only the dessert bar gave us reason for interruption and that was a welcomed interruption. The bar at noon featured all chocolate concoctions. I admit to at least two visits to the buffet. Many have called chocolate the perfect food. Some argue that chocolate is actually good for a person because it comes from a bean and a bean is a vegetable. Granted it's a cocoa bean, but still a bean nonetheless. They also stress its healthiness because chocolate is processed with milk making it a dairy product. Finally, its stock rises as a healthy food if you add fruit and nuts. Experts have also known for centuries that the answer to being stressed is desserts. Why else would "stressed" be "desserts" spelled backwards?

The buffet featured all things chocolate, a smorgasbord of delights including chocolate candies, chocolate torts, chocolate cakes, chocolate dipped fruits and nuts, chocolate cheesecakes, chocolate cookies, chocolate puddings, chocolate covered sushi and chocolate added to items I couldn't pronounce but still sampled at my own risk. It should be added that the application of guilt to the sampling of food, especially chocolate on a cruise is illegal, immoral and in just plain bad taste.

The main relaxation deck gradually filled with sun worshipers who had either returned from shore excursions or finally woke up from the previous night's reverie. As the crowd grew, Beth and I eventually relocated to the Serenity Deck for more peace and quiet.

We talked very little throughout the day. We mostly read and napped and baked under the warm sub-tropical sun.

I woke to the gentle movement of the ship and to the rustling sound of Beth gathering up her things. "I'm going to my room and start getting ready for dinner."

"Is it that time already?"

"Yeah, it's nearly 4:30."

"Okay. I'll walk you to your room."

"No. Stay here. I know how much you enjoy watching the ship come and go from a port. Pick me up a little before six."

"Okay." I gazed at her for as long as she was gaze-able and then some. She was even more of a pleasure watching come and go than any port I had ever watched come or go. I started gathering up my stuff when I heard a familiar voice.

"We need to talk."

"Good afternoon Lou. It's good to see you too!"

"Yeah, save the niceties. Let's go some place quiet. How about your room?"

"Sure."

Lou was silent until we both sat down in my stateroom. "The Russian's dead."

"What?"

"The Russian, Alexi, he was killed this afternoon."

"How? Where?"

"It was a hit. He and Ms. Zabbarova we're on shore for that meeting with the drug locals that I told you was going to happen. My partner Mike and some other assets already on the ground followed them. They were watching the meet from a distance when a sniper took out Alexi. After the shot everyone scattered. As far as we know, there was only the one shot and only Alexi was hit, but we're still investigating."

"Are the local authorities involved?

"I doubt it. Even if they are called in, it will be for cover up purposes only."

"Who did it?"

"We don't know that either. My boys filmed and recorded the engagement. Even as we speak, the techs back in Washington are going over that stuff with a fine tooth comb looking for any clues."

"Do you think it's tied to what happened on the ship?"

Bender's jaw and lips were working. "It's a classic tit for tat play – they hit us and we hit them kind of thing. The problem is I got no proof and I got no real motive for that. If I knew for sure that the Russian was after a Gambolini but accidently hit a mistaken look-a-like, then I would conclude that Lorenza passed this fact on to Frankie and Frankie ordered Emilio to take out the Russian as a payback."

"You don't think it's that simple?"

"I know it's not. Neither Lorenza or Emilio left the ship today."

"What about the other Russian, Jabberov, where is she?"

"Ms. Zabbarova? She's back on the ship."

"That's odd. I would have thought she would have run or what's the phrase, gone to ground or gone to the mattresses or come in from the cold or whatever the spy-speak is."

"I agree it is a bit odd, unless she didn't have any assets in place to help her out."

"Maybe she arranged the hit. Maybe she's tired of playing second fiddle to Alexi."

"Maybe."

"Or the deal went bad. The locals felt a double-cross coming or the Russians have been threatening them or playing hardball or changed the deal and they needed to send a message."

"Yeah, all possible scenarios," Lou took a deep breath and exhaled. "That's what makes my job so much fun. Right now every idea I've thrown at my wall has struck and all I got is one big mess."

"So what's next?"

"I wait for the experts back home to pass along any meaningful tidbits they glean from the audio and video we sent them and then I will go and introduce myself to Ms. Zabbarova."

Fifty-four

Dinner passed without incident. I told Beth about the Russian. She expressed both delight and disappointment in the knowledge that her sister's murderer had himself been murdered – *those who take the sword shall die with the sword.* Alexi had received an eye for an eye and a tooth for a tooth justice, well not quite. He went quickly. He never had time to prepare. A high velocity round arrives before the sound of the explosion that launches it. Anne and no doubt every other victim of his personal sense of justice died much more slowly than he did and with a great sense of terror in their minds and being. Alexi, unfortunately, missed his moment of terror. That was a shame.

There would be no quiet evening of discovery for us. No post-dinner hand in hand stroll. No chance to relax and hopefully witness an entertaining show on the big stage, and no margarita. It had been looking like today would be the day, but that too would be postponed.

Lou had phoned just as I was leaving my stateroom for dinner and requested some more of my time. I was torn between a growing loyalty to him and the case and my growing feelings for Beth.

I wanted to spend my waking moments with her and do the work necessary to discover the truth about those feelings and where they might lead me and us. Right now I wasn't sure if we were far enough along in our relationship to know much of anything about us for certain. What I felt assured of was that I wanted to be with her, that I enjoyed being with her and that my time to be with her on this cruise was rapidly running out.

I had already begun thinking about a possible post-cruise relationship and was developing viable scenarios about how that might work. Unfortunately those mental exercises were becoming distracting.

There is a fine line between worrying and fretting about the future and planning for the future. A person can't plan for what he can't control. And a person certainly can't control another person's feelings or desires. So I kept telling myself that any future with Beth was out my hands, that I shouldn't become anxious about it because it was too far removed from the present. After all there is enough going on in the present to use up more energy and resources than I probably have at my disposal. "Do not worry about tomorrow, for tomorrow will worry about itself. Each day has enough trouble of its own. . .

. Look at the birds of the air; they do not sow or reap or store away in barns, and yet your heavenly Father feeds them. Are you not much more valuable than they? Who of you by worrying can add a single hour to his life?" (Matthew 6:25ff.)

I try to live by that Biblical counsel. It's great counsel. When I am able to trust that counsel then every tomorrow is secure and every today passes smoothly. Living without worry is not easy for any of us because we are creatures who don't deal well with the unknown. We like to be in control of both our present and of our future. We don't like surprises and we don't like uncertainties. Hence we worry and fret. The more the uncertainties pile up, the more we worry. The more we worry, the more uncertain the future looks. We create an ugly and vicious cycle. We are like the car stuck on ice. It is frantically spinning its wheels, burning up all kinds of energy, but getting nowhere fast. Worry makes us useless and unproductive. It often drains us of our energy and the will to accomplish anything good.

Worry is also linked to responsibility. Every time a person adds a responsibility to his or her life, the less time that person has for each of those responsibilities and the better that person must become at juggling those responsibilities. If the juggler doesn't become better then worry enters the picture and further distracts the overwhelmed person from fulfilling any of his responsibilities.

In recent days I had added a couple of balls to my routine during a time when I had been intentionally eliminating balls from my life. My involvement with Beth was a big ball in itself. That relationship had then unintentionally involved me in this case and with her family and then with Lou Bender and now two murders. This involvement was not just threatening my time with Beth; it was taking away that time. Some people call it "being busy." It doesn't matter whether you call it "being busy," "having too many responsibilities" or "too many irons in the fire" or "juggling too many balls," the result is the same. Quality and quantity time suffer. Relationships with the significant people in your life suffer.

A busy father, we'll call him Ted, assured his own father that while he didn't spend much time with his son, the time that he did spend was quality time and that quality time was more important than the amount of time. One day Ted's father invited him to lunch at the city's finest restaurant. When Ted arrived his father said, "I have already ordered the absolutely best piece of meat this restaurant has to offer." Ted asked, "What's the occasion?" His father replied, "Can't a father do something nice for his son once in a while." The waiter brought the main course and set it down in front of Ted and took off the cover. On the plate was a cubic inch of steak. "What is this?" Ted exclaimed. "That my boy is just what I promised you, the best piece of meat in the city." "But is this all I get?" Ted com-

plained. His father replied, "Haven't you always said that it is the quality and not the quantity that matters most?"

For relationships to develop properly and to be maintained properly the people involved must spend a significant amount of time together in many different settings. Relationship development is about quality and quantity. Because of all the things vying for my attention I was not able to provide my budding relationship with Beth the quality or quantity time it deserved or needed.

The easy way out, the lazy way out, would be to walk away from all of those responsibilities contending for my attention. It was tempting, but I was in too deep to follow that course. I would have to become a juggler for a while. I would have to prioritize. I would have to communicate. I would have to find satisfactory solutions in a difficult situation. But that was nothing new for me.

Before I could break the news to Beth that my after dinner plans did not include her, she broke the news that her after dinner plans did not include me. I could sense the same frustration in her.

"Is something wrong?" I asked as I sipped a delicious navy bean soup and fingered shrimp cocktail.

"It's Genette. I've been trying to get her to talk about my sister's funeral arrangements. The ship needs to know them so that they can release the body when we arrive back in

Miami. The more they can settle before we dock the quicker the whole ship can clear customs. She finally agreed to talk with me right after dinner. I'm sorry."

I assured her that this was more important and gave her my own bad news. We finished dinner. I walked her to her room. We hugged each other for encouragement and made tentative arrangements to meet later. Beth inhaled deeply and then exhaled. She smiled at me, stuck her card in the door and disappeared.

Fifty-five

Bender opened the door to his stateroom. He motioned for me to come in with the same hand that was holding a drink, "Can I get you something?" He held out his drink to me then used it to point to a small bar he had set up in his room.

"No. I'm fine, thank you."

"Have a seat." Lou pointed to the sofa. He took the higher desk chair. If this were a friendly come on over and watch the game night out, the seat selection would be meaningless. However, if Lou had a different agenda, then perhaps his choosing the higher level chair would indicate that he wanted to be in control of the discussion. Either way I didn't know Agent Bender well enough to relax in his presence.

Lou sat slumped forward in his chair staring into his drink while swirling it gently around and around. His jaw and lips were keeping the same rhythm.

"So Lou, what's on your mind?"

"Huh?"

"What did you want to talk about, something regarding the case? Did you meet with the Zabbarova woman?"

"Uh . . . no, I haven't talked with her yet. I'm still waiting for the report from Washington." Silence. His posture remained unchanged.

"Anything from Mike or your investigators at the site?"

"No, nothing new."

It was fast becoming obvious to me that something was bothering the FBI man and it wasn't the case. He had invited me up here to talk about an issue that wasn't easy for him to talk about. He apparently wanted me to dig it out of him. This was a new side of the man that I hadn't seen before. Digging into someone's psyche presented a potential problem for me. I'm more of a listener and observer than an inquisitor. I have never liked the twenty questions game, but it looked like I was going to have to do some probing.

His demeanor suggested that he was troubled by something going on in his life; something that had been building for a while and that had just reached a tipping point. Some might say that a straw had been recently laid that broke the camel's back. People wrongly think that it's one crisis that creates a problem. The reality is that there has been a whole string of crises which have led up to the one that gets blamed. The crises were the bigger problem, but the straw would be useful in helping us get to the real issue.

Agent Bender was too proud or too ashamed or too something to come right out and tell me what was weighing on him. In that respect he was typical of many men. Men are problem solvers. Men do not like to admit weakness. Men don't like to think of themselves as victims. Men don't like to fail; especially men like Lou Bender who are gun carrying, defend and protect ex-military, macho types.

I felt like I was in an ironic situation as I asked myself: How do I get someone to talk who doesn't want to talk? An important part of Lou Bender's job is to get people who don't want to talk to talk. Now the shoe was on the other foot. The master inquisitor did not want to give up his information. How should I approach him? How would Lou approach Lou? I smiled inside at the thought. I wouldn't need torture because he was already experiencing a personal hell. I knew that he was a man who liked to confront people so I needed to confront the confronter.

I figured that whatever was burdening him had to be tied either to some conflict in his career, some issue with his parents or children, a personal health crisis, marital discord, or a loss of manhood. I went after the most likely.

"Is there something going on at home with your wife, Lou?"

The swirling, the pursing and jawing all stopped. Bingo. I would have paused to pat myself on the back but my deduction was not all that brilliant. In truth it was unfortunately the most likely of the options.

"Talk to me, Lou, what's going on? Did something happen today?"

He still hadn't looked up, but his nervous habits slowly returned. This might be tougher than trying to tenderize a ninety-nine cent a pound round steak. Silence is often a counselor's best friend especially when he doesn't know what to say next. I decided to wait him out. He needed to talk more than I needed to talk so I would sit and calmly stare at him until the pressure became too much for him to bear. It wasn't long before the silence got to him, although long is relative. When you are in that situation even fifteen seconds of silence seems like an hour.

"I shouldn't be wasting your time with this. It's nothing really."

"Yeah, I can tell. Nothing's bothering you. What's your wife's name?"

"Rachelle.'

"Did you talk with her today?"

"Yeah, just after we talked before."

"What did she say? Tell me what did you talk about?"

Lou stood up. He drained his glass and slammed it down. He started pacing in the small room. "She said that she needed some time to think. She said that she was going to move out of the house."

"Were those her exact words or is that what you heard her say?"

"Huh?" He stopped his pacing and stared at me.

"I said, were those her exact words or is that what you heard her say?" Lou gave me a somewhat confused look. "There's a huge difference between someone saying, 'I'm thinking about moving out' and 'my bags are packed and in the car and I'm on my way to an undisclosed location and I don't want you contacting me except through my lawyer.'

"There's also a huge unknown in what her motive might be. She could be merely trying to get your attention or she might already be completely fed up with you.

"And there's your own state of mind. What did you want to hear? What were you expecting to hear? Do you think she should leave you? Do you want her to leave you? So tell me, what were her exact words?"

"I don't remember." Lou looked away and returned to his pacing.

"What?" I decided to substitute drama for sympathy at this point. "Someone with your interrogation, communication and investigation skills doesn't remember what his own wife said during a conversation that may or may not include ending your marriage. What is wrong with this picture?"

Lou stopped, turned toward me and became defensive. "Don't you be standing in judgment over me. You don't know what it's been like to be married to that woman. I haven't been good enough for her or her family since the day I married her. I can't . . ."

I sat back in my chair and let the man vent. This was more to my liking, listening as people became historical. That's right, historical – the blow by blow recounting of every offense suffered and logged since the day of trouble began. People love to remember and use what they remember to beat one another up over and over again. In my experience, men are pretty good at this but they are not in the same league as women.

Women in addition to mastering the art of documenting and recording for all posterity every past spousal transgression, failure, wrongdoing, indiscretion, infidelity, broken promise, suspicion and misconduct either in thought, word or deed also can turn on the hysterical. By adding her emotions to the mix the female hopes that if the facts as she sees them do not sway the therapist or judge or whoever to her side, then certainly her tears and dramatics will. A man's emotional repertoire is pretty much limited to tears, anger and a protruding lower lip. He comes in a distant second on the hysterics effectiveness meter.

Lou went through his list of trials that he endured, a list that he was convinced no man should have to endure. He was the unappreciated great provider. He worked his butt off to give her a good life. She complained when he worked late and complained when he was home. She nagged him about his dangerous job. He couldn't help it because he had to cancel so many events with her and their kids. She nagged him about the list of jobs to do. She accused him of unfaithfulness because he worked late, but he swore to God that he hadn't ever been unfaithful. He must have vented a good fifteen minutes. He talked and he paced. Finally he took a deep breath and sat down.

Fifty-six

"You've been under a lot of stress at home." I offered in a genuine sympathetic tone.

"Damn right I have."

"What's your plan?"

"I don't have a plan." *Where do I go with the conversation now? Perhaps I need to get him thinking positively instead of negatively.*

"How long have you been married?"

"It's coming up on twenty years."

"Tell me about your kids."

"Jordan is a junior in high school. Tommy is a freshman and the twins Paul and Dinah are in sixth grade." I could sense some pride.

"That's a handful. What are they interested in?"

"Jordan plays the piano. She's really good. She was giving a concert this week when I drew this assignment. I can't remember the last recital I was able to attend." Silence.

"How about the others?"

"Oh, yeah, Tommy's my brainiac. He absorbs knowledge. He has a photographic memory. The kid has computer skills that would make the boys at Langley green with envy. He's skipped some grades and somehow is already taking courses for college credit. The twins are my athletes. They're in sports year round. They're playing baseball and softball right now."

"Sounds like Rachelle has a lot on her plate."

"Yeah, she's done a great job with the kids, that's for sure."

"How long have you been with the FBI?"

"About twelve years."

"And before that?"

"I was a cop and a detective."

"When you married Rachelle were you a cop?"

"Yeah."

"How long had you known her?"

"We've known each other for years. It was shortly after her father became the pastor of the church my family attended. We became friends in the youth group and we were classmates throughout high school. We didn't date or anything. We both went off to college. She became a teacher and I got a criminal justice degree. About the time we graduated, we had our first date. About two years later we were married."

"When you were dating and in those initial months and years of marriage, what was it that Rachelle did for you or to you that lit you up? What was it that made you feel loved by her?"

Lou leaned back on his chair and put his hands behind his head to think. He closed his eyes. A faint smile appeared on his face. "Seeing her, watching her walk up to me and wrap her arms around me. Holding my arm, running her fingers through my hair, slipping my shirt out of my pants and running her hands up my stomach and chest, then reaching for my belt buckle and . . ."

"I get the picture. You like to be touched. Having your wife touch you tells you that you are loved. When she withholds that touch from you then you think she doesn't love you. I take it you haven't been touched much lately."

"You're right on there. I might as well be a monk. We haven't made love in I can't remember when. We don't even kiss good night."

"Let me ask you another question. When you were dating and in those initial months and years of marriage, what was it that you did that lit Rachelle up? What was it that made her feel loved by you?"

This time Lou leaned forward in his chair. This would be harder for him to answer but he seemed to know where I was going and he wanted to go there too. After a moment of staring at the floor and rubbing his mouth with his hand he had an answer. "She liked to do things together. She liked to go places, especially to parks. She liked to go for walks or canoeing or hiking. She liked to hold hands and sit and go watch a movie. She liked to play games. She would always become sad and disappointed when I would pull a double shift, but she would brighten if we could arrange to meet during my breaks."

"When was the last time you lit her up like that, Lou? When was the last time the two of you did something together that you knew she enjoyed doing?"

He looked up at me with a pair of pathetic looking eyes that suddenly filled with the tears of genuine repentance. I let Lou cry until he was finished. "Do you think it's too late to save the mess I've made?"

I was impressed. Most men would continue their prideful and lazy ways and continue to blame their wives for their marital woes and expect them to come crawling back. Lou realized his failure and the consequences of that failure. He also realized the burden of his responsibility.

If reconciliation is going to happen between two people then both must eventually accept culpability. However, the reconciliation process will not begin until at least one person is willing to swallow their pride and takes the first step toward mending the brokenness. The process will begin by whoever of the two chooses to be the more humble; whoever of the two chooses to be the more loving and whoever of the two chooses not to be a fault finder. Love, not blame, must become central. "It's not what I think Lou, it's what you think?"

"Will you help me try and fix it?"

How could I refuse, I'm in the healing business.

A husband and wife came for counseling after 20 years of marriage. When asked what the problem was, the wife went into a passionate, painful tirade listing every problem they had ever had in the 20 years they had been married: neglect, lack of intimacy, emptiness, loneliness, feeling unloved and unlovable, an entire laundry list of unmet needs she had endured over the course of their marriage. Finally, after allowing this to go on for a sufficient length of time, the therapist got up, walked around the desk and, after asking the wife to stand, embraced and kissed her passionately as her husband watched with a raised eyebrow. The woman shut up and quietly sat down as though in a daze. The therapist turned to the husband and said, "This is what your wife needs at least three times a week. Can you do this?" The husband thought for a moment and replied, "Well, I can drop her off here on Mondays and Wednesdays, but on Fridays, I go fishing."

Bon Voyage

Lust

Envy/Jealousy

Anger

Sloth

Gluttony

Greed

Pride

Debarkation

Fifty-seven

This cruise ship really sucks. In fact, every cruise ship sucks. I mean that quite literally. The ship itself consumes huge quantities. The people on the ship consume. Together they suck up tons of resources.

Cruise ships come in many different sizes. The majority of the ships that are operated by the main companies servicing the United States normally accommodate about three thousand passengers, give or take a thousand. In addition the passengers are serviced by about fourteen hundred crew give or take five hundred.

The world's largest cruise ship, the *Ocean of the Sea (OOTS)*, launched right at the end of 2009. It weighs two hundred and twenty thousand tons and has room for five thousand and four hundred passengers who are cared for by two thousand, one hundred and fifty crew. In order to house that many people, it has eighteen decks. In addition to the normal amenities which are more than most small cities, it features the first ever cruise ship carousel. The *OOTS* measures nearly twelve hundred feet in length (that's four football fields) and a width of over one hundred and fifty feet (that's one-half of a football field). It has a thirty foot draft making it inaccessible to many ports.

By comparison Noah's ark was four hundred and fifty feet long (about one-third of the *OOTS*) and seventy-five feet wide (about one-half of the *OOTS*) and forty-five feet high with three decks. Granted Noah only needed to house eight people; however he was required to fill his ship with one pair of every unclean animal and seven pair of every clean animal, each according to their kind. He was instructed to include every creature with the breath of life in them. That meant wild animals, all livestock, every animal that moved along the ground, every bird, and every creature with wings. Some might have figured Noah a fool for building such a giant ship so far from water and he no doubt took his share of ridicule, but I suspect he was smart enough to select young, immature members of each species to come aboard in order to conserve precious space.

Noah also needed at least a year's worth of supplies — food for his family and for his zoo. They were on the ship fifty-three weeks. However the flood had dramatically reshaped the earth's surface and pretty much destroyed all vegetation on it. This made finding fresh food, unless you liked fish and sea weed, scarce for several more weeks and perhaps months after the animals were released.

The giant cruisers store only people food and only enough for the length of the cruise and for about four emergency days.

Emergencies do happen. A home port might close temporarily due to weather. That happened to Amy and me once as we tried to dock in Mobile. Rain, fog, wind or high waves can keep a ship out a partial or an entire extra day. A hurricane can force a ship to divert its course and add several days to its scheduled itinerary. Mechanical failure could likewise cause delay. Those experiencing a delay receive some bonus cruise time. Those waiting for the ship to dock lose precious cruise time but are usually compensated in other ways.

We don't know how much Noah's passenger's consumed but an average cruise ship over the course of a week will scarf down some of the following from a list of fifteen hundred different food and drink items:

Twenty-one hundred pounds of prime rib

Ten thousand pounds of chicken

Six hundred and thirty pounds of lobster tails

Four thousand steaks

Six thousand hot dogs

Seven thousand eight hundred hamburgers

Thirteen hundred pounds of salmon

Sixty thousand eggs

Fifty-two thousand slices of bacon

Two thousand two hundred pounds of coffee

Three thousand pounds of butter

Ten thousand five hundred boxes of cereal

Fifteen thousand Danish pastries

Eighteen thousand cans of soft drinks

Eighteen thousand bottles of beer

Four hundred bottles of champagne/sparkling wine

One thousand eight hundred bottles of wine

One thousand liters of alcohol (rum, vodka, tequila, gin, etc.)

Fruits and vegetables

All of this and whatever else by way of food that is needed is stocked at a cost of about $350,000 for the seven days plus the four emergency days.

If you have never cruised you need to try it once just for the food experience. Eating is possible for most or all twenty-four hours of the day, depending on the ship. Your choices vary from elegant dining to buffet lines to room service. Every food item except certain specialty treats like a birthday cake, dessert liqueurs or fancy coffee concoctions are included in the price. Some cruise lines offer twenty-four hour pizza bars and ice cream service and mid-night buffets. And it is all excellently prepared and served by highly trained staff working around the clock. An average ship will probably have nearly one hundred and fifty working the galleys and over two hundred serving as wait staff so that the average passenger can pig out to his/her heart's content or demise.

If food isn't your fancy then maybe drinking is. Through the miracle of your key card and the ever present bar staff and the absence of alcohol police, passengers are free to drink whenever and whatever they want. Some do. For most, it's adult beverages. For others it's soda, pop or soft drinks (which is the same thing depending on what part of the country you hail from). For a few, like me, we stay with the free stuff, i.e. coffee, water, lemonade, hot chocolate and tea. I'm sure that the sale of alcoholic beverages is a big money maker for the ship so it is not surprising that there are daily drink specials, morning drink specials, wine with your meal drink specials, and souvenir glass drink specials.

The key card is an ingenious plastic device about the size of a credit card that allows a passenger to operate sans cash while on the ship. Every charge is quickly, conveniently and effortlessly added to your account, sight unseen. While there may be some morning after headaches from all the drinking that goes on, my guess is that the biggest headache comes on the last morning of the cruise. That's the day passengers wake up and discover the bill for the cruise's expenses under the stateroom door. The printout lists the items that have been charged to the key cards.

As I have walked the halls on those early mornings, I have noticed bills several pages long. There may be a whole lot of consuming of food that goes on during a cruise, but there is also a whole lot of consuming of drink that goes on too. I have often been tempted to read the bottom line of one those print-outs just to satisfy my own curiosity about how much people actually spend on these cruises, but so far I have resisted the temptation since that information is none of my business.

If drink isn't your fancy then maybe shopping is. The bigger the ship is, the more stores that are packed into its atrium or mall. Some folks are born to shop, others like to pick up souvenirs of their trips or grab the duty free items that ships provide while in international waters. One gets the impression that diamonds and gems along with silver and gold chains are as cheap on a ship as they are anywhere in the world. I am not convinced of that fact even with the advertized sale prices.

If shopping isn't your fancy then maybe gambling is. Cruise ships have what I assume to be full blown casinos with some game for everyone. There are blackjack tables and roulette wheels and slot machines and other games of chance. I suspect this too is a money maker for the ship. It is the one place where people flash cash in addition to their key card. I usually walk through the place and observe the action. People are really intense as they watch cards and place bets and wait for matches. I'm amazed at the speed at which people play. I suspect that if I knew what they were doing, the games would also slow down for me.

If gambling isn't your fancy then maybe shore time is. The cruise lines arrange excursions for their passengers with local vendors whom they trust. Interested passengers can select from a list of attractions, pay their money, walk off the ship and meet a guide. These tours offer a variety of experiences from horseback riding in jungles to snorkeling along coral reefs to playing with dolphins and stingrays and sea turtles to visiting ancient ruins to shopping tours to museum tours to a day at a beach resort to a golf outing to parasailing to deep sea fishing and on and on. I have been on many of these tours and have enjoyed them all equally.

Some folks prefer to arrange their own tours or to simply walk around the area where the ship docks or to hire a taxi or motor bike and go where they want to go. There are two things to keep in mind. One is to be back before the ship leaves. The only person it will wait for is the Captain and he doesn't get off the ship. If you miss the departure you are one hundred percent responsible for finding your own way home or to the next port. The second is to respect the warnings that your cruise director gives you about the port. He or she may advise against renting equipment or going off alone on walks or shopping in certain stores. That counsel is provided for good reason.

There is a lot to consume on a cruise ship. Be careful not to so over indulge yourself on the sun and fun and other good times that your dream cruise turns into a nightmare for you.

Fifty-eight

I found Beth sitting by the window on the Lido Deck drinking a cup of hot chocolate. I stood and watched her for a moment before I walked over to join her. She was lost in thought. "Hi," I said.

She smiled. I hesitated before deciding whether to sit down.

"You look tired," I observed. "Rough night?"

"Yeah, I had a major run in with Genette." I was faced with a decision. Should I sit or should I go. Kenny Rogers knew when to hold 'em, knew when to fold 'em, knew when to walk away and knew when to run. Where was Kenny when you needed to know what he knew? I was mentally exhausted from my marathon session with Lou and the last thing I wanted was to deal with someone else dumping their emotional garbage all over me. But this wasn't just anyone. And even if it wasn't Beth and happened to be a complete stranger, because I was here, I would be available. I needed to be available. I sat down. "Tell me, what happened?"

None of it was good. Genette still didn't want to talk about the funeral arrangements and they fought. Beth stopped abruptly. "Let's walk."

We worked our way through the casino. Business was booming. I had been to a casino once in my life and that wasn't to gamble but to take advantage of the $6.99 all you can eat buffet. Prime rib, lobster, shrimp, sushi – no way they made a nickel off me. I felt bad about only eating and not supporting their small business through gambling, but they put the price up and I agreed to it. I admit I stuffed myself. I ate more than a reasonable person should have eaten and felt miserable for several hours after, but at least I didn't throw it up and I didn't leave food on my plate. Mother would have been proud. *Jonathon only take what you can eat and then eat everything you take. There are people starving to death in Africa and could use the food you waste.* It never dawned on me as a kid how my leftovers could get to Africa anyway.

I don't gamble. I don't encourage people to gamble, in fact I discourage gambling. I've seen too many people lose what they can't afford to lose in the hope that they will win what they won't be able to handle if they were to win it.

There are a couple of aspects to gambling. All gambling involves risk. Most gambling is about trying to get something for nothing. It usually involves a get-rich-quick mentality that many times has a get-poor-quick result.

Another facet to gambling can be understood from the perspective of a farmer or businessman. He plants a crop or introduces a product expecting a successful venture but is realistic enough to plan for a different result. These kinds of gambles contain risks but also include an element of control and the results are not exclusively left to chance or to a pair of dice or cards or wheels or other games that are certainly rigged in favor of the house.

Certainly some gamblers lose nothing but chump change or their entertainment dollars and can walk away after doing so, but many who gamble are laying down the very dollars needed to buy necessities for the kids. Those who can least afford to be risky are the ones who are pressured to risk the most. Even the government encourages this kind of irresponsible living by claiming that their lotteries are helping kids as they raise money for education. If the money were actually going to educate our children then we might be smart enough to figure out that the government isn't smart enough to do much of anything very efficiently.

You heard about the man who went to Las Vegas in his $70,000 Mercedes. He came home in a $700,000 Greyhound bus.

Fifty-nine

I led Beth out of the casino toward the fresher air and the quieter space of an outside deck. We said nothing as we took in the lovely evening. Beth was the first to break the silence and when she did she sounded somewhat ominous. "We need to talk."

"Sure. Where would you like to go?"

"Some place where we can be alone."

I pointed to a spot not far from where we were. Beth nodded her head in approval.

I watched her stare out at the passing waves for a moment before she spoke. "There's something that I need to tell you."

Oh, oh. I was about to be on the receiving end of an, it's been a wonderful couple of days but it's time to move on speech. I know that I'm sometimes not the quickest person to pick up the obvious clues that are happening around me but I hadn't seen this coming at all.

Beth turned to face me. "My argument with Genette was pretty bad today. So bad, that she threw me out of her room.

I didn't have any place to go. I checked with guest services and the only room on the whole ship that is unoccupied is my old stateroom. I can't go back there, besides it's still a crime scene. I hope you don't mind, but I had my things moved into your room."

I stood there frozen in time not knowing whether to laugh or cry or yell or cheer or throw up. Finally I spoke. "You what?"

"I moved into your room. It's just temporary. I know how you feel about such things. I would have asked you first but we couldn't find you and so Sashi helped me cut through all the red tape and I moved my stuff in."

I inhaled a deep breath, formed a small circle with my mouth and slowly exhaled, hoping to give my muddled emotions a chance to realign themselves and my mind an opportunity to process the unexpected announcement. Beth was sensing my discomfort.

"I will sleep out on the ship's deck somewhere. I just need some place to put my things and to get cleaned up."

That comment seemed to snap me out of my daze. "No, no you can't do that. You can stay in the room. The deck is no place for a woman to be sleeping." I was about to add a most chivalrous comment but stopped. Any offer by me to sleep on the deck would only heap unnecessary guilt on an already burdened woman. But I had to be a bit gallant. "You can have the bed. I'll take the couch and no arguments." As I said that

I put up an index finger in warning that I meant it and I did. "Tomorrow we'll see what other options there might be."

That earned me a most generous embrace and a "thank you." When we finally unclenched I tilted her face back by the chin to share a kiss when I noticed her watering eyes, "Why the tears?"

"You are too good to me. I don't know how you do it. People keep taking and taking and taking from you and you just keep giving without complaint, without getting angry. How do you it? Why do you do it?"

"It's not me, Beth. Believe me, if I had my druthers I would take all I could take too."

"But you don't. Most of the people in my life are hard and cruel and stubborn and self-absorbed, but you're not. You're soft and kind and patient, but still strong."

"I appreciate your generous words, although I'm not sure that you're entirely accurate. I do work hard at trying to be those things, but in my own mind, I have a long way to go in becoming the kind of person that I would like to be. What has been a real blessing for me has been the example of so many giving and caring people who have touched my life over the years. They have demonstrated through words and actions the secret to the better way of living. I know that it's a lot easier being a taker than it is being a giver, however being a taker is a whole lot less satisfying in the long run."

"You'll have to tell me that secret."

"It's not really a secret, Beth. I'll be happy to tell you about it when all this mess going on around us finally settles a bit." A faint recollection of a Proverb or maybe it was a verse of a Psalm flashed through my mind – "Whoever listens to me will live in safety and will be at ease, without fear of harm."

Sixty

I knew that I had my work cut out for me tonight. It was not smart for a sexually deprived and alive man to be sharing a room with a beautiful woman who had on previous occasions made provocative overtures of lovemaking. Granted neither bed afforded an ideal venue for such activity but venues had not once in recorded history deterred determined lovers. My determination was to resist any and every temptation. It would be an uphill battle, the most difficult type to win.

Through the flip of a coin we determined that I would use the bathroom to get ready for bed first. This allowed Beth time to finish unpacking her things and rearrange mine according to her needs. Apparently she was fairly confident that I wouldn't refuse her request to move in with me. Housekeeping was obviously certain that I would grant her request. They had both beds made up and pulled back with pillow chocolates in place. Tonight's towel animal was ironically a monkey.

I gathered up my pajamas, entered the bathroom and then closed and locked the door. I took my time ridding myself of the day's internal and external grime. I debated the merits of switching to a cold shower and decided to forgo that horror. With my night time garb completely in place and everything in the room in good order for Beth, I took a deep cleansing breath, unlocked and opened the door and stepped out into the room.

I wasn't sure what I expected to see. What greeted me fortunately was Beth still fully clothed sitting at the dressing table and arranging her personal items. The room was neat and tidy. Her suitcase and clothes were nowhere to be been.

"Next," I offered.

Beth smiled and gathered up what she needed and took her turn in the bath room. I heard the familiar "click" of the door locking. She either didn't trust me or was sending a not so subtle message about my lack of trust in her.

I crawled into my new bed. It wasn't so bad. I propped up my pillows, read my evening devotion and then opened up the novel that I had started during the cruise. Beth came into the room before I had made it through one page.

Thankfully she was wearing pajamas and not a see through nightgown or negligee. I looked back at my book and tried to picture myself in a situation similar to being in college with a regular roommate, or akin to being on an all men's retreat. I looked back up at Beth. Yeah, right, nice try. But keep telling yourself things like that Coop and you might just survive the night!

Sixty-one

Beth turned out the overhead lights leaving only the reading lights burning. She crawled into what used to be my bed and opened her own book. I was at first hurt that we shared no good night hug and kiss but then quickly counted that omission as a blessing to my internal battle.

It wasn't long before she said, "Thank you for letting me stay here Coop. I don't know how I'll ever repay you."

"You don't owe me a thing. If anything these last couple of days you've given me have put me in debt to you."

"How can you say that? I've brought you nothing but trouble."

"Well, I grant you there have been a few bumps and bruises since I've met you but the perks have more than compensated for the quirks."

"I wouldn't call getting beat up and involved in a murder and now having someone kick you out of your bed quirks."

"All right, if you really want to make it up to me here's what you can do. Go and get me a bowl of soft serve."

"Come on, I'm serious."

"I know you are and I appreciate it. Look, until you came along there hasn't been anyone who I really cared about and who I felt really cared about me since my wife died. When people really care they don't want things from each other, they want to give things to each other. Maybe that's where we're at right now. I don't want anything from you other than your presence, your time, your attention, your honesty, your interests, your next tomorrow and the details of your life. I want you. I want to know who you are and what makes you tick and what you've done and what you want to do and how I can help you and how I can fit into your life and your hopes and your dreams and how you can fit into mine. But I don't want to rush into it. I don't want to miss the adventure of the moment. And I don't want there to be any hint of obligation. I don't want you to feel like somehow you owe me for something I've done for you or that I owe you for something you've done for me. We both need to be free to care about each other. Does that make any sense?"

"Yeah, except when you've lived your whole life under obligation, it's not easy to change your ways or your thinking or behaving."

"How right you are."

"So how do I do it?"

"You're not going like my answer. It's a process of discovery and gradual change." We both laughed softly. "This time I'm totally serious. It's first of all discovering that the ability to live a full and free life is a gift of God's grace and working. And second it's realizing that any change rarely happens overnight. It usually evolves over time and through a variety of life experiences."

"Are you too tired to talk more about this tonight?"

"I'm willing if you're willing."

Sixty-two

We each changed positions in our beds so that we could face each other. I began. "It might be helpful to look at relationships like rooms in a house. Initially when people meet they are very superficial toward each other. It's like conversations that you have on the front porch – 'Hey, good to see you . . . How is the family . . . Can I borrow your clippers . . . Would you like some tomatoes from my garden?' Some people never progress in their relationships beyond the porch. They are comfortable there and don't want to risk taking the relationship to a deeper level. They don't want to invite this person into the more private space that lies beyond the front door. And that's okay.

"But when you do decide to take that risk to your comfort zone and extend that invitation, understand that the relationship changes. Once you invite someone into your house or into your life, you open yourself up for inspection on the one hand but for opportunities of friendship on the other. The least threatening of these rooms is probably the living room or front room. This is where we invite mostly strangers or new acquaintances or salesmen or neighbors and the like to visit with us. It's a fairly sterile room. The conversation is mostly superficial but some of the exchanges are personal and you begin to determine whether to invite them deeper into your home and life as friends or whether to keep them as occasional acquaintances."

Beth picked up the analogy. "I see where you're going. When you decide that you like a person or maybe even can trust a person you open up more of yourself to them just as you open up more of your home to people you like and trust. The more that you find out about someone the more comfortable you get with them and the more personal you are with your sharing."

"Exactly. As comfort and trust grow you take a person into the more private places of your home or heart. In your house that might be the family room. That's where you play games, where you laugh, where you spend time, where you tell stories, where you discuss life issues and even where you have arguments. There you are more authentic. When you bring non-family members into your family room, you are inviting them to become a part of your real self or family.

"As you do that, the relationship changes. One change is that you will find yourself becoming more and more obligated to them, especially in a tit for tat kind of way. What they do for you must be duplicated by you for them. These are the people you ask to become involved in your projects and you are the one that they ask to be involved in theirs. It is hard for either of you to say no but then you don't want to because you are pretty good friends, almost family."

"I know what you're talking about," Beth chimed in. "I've had a number of friends like that. And you're right about the obligation thing. Why is it that we have this need to rub each other's backs? Whenever someone does something for me, especially a friend, I immediately feel obligated to do something for them. The same is true with gifts. I love giving gifts to people, but they always give me something back. I don't want anything back. Why do they do that? Why do we get caught up in this obligation game?"

I smiled and chuckled slightly before continuing. "I'm thinking that would be a good subject for an all day paddle boat ride sometime. But you've picked up on my point about how quickly relationships obligate us and then frustrate us, and we've only made it to the family room." I laughed again.

"Let's go to the dining room. We invite even fewer of our friends to eat with us. It's around food and the table that people share even greater intimacy. The stories become more personal probably because there are fewer distractions at meals along with more contentment. Food, wine and music soothe us and the noise of the TV and game playing is absent. The tastes and smells of food tend to stir up powerful memories in people. Memories lead to stories and stories reveal secrets. The more people reveal about themselves the more power obligation has. The more we become obligated to each other, the more we will sacrifice for each other and the greater the demands we will make on each other. As long as people continue to nurture their friendship and the demands are mutual, then the sense of obligation will not be burdensome. If, however, one or both parties abuse each other or don't nurture the friendship, then the odds are good that the friendship will deteriorate."

"Tell me about it," Beth offered. "I had a business associate, actually a client just like you are describing. We became great friends. We had a lot in common. We would go out to eat often, just the two of us, and it wasn't business related. We did other things together. It was her idea that I take that Alaskan cruise. But as time went on she kept asking for more and more from me. At first I didn't mind. But then I got to a point where I thought she was taking advantage of me and when I said something to her about it, she became defensive. She suggested that our friendship must not mean anything to me and the next thing I knew she pulled her account and I never heard from her again."

"She never told you why, never gave you a reason?"

"No. She wouldn't return my calls, my emails, nothing."

"I'm sorry to hear that."

"I think I understand it a little better now after listening to what you said. I've shied away from other friendships like that because I thought that it was something I did, something in my character."

"No," I assured her, "You were a victim of obligation gone amuck. You weren't the first and you won't be the last."

"Are there any more rooms?"

"Just the bedroom."

"Oooh, that sounds interesting."

"It is, but you may not like my spin."

"Try me."

"The bedroom I believe is the room reserved for two people, one man and one woman who are committed to sharing the greatest possible intimacy and privacy with each other and without obligation. Entrance is by joint consent and only after a serious and clear mutual understanding and commitment has been made. There must not be any secrecy or obligation in this room or in this relationship. If there is then the peace, harmony and happiness of the relationship will be jeopardized and the whole house will experience turmoil."

"So how do you keep secrecy and obligation out of this room?"

"That's the sixty-four thousand dollar question, isn't it?"

"I've never had an obligation free relationship."

"You haven't? That's too bad. But I'm happy to announce that you are on the cusp of one right now!"

"What do you mean?"

"I mean that I'm offering you the one that I've been a part of one since my baptism."

"I don't understand."

"Since God made me his child I am in an obligation free relationship. He loves me unconditionally and his power is at work in me so that I might treat you the same way. "

"I don't know what to say about that."

"You don't need to say anything. You only need to accept it."

Beth was silent for a moment. She was obviously processing

"I have wanted to be close to somebody my whole life, but I don't think in reality I've ever made it out of the family room."

"You're doing a lot better than you're giving yourself credit for Beth."

She smiled. "Thank you, but I don't feel that way. I struggle so much with intimacy and obligation. I've always wanted intimacy, but I've never found it. And as much as I hate to admit it, I'm still living mostly by obligation."

"Beth, intimacy is one of those words and concepts that has really been undressed of its meaning by modern culture, pardon the pun. Probably the top five answers on Family Feud for what intimacy means to people would all be *having sex*. Having sex is a small part of intimacy. It is really one fruit of intimacy. But for most people intimacy equals sex and sex is mostly the exchange of emotional energy, passion and bodily fluids, and that can happen in any room of the house with any person at any time. When sex happens apart from true intimacy, there will be obligation like you wouldn't believe.

"Intimacy is so much more. Intimacy is two people who not only share a life journey but want to create one life journey out of two. Right now my life journey is a solo journey. I miss the shared journey that I had. My life feels incomplete. My bedroom is empty. I have no one to share my life journey much less to help me create one. I have no one person to focus my care on and there is no one person focusing their care on me. Not that I need that to survive or to be happy or productive. What I'm saying is that I prefer the life I had. I got used to that life and I liked it a lot and I don't like not having it. God told Adam at the beginning of time that it's not good for man to be alone. That bit of wisdom has my 'amen.'

"Don't take me wrong. I have a lot of people who care about me and my well being and I have a lot of people that I care about. Way at the top of the list are my wonderful, loving children and grandchildren but they are not bedroom candidates."

"You are talking all around marriage Coop without saying the word."

"Yes, I guess that I am."

"Should we be talking about marriage after only knowing each other for a few days?"

"What do you think?"

"I'm not ready to think about it. What about you?"

"I'm not either if you mean making plans, looking for rings and seeking permission from your father. That's something that shouldn't happen for months if it happens at all. But what should happen right now is that we accept the possibility that marriage might happen and freely discuss it whenever the topic comes up. Unless we understand each other's understanding of every life issue including what marriage is and isn't, then we're not ready, if and when the time comes, to make marriage plans anyway."

"You're saying we should keep on discovering!"

"That's the ticket, Beth. And no topic is off limits even those you feel obligated to keep hidden."

Sixty-three

We decided to interrupt our discussion with some much needed sleep. I made one hopefully final bathroom stop before morning while Beth replaced herself in a prone position under her covers. I crawled back into my bed and was preparing to turn off the reading light when the phone rang. Since I was closest to the phone I got up to answer. As I did Beth said, "I wonder who that could be at this hour?" I shrugged.

A phone ringing at this time of the night or morning is never good news unless it's a wrong number.

Ole answered the phone and hung up after a brief moment without saying a word. "Who was it," Lena inquired. "Someone must have thought this was the lighthouse station," Ole replied. "Why did they think this was the lighthouse station?" Lena asked, "I don't know, Lena. All he said was, 'Is the coast clear?'"

I picked up the receiver. "Hello." I listened for a moment and then hung up.

"Who was it?"

"It sounded like Lou Bender."

"What did he want?"

"All he said was, 'Good, you're awake. Don't go anywhere.'"

Sixty-four

I went into the bathroom for a glass of water. As I stepped back into the room I heard a knock on the door. When I opened it, Lou Bender stood in the opening. "We need to talk," he said as he pushed his way into the room.

"You know Lou," I said to his back, "it's always 'we need to talk.' Why can't you ever say, 'good evening' or 'may I come in' or 'I am so sorry for bothering you this late.'"

"You want pleasantries? Sign up as a contestant on the *Price Is Right*." He caught sight of Beth for the first time. "Oh, ho, what have we here? I hope that I haven't interrupted you kids?"

"If you were interrupting anything I would never have answered the phone." I tried to sound a little irritated and tired, which I was. I thought about providing an explanation for our room sharing, but decided to let the thought die of natural causes. "So, now that you're here, have a seat and tell us what can't wait until the sun comes up."

Lou's jaw started working as he looked first at me and then at Beth and then back at me. He was apparently trying to decide if Beth should be included in the discussion.

"Is this about Rachelle or the case?"

"The case."

"Do you want to talk here or should I get dressed and we go . . ."

"No, here is good. I got the report on the Alexi hit back from Washington."

He talked us through it. There wasn't much to talk through. The transcript contained nothing of value. The participants were all comfortable in their roles. No one appeared nervous or fidgety. When the shot came and Alexi went down there was genuine surprise on everyone's face. After the shot, everyone scrambled to find safety. Lou was ninety-nine percent sure that Alexi was specifically targeted by the shooter. He was also confident that his murder had nothing to do with the drug meet other than whoever took him out knew that Alexi was going to be there and used the meet to put a bullet through his brain.

"So you're telling us that whoever wanted Alexi dead had to know his travel plans far enough in advance to be able to arrange this hit."

"That's what it looks like."

"What scenarios does that conclusion still leave stuck to your wall?"

Bender pursed his lips, looked at Beth and then at me. "Retaliation for Ms. Malone."

Sixty-five

Beth was the first to break the silence. "How do you figure that his death is retaliation for killing Anne?"

"It's mostly a hunch at this point, but it's the only hunch that makes sense. Alexi kills Anne either intentionally or by mistake thinking it's you in order to send a message to Frankie or the Gambolini family. I tell Lorenza and Emilio that he did it and they arrange the payback."

"Do you have proof of that?" I asked.

"I'm working on it. We're still tracing phone records but from what we've been able to gather so far through NSA and Interpol and some other cooperating agencies, it seems like we're on the right track."

"What have you learned?"

Lou hesitated before he continued. "We know that Lorenza called Frankie every day since he boarded the ship. He also called right after I informed him of Ms. Malone's murder. Interestingly it was to a different number although to the same residence. Even more interesting, it was to a secure line. He called Frankie again after my second conversation with him. It was during that conversation, I implicated Alexi in her murder."

"Why all the cloak and dagger, with the different numbers and secure lines?"

"I don't know for sure. Phones are fairly easy to tap and Lorenza may have felt that the main line was compromised."

"You can tell if lines are secure and monitor calls and whatever even after phone calls have been made?"

"Oh, yeah, I can't begin to tell what we can do. Big brother has eyes, ears, noses and fingers everywhere."

I kind of figured all of that was true but I still shivered inside at the thought of how modern technology, while it has made life easier, has really invaded and threatened our privacy.

Lou continued. "Things get more interesting. Lorenza's next call is to a number in Italy. That is followed by a call to someone in Mexico. We're trying to locate any recordings of those calls but the red tape and the hoops we have to jump through are making it next to impossible."

"If I understand correctly, Lou, you're saying that Lorenza must have felt that Anne's murder was offensive enough to either him or the family to warrant this eye for an eye payback. There was no mistaken identity."

"That's the explanation that best seems to fit the facts that I have at the moment."

"One problem with that," Beth chimed in. "Anne wasn't a part of the family. To my knowledge she never once set foot in the home place. In fact she even refused to come and see me. She never liked my choice in a husband."

"That is a problem or at least a mystery yet to be solved. From where I sit either she was intimately involved with the family or I got a whole bunch of circumstantial pieces that have to fit together in some other way that I'm not seeing."

"Lou," I said, "Be honest with me. Do you believe that Beth is still in any danger?"

"No. I don't believe that she is or certainly an attempt would have already been made on her life." I hoped that he was right.

"There's something more that I must tell you before I go."

"What's that?"

"Emilio and Svetlana have spent the evening together, drinking, dancing, gambling and indulging in all the pleasures that this ship provides including, I might add, engaging in whatever Mafia bad boys and girls do behind a locked door with a do not disturb even if we hit an iceberg sign on it."

"What's that all about?" I queried with obvious shock in my voice.

"I'm gonna have to find out." Lou got up and moved toward the door. He turned. "Would you be surprised if I told you that this is not the first occasion that they have spent some time together?" Lou smiled, gave us a mini salute and left my stateroom.

Sixty-six

It was a short night for sleep. In spite of the diminished hours I still woke up at my usual time. I was surprised at how soundly I slept. Usually when a lot of information is dumped on me just before sleep or I go to bed right after a long meeting, a difficult counseling session or a disturbing phone call, my mind won't shut down. This time it did. No doubt I was more tired than I presumed that I was.

I got up quietly without turning on any lights and went into the bathroom to get dressed. I did my best not to wake Beth. I left a brief note and then eased out of the door for my morning ship's ritual.

To my surprise I met Lou at the coffee machine. "You're up early."

"Your faithful government servants never sleep."

"Yeah, but do they ever get anything worthwhile done?"

Lou laughed and I laughed with him. I was really starting to not only like the guy but also respect and trust him.

"I didn't get a chance to ask you last night if there was anything new with your wife, if you've talked any more with Rachelle."

Lou smiled. "Do you have time to sit and talk?"

"Are my ears deceiving me or are you actually being polite?"

"Don't push your good fortune Meyerhoff."

"Okay." I held out my hands in surrender. "Let me grab a Danish on the way."

As we prepared to sit Lou pulled a book from his pocket and threw it on the table. It was the one I had recommended that he read: *The Five Love Languages* by Gary Chapman. The subtitle is: *How to express heartfelt commitment to your mate*.

"Where did you get that?" I asked, not hiding my surprise.

"I work for the FBI, remember? There's not much that I can't get my hands on when and where I want it."

"Have you had a chance to get into it much yet?"

"Yeah."

"What do you think?"

"What he says makes a lot of sense." Lou headed for the coffee machine.

Dr. Chapman's contribution to building better marriages is the realization that love can be expressed and understood in numerous ways or languages and that not everyone feels loved or expresses love in the same way. He identifies five different languages of love or five different ways in which people prefer love to be given and received. Those five are quality time, words of affirmation, gifts, acts of service and physical touch.

He contends that each spouse in a marriage brings an empty emotional love tank that needs filling. The husband looks to the wife and the wife looks to the husband for that filling. When the tanks are full then the married life is generally good. When the tanks are empty then the married life is accompanied with difficulties.

This concept has interesting applications when couples discover that their marriage isn't happy. The husband may be wired in such a way, as I learned from Lou, that physical touch is what fills his tank. He assumes that his wife is wired the same way and that physical touch is what fills her tank. If she is wired in that way then this aspect of their relationship will be pretty well tanked up. However, if she isn't wired the same way, which I learned that Rachelle wasn't, then more than likely this couple will "fall out of emotional love" for each other. To keep that "falling out" from happening, couples need to "speak" their spouse's unique love language to each other.

Even if both spouses do speak the same language that is no guarantee of marital bliss because a love language, like physical touch, for example, has many dialects or better different ways of being expressed. One partner may prefer hand holding and snuggling while the other desires experimenting with every sexual position and toy known to mankind.

In his book Dr. Chapman describes each of the love languages and practical ways to implement them. He also helps a person discover what their primary love language is through a self scoring profile. This book is valuable because it can help spouses inform each other how they can more effectively and specifically fill their tanks and make them feel loved.

You should also know that these same love language principles apply to children. Every parent with even an ounce of perceptive power knows that each new child born into the family is different to raise than the one before. Each has a different personality, different potential, different gifts, different thought processes and Chapman argues, a different way to feel and be loved. Figuring out early on what makes each child feel loved will save parents a lot of grief, not all grief, but a good portion of grief nonetheless.

One last comment. It's easy to fall into love. It's easy to fall out of love. It takes commitment to be in love. But those who are in love, those who choose to remain in love are most to be envied.

Sixty-seven

Lou returned to the table with two fresh cups of coffee and sat down. "I called Rachelle last night after we talked and I apologized to her. I told her that I had talked to you and I pretty much related our entire conversation to her. I asked if the way I had ignored her was what hurt her the most. She said it was. I told her that what I had done was selfish of me and wrong of me and that I should have known better. I asked her to please wait until I got home before she made any decision about leaving so that we could talk about this in person, but I also told her that I would understand if she couldn't.

"As I talked with her, I couldn't believe that I was saying the things that I was saying. It was like it wasn't me talking. I kept waiting for her to come after me with both barrels, but she didn't, she listened and then apologized herself for things she said she's done to me." Lou looked down at the table slowly shaking his head.

"How do you feel right now?" I asked.

"I want to get off this ship and hurry home to see her, to see my kids."

"No, I didn't ask what you wanted to do. I want to know how you feel right now."

"I feel scared, yet alive."

"Talk to me about scared."

"I guess I'm afraid that I might not be able to follow through on what I need to do to hopefully save my marriage. I'm afraid Rachelle isn't really committed to saving it either. I'm afraid that I'll do just enough to make a temporary fix and then I'll get caught up in work again and everything will go to pot."

"Those are all honest fears. It's good that you are aware of them. Tell me about feeling alive."

"I feel excited and energized, like I'm starting out on a whole new adventure, like I'm a kid again."

"Where do you think that's coming from?"

"I don't know. I hadn't thought about it coming from any-where. I guess it started after we talked, after I was able to admit my mistakes to you and to myself and then to Rachelle and have her admit hers to me. I think your words about rec-onciliation, forgiveness, humility and blame and then taking the first step have also been working that change in me."

"You're right. That's what's been happening. You are becoming a new person inside. Honest repentance does that to people. When you face your pride and selfishness and accept responsibility for not just blame but then for healing you open up all kinds of possibility for good to happen mostly inside yourself and sometimes with others. That new spirit that is coming alive in you will help keep those fears in check too."

"You think so?"

"I know so. You've already done the hardest part. You've smashed the wall that's kept you and Rachelle apart by admitting your pride. Now comes the part that's actually easier but requires perseverance. You must now do the work of both picking up and clearing away all the rubble from the mess you've made and then start building a new life together."

"How do I that?"

Sixty-eight

"To use Dr. Chapman's terminology, you can't do it on an empty tank."

"You can't do what on an empty tank?" Beth walked up to our table. We both stood to greet her. I gave her a good morning hug. She felt good. I brought her up to speed about what Lou and I had been talking about and she asked if she might join the rest of our discussion. I certainly didn't care and Lou welcomed her with open arms.

"Can I get some coffee first?" She said.

"It looks like the breakfast buffet if open," Lou observed, "Let's get something to eat."

This being the last day of the cruise we loaded up with eggs and sausage and French toast and hash browns. Although there were a goodly number of calories on our plates, those additional calories would not make a significant impact on the total weight gain for the week.

Between mouthfuls Beth looked at Lou and asked, "Have you learned anything more since we talked last night?"

"No. I haven't."

"You hinted just before you left that Emilio and Svetlana weren't strangers and were maybe even lovers. What did you mean?"

"The Bureau sent a couple of surveillance pictures of the two of them together as well as some reports of them meeting at restaurants, coffee shops and a motel."

"How long has this been going on?" I asked.

"For about three months, as near as we can tell."

"Do you know if they planned to meet on this ship?" I continued.

"Nope."

"So maybe Emilio got the information about Alexi's meeting from Svetlana, maybe she even helped him arrange the hit to get rid of him." I liked coming up with off the wall ideas for Lou's wall of ideas.

"I don't think so. We watched both of them from the time of Ms. Malone's death and they didn't contact each other either in person or by ship phone or by any other phone that we're aware of."

"Yeah, but you said that the hit on Alexi was arranged ahead of time."

"I did, but not by the two of them. If it were their doing then how do you explain Lorenza's phone calls first to Frankie, then Italy, then Mexico?"

I shrugged my shoulders in defeat. As I did my eyes caught sight of a familiar face. Speak of the devil. It was Lorenza walking two paces in front of Mike Andrews.

Sixty-nine

"Agent Bender, I got a little problem." Lorenza looked at me and Beth and then back at Lou. "Can we go some place a little more private?"

"Is this about Emilio?"

Lorenza was taken aback. "Yeah, it is. How did you know?"

"Sit down Lorenza. These folks know just about everything I know." Lorenza sat down. Mike remained standing. "Start talking my man."

"Well, like I was telling your partner." Lorenza shifted his gaze from Andrews to Lou. "Emilio left shortly before dinner time. He said he had some business to take care of and he still hasn't come back to the room."

"Do you have any idea what his business was?"

"No, he didn't tell me."

"Did it have anything to do with a woman?"

Lorenza responded to Lou with a quizzical look on his face. "Why would you suggest that? I don't think Emilio has spent a day with a woman since his mother, God rest her soul, died."

"You're serious."

"Yeah I'm serious. What's this about?" Lorenza looked nervously back and forth between us. "Hey, don't be thinking that Emilio isn't all man. He is what we call celibate, like a priest. He's just not interested in going out with women and don't have time for women."

"So you wouldn't believe me if I were to tell you that he spent the last fifteen hours with a woman and that he is still enjoying her company locked inside her stateroom?"

"No, not Emilio?"

"Believe it. It's true."

Lorenza took some time to process what Lou had just told him. "No, why would he do this?"

"That's the question I was hoping that you could answer?"

"Who's the woman?"

"Does it matter?"

"No, I guess not."

"How about if we play a little more, *Let's Make A Deal*, Lorenza?"

"Whattaya got in mind?"

"How about I tell you who the woman is, if you tell me why you arranged to have Alexi offed?" It was obvious from his expression that Lorenza did not see that one coming. "Before you deny it, I have all the proof that I need to put you away as a co-conspirator to his murder. I've got phone records and conversations. Now I am also a man of my word. The promise I made to you still stands. The world is better off without scum like Alexi, but I still need answers. Why was Ms. Malone so important to you that you had to go after Alexi so soon after she was killed?"

Lorenza sat with his hands folded on his lap. He was perfectly still except for his thumbs rubbing each other. His mind was no doubt searching frantically for an escape. "You are right. I did arrange to have Alexi taken out. It is no secret that the Russians are moving in on our territory and they decided to send us a message. They weren't smart enough to get the right woman. But it didn't matter. Frankie, give him credit for once, agreed to send a stronger message back."

I noticed that Lorenza never looked Lou in the eye until he spoke his last sentence. To me when you don't look someone in eye that means either shame or you are telling a lie.

Lou and Lorenza talked a while longer about some of the phone calls and other details but Lorenza was not about to rat out anyone specifically. Eventually they got back to Emilio and his girlfriend.

"I've told you what I know and what I can, now who's the woman?"

"You told me in previous conversations that you never met Alexi or Svetlana before this cruise. Do you still stand by that statement?"

"Yeah, I know them Russians all look alike but I swear on my mother's grave that I never met those two before or saw them before."

"Would Emilio have attended any meetings that the family had with those Russians that you wouldn't have attended?"

"No. I know it may be obvious to everyone but you, but I'm the brains and Emilio is the muscle. He don't go nowhere by himself. Frankie don't trust him. Even Tony didn't trust him to make good decisions. What's this all about?"

"Emilio spent all night with Svetlana Zabbarova."

Seventy

Lorenza said something in Italian as he slammed the table with his fist and sent our dishes jumping. None of us required a translator for his remarks. He was ready to leap out of his chair when Andrews pushed him down.

"I need for you to get yourself under control," Lou ordered.

"I am going to kill that mother . . ."

"Lorenza." Lou interrupted. "We need to think this through calmly. We need to figure out why he's seeing her and why he's kept it from you. There's got to be a reason."

"Yeah, you're right." Lorenza looked at Beth and apologized for his choice of words and his outburst of temper in the presence of a lady.

We spent the next thirty minutes or so discussing this strange situation and working to develop a strategy with which to proceed. Lorenza would go back to his room and wait for Emilio. When Emilio returned he would not interrogate him any more than normal about his absence nor would he let on what he knew. If Emilio were forthcoming about his whereabouts he would of course gather all the information that he could and they would turn it over to Lou. If Emilio remained silent then he would get a message to Lou and Lou would come to the room and attempt to get the information himself.

Bender's communication device buzzed. He got up and walked a few steps away from the table before he answered it. He closed the phone and walked back.

"That was Sashi. It seems like the prodigal son is returning home. Lorenza, I suggest you head back too. I'll be waiting for your call. You've got your story straight, right?"

"I'm good."

I invited Beth to step outside with me for some much needed morning fresh air before I headed back to my room to get cleaned up and properly dressed for the day. We were greeted by a sky that appeared filled with the promise of a lovely last day at sea. There were also several ships that greeted our gaze. I counted at least three huge cargo vessels weighted down with supplies to support body and life somewhere in the world. I identified one oil tanker hauling fuel to either keep people warm or to motor them wherever they chose to be motored. And I counted one other cruise ship. Another three thousand or so people like us enjoying some of the finest pleasures available to average folks. So much stuff, so much abundance, so many with so much more than they knew what to do with, so much going to waste while so many were dying of hunger, dying of cold, dying of lack.

Bon Voyage

Lust

Envy/Jealousy

Anger

Sloth

Gluttony

Greed

Pride

Debarkation

Seventy-one

While waiting for Beth to finish assembling herself and her things for the day I decided to turn on the television in the stateroom. The *Festival* had a channel dedicated to showing the vessel's location relative to its itinerary in the Caribbean. In addition to the geographical map, the screen displayed the speed at which we were traveling, our actual GPS location, the wind direction and a couple of other pieces of information useful to people who like that kind of information, people like myself. I check this station often during a cruise if it's available.

I decided to also look for a twenty-four hour news channel. Since we would be docking tomorrow I thought that it might be prudent to learn what might be going on in the world, if the world was still going on.

After listening to the anchor and watching the news ticker for several minutes I resolved that nothing much had happened to the world during my absence. There were no new wars, no major natural disasters, no assassination attempts, no unusual weather and no new scandals affecting Hollywood, government or the sports world being reported. It is interesting how a person can escape the business and busyness of the world for six days and not really miss anything. Life goes on with or without us.

The new news was eerily similar to the old news. The oil producing countries were meeting and considering raising the price of a barrel of oil. A first round draft choice who had never played a minute on the professional level was holding out for the sole purpose of evidently earning the distinction of becoming the highest paid draft choice in his sport ever.

The U.S. Congress, in order to fund increased spending measures, was considering raising taxes on everyone who made more than $40,000 per year. Our out-of-touch legislators were also planning on hitting businesses with additional taxes as well as adding taxes to certain luxury products and the old standby, cigarettes. For some reason they never seemed to excessively tax or attempt to regulate much less reign in the alcohol industry. Could it be because people in government or their top contributors liked to drink?

Hollywood's film makers, although they were having their best box office in several years were complaining that they didn't have enough money to produce the kind of films they claimed that the public wanted. The NFL announced that ticket prices would on average only increase by fifteen percent for the upcoming season.

The journalist reporting most of this breaking news was earning seven figures himself, having received that settlement as a result of a network bidding war over his services about a year ago.

Just before I turned the set off, a young up and coming, on location reporter, detailed yet another ponzi scheme impacting unsuspecting investors. Her last comment before signing off was, "Money is indeed the root of all evil." Editorial comments like that as part of a news story is one of several reasons why I rarely watch television news, listen to radio news or read newspapers. If a person is going to quote an authority for millions to hear, at least get the quote correct. Someone shouldn't use misquotes along with a position of influence to mislead people or to promote a personal agenda, ideology or point of view. There is nothing wrong with having a point of view or an agenda. But if you want to express your opinion or personal bias, then be honest with your audience and tell them you are editorializing and not reporting fact.

In this case, the truth is that "the love of money is a root of all kinds of evil" (1 Timothy 6:10) and not that money is the root of all evil. People misquote this Bible truth all the time. They do so in the way the reporterette did, by leaving out the word "love" and/or by not emphasizing the indefinite article "a." The indefinite article calls for an understanding that the love of money is one of many roots of evil and not the only one by a long shot.

My favorite abuse of this verse though is from those who claim that it is not the love of money but rather the lack of money that is the root of all evil.

Almost every story from that newscast was about people wanting more. It's not the wanting itself that is necessarily bad. What makes the wanting bad is when the wanting is accompanied by dissatisfaction, discomfort and a desire to have more at someone else's expense. When wanting is accompanied by the hunger to accumulate or by the sense of privilege or by the demeanor that some have that they are owed or by the quest for power, control and influence, then we conclude that greed is at work in the wanting.

Greed is characterized by an obsessive desire to both acquire and to then to retain what has been acquired. A greedy person wants to obtain more and isn't concerned about how he obtains it. The end justifies the means. Being greedy is not just about gaining material possessions. People are greedy for intangible things like fame and recognition. One of the best ways to combat a covetous spirit is by developing a thankful and contented spirit and practicing generosity and mercy. This change in the Scrooge-like attitude seems to best happen as a result of a midnight visit from Dickens' spirits of Christmas past, present and future.

Avarice or at least the far reaching effects of discontent in our culture was brought home to me in a study that impressed me a number of years ago. I don't have the source information any longer but essentially the paper I read summarized a research sampling of a large number of people from across socio-economic lines. The one detail that I remember concluded that groups of people from the poorest to the richest gave the same answer to the question, "What do you need to make your life better?" Every group regardless of their level of income answered, "A few more dollars."

The study suggested that people believe a little more can only help them and not hurt them. That would be an interesting discussion to have some time. Does more help or hurt a person? I can think of all kinds of examples of how wanting more and accumulating more tends to hurt us while giving up things or losing things tends to help us. On the one hand consider lottery winners. Very few report in the years following a big windfall that they were glad they won. On the other hand consider two income families who have been forced to cut back to one income. Most of them report renewed family vigor and life.

Greed leads people to rob, to murder, to deceive, to lie, to undermine, to cheat, to betray, to cover up, to shift blame and a host of other dubious acts. We can easily understand when bad people do these things, but how about when supposedly good people do them? When fathers and mothers do them to their children, or friends do them to their friends, or neighbors do them to their neighbors, or church members do them to fellow church members? Then it's not so easily understood. A lot of wars in our world's history have been started, not to mention a lot of family relationships shattered, all because someone wanted and took what belonged to someone else. The hunger for stuff that is here today and gone tomorrow has caused a lot of grief. The hunger for stuff that no one brought into this world and that we're told no one will be able to take out of this world has put whole nations into turmoil and enslaved countless innocent people.

Three clergymen split the cost of a lottery ticket and they won the grand prize of a million dollars. Before picking up their winnings they had to resolve the issue of how much God would get and how much they would get to keep.

The first minister suggested, "Let's draw a circle and throw the money up in the air. Whatever lands inside the circle we'll keep and whatever lands outside the circle we'll give to God."

The second minister said, "You know it's a little windy today. I think we should throw the money up in the air and whatever lands inside the circle we give to God whatever lands outside of the circle we keep."

The third minister said, "I think we should simply throw the money up in the air and whatever God wants he can keep and whatever falls to the ground is ours to keep."

Seventy-two

Beth and I left the stateroom and went directly to the serenity deck. We had no trouble finding two lounge chairs together in a prime spot. It was fairly early and most of the passengers were still sleeping off last night's carousing. The sun was strong and warm and there was just a breath of breeze.

I shifted the chairs so that we would be close together, adjusted the angle of the chaise, took out my book from my travel bag, slipped off my t-shirt and sandals and lay down on my back for a day of relaxation. I would wait until a little later to apply some sun screen. I hurried to get into this position because I wanted to focus my attention on Beth as she went through her unpacking to sunning ritual.

I was glad that I had not dawdled. She deliberately pulled a book from her bag as well her sun screen. Then she pulled up and over her head the delicate garment she was wearing over her swimsuit. Swimsuit was a very generous name for her attire. She apparently was planning on tanning the maximum surface area allowed by the international cruise line tanning federation. Who was I to argue? She leaned over, picked up her sun screen and began a slow and careful application process to her skin. I didn't get any of my book read for those several minutes.

When she finally finished and lay back side down on her chaise, I swear that the temperature on that portion of the deck had climbed twenty degrees. The smile on her face as she turned to look at me told me that she thoroughly enjoyed the agony that she had just put me through.

"You look great today." I told her.

"Thank you. I feel good." She took my hand. "Thanks again for everything. It's been a wonderful week." She turned and we lightly kissed. As she pulled back a shroud of gloom appeared on her face.

"What's wrong?" I asked.

"I can't stop thinking about what's going to happen after tomorrow."

"Let's not spoil today by worrying about or even thinking about tomorrow. Let's just enjoy today. Tomorrow will take care of itself, okay?"

"Okay." We squeezed hands, let go of each other and turned to our respective books.

Seventy-three

"Do you think that Lou and Rachelle will work out their troubles?" Beth broke a period of silence between us.

"Not without more of my brilliant counsel and help." I responded in a somewhat pompous voice.

"I'm serious."

"I certainly hope they work things out. Even if I knew more about their situation it's next to impossible to predict what might happen to them. There are too many unknowns and too much mystery in relationships to ever say for sure."

"We never had a chance to talk about what marriage is earlier this morning. Can we do that now?"

I closed my book and turned just enough to face her. "Sure."

"So what is marriage?"

"What do you think it is?"

"Well it's when two people love each other and want to spend the rest of their lives together."

"Okay. Sounds about right, anything else?"

"Well there's the commitment of for better or worse and 'til death us do part."

"Yeah."

"Ah, and there's compatibility and common interests and working together, there's sex and ah, building a family and ah, understanding each other and putting up with each other and ah, things like that . . . and intimacy and discovering life together!"

"That it?"

"Yeah, pretty much. What do think?"

"Well I think that there are two ways to look at marriage. One way is to see it as something that society and culture has created on its own. The other way is to view it as something that has been established for us and given to us as a trust.

"If marriage is a product of the human mind and societal need, then the discussion about marriage will focus on the questions of who, what, why, where and how. Society will try to understand the dynamics behind people falling in love and what to do about uniting those lovers. They will be concerned about how to protect the unions, the property in the unions, the children of the unions and other issues germane to pre-serving the unions. Should a married couple fall out of love then society has to figure out how to dissolve the union while still protecting the various parts that made up the union.

"And so the discussions today center around marital rights and contracts and legal unions and taxes and alimony and pre-nuptials and children's rights, and of course who can and who can't get married, and what's fair and what's unfair, and so on and so forth. In all this we avoid discussing what the real essence of marriage is. We never get around to understanding marriage's purpose for life, which I happen to believe has a divine origin and intention to it."

"You're saying that marriage is instituted by God," Beth offered. "But what if people don't accept that there is a God or care that marriage might have a divine purpose?"

"Anyone can believe whatever they want, I don't care. If you think that you've got a better way to live, more power to you, just let me live my way. Or better yet, give me a chance to hear you and your way out, and then take the time to listen to me and my way. I think that my way will wipe the floor with your way."

"I'm listening. What is your way?"

"Well if you really want to understand marriage, you first have to understand where you came from."

"You mean your background, your country of origin?"

"No, I mean the beginning of life. Did life originate from a rock that over billions of years turned into a liquid from which a single living cell appeared, which cell eventually through countless mutations and exposures to external forces evolved into the male and female humanoid species that we are today? If you believe that life began and developed that way then marriage or relationships between the sexes of our species can be anything you want them to be. Since you and I and people like us are for the most part the highest evolved members of the animal kingdom, our behavior need not necessarily be any different than what we might observe anywhere in the animal kingdom.

"If however you believe that you were personally, purposefully, and uniquely created by the God who also created and rules the universe, and that your life is supported and sustained by him, and that you will be held accountable by him, then it follows that there are differences between the animal and human species. It also follows that not only are there differences between us and animals but that humans have standards by which relationships between the sexes exist and might prosper. Does that make sense?"

"Yes, I hear what you are saying."

"People get all worked up when you raise the issue of creation versus evolution. Certainly those two views of origins have a different understanding and explanation for the evidence that is being uncovered in the world around us, but for one side to claim that it is science while the other is religion is a very false and misleading notion. The bottom line is that the assumptions and hence the conclusions of the evolutionists and the creationists make them both religions because both require faith. Which explanation of origins is easier to believe? That we evolved by chance over billions of years from a rock nobody can explain where it came from or that a divine being who nobody can explain made it all?"

"You're asking me?" Beth inquired. "Neither one is believable."

"Exactly, and since there were no human witnesses present we have to accept any explanation of the beginning by faith.

"I choose to believe that I am a creature who was divinely created. Someone else may believe that his first ancestors were a rock. Who's right? It doesn't matter really. What matters more is how that belief guides each of us. I believe that I matter to God and to his world. I believe that I have been carefully and purposefully knit together in my mother's womb by a gracious and divine architect. I believe that I am an important piece in his plans. I believe that he is taking me on a journey through time and into eternity. Part of my journey is to figure out my place in those plans and accomplish the greatest good during the time that I have. I know that it includes serving him by loving and caring for my fellow travelers.

"My other option is to believe that I am a product of lower life forms. From that perspective life focuses on me. I am accountable to me. There are no absolutes governing my behavior or choices. I can adopt one of many different life philosophies. I can be a stoic, like Spock on Star Trek. I can be a fatalist and just accept whatever happens. I can be an epicurean, someone who lives life to the fullest – eat, drink and be merry for tomorrow I may be dead. I can be a relativist. I can be a bully. I can be a hermit. I can be counter-cultural. I can try to become powerful, wealthy or famous. I can write my own rules for living, even choose my own sexual orientation if I want. The point is that life revolves around me, myself and I. If someone gets in my way then I ignore him, use him or run over him unless I need him in which case then maybe I will help him.

"That sounds pretty unfeeling and uncaring."

"I don't intend it to be. I'm only trying to illustrate logically the two competing world views."

I went on to describe to Beth some of what I believed about origins based on the first two chapters of the book of Genesis from the Bible. She was familiar with the stories of creation from her days in Catholic school.

I emphasized mostly the truth of our uniqueness from those chapters. I suggested that while we may have many similarities to the members of the animal kingdom we are not linked to the animal kingdom. We are instead linked to the Creator and each other. We were made in God's image and no animal can claim that distinction. The Creator took time and care to fashion the first man from dust and then put his breath in him.

Later he took a piece from the man's side in order to fashion the first woman.

"For me it is far more comforting to believe that I am a part of something divine and something purposeful rather than to accept that I am just a bunch of chemicals that have bonded together in a random, impossible to explain way. I may be here today and gone tomorrow, but I am here for a purpose and I am loved while I am here."

Little Johnny heard the preacher telling the people gathered at a funeral that the deceased had come from dust and now that he had died, the man would return to dust. That would be the fate of everyone.

That evening after Johnny's mother had tucked him into bed for the night she heard him calling to her in a loud voice, "Mommy, come here quick!" She ran up the stairs to his room and saw him on the floor by his bed. "Johnny what's wrong?" "Look, under my bed," he said pointing to a thick layer of dust. "There is someone here and he is either coming or going!"

Seventy-four

"**W**hat does all this have to do with marriage?" Beth asked.

"The first point of emphasis from the story of creation is that God determined that the man he had placed in the world to care for it needed a companion, a helper, someone to share his life journey and responsibilities. The man as far as we know wasn't lonely or wasn't complaining. God decided to provide something more for the good of the man he loved.

"The second point of emphasis is the way in which God provided the companion. He didn't get the material for her from the ground; instead he took it from the man himself. From one substance, from one hunk of humanity God created two. The first man and the first woman were, with the exception of some hardware and plumbing differences, equals. She wasn't made from material originating in his head or feet which might indicate competitiveness or subservience, but with material from his side which again argues for equality. The essence of marriage is fundamentally based on the man and woman accepting each other as equals.

"Second they were each whole. They had their own identity as male and female. They didn't need each other to survive. They could stand on their own with God as their provider. The symbol of marriage in our culture emphasizes this truth. It is two rings that interlock. Each is a whole circle symbolizing in my mind a whole person, an independent person who chooses to join with another independent person. Two strong links who join to create a strong chain.

"Too many marriages begin with dependant people, with people who aren't whole, with people who are needy, with people who are incomplete, with people who are looking for another person to complete or fulfill them. They are more like half rings trying to connect and the result is a non-chain or a weak linking. They marry for the wrong reason. They marry because they're fed up with living at home or because all their friends are already married or because there's a pregnancy or because they think they're in love or because there's money or because of security or because of social status or because of any number of self-centered reasons. What too often happens is the reason for marrying grows thin and a troubled, unsatisfied relationship results."

"That's exactly what happened to me," Beth offered, "and I might add to my sister and most of my friends. But at the time we thought we had it made. We were in love and we're convinced that we would be married forever, 'til death us do part." I sighed in agreement and continued on.

"The next step in the story is that God brought the woman to the man and in the same act brought the man to the woman. She is his gift to the man and he is his gift to the woman. They celebrate each other.

"Recognizing that God brings a man and woman together for marriage and gives them to each other is a critical part of the essence of marriage. If I look at my wife and think about how I swept her off her feet or how I found her or how I own her or how I might have rescued her or whatever other claim I might make on her then that attitude might potentially lead me to believe that I could find someone better. Or that perhaps when I first chose her I was young and impetuous and foolish in my choice of her and now that I'm older and wiser I am able to make a better choice. If on the other hand I see my spouse as a gift to me I won't question my choice but will be much more eager to spend the rest of my life unwrapping her and discovering that I will never live long enough to be able to remove all the paper."

"Is that what people mean when they say that a marriage is made in heaven?"

"I'm not sure what people mean by that."

"I think they mean that God arranges a person's mate."

"Humm , , , that's an interesting thought. How would a person know if he or she found the one that God had picked out?"

"I don't know how it works. It just seems that some couples are meant for each other. Some seem really happy and some, you know, are a disaster."

"God certainly has his hands in bringing a man and woman together but you must remember the man and the woman have a big say too in the outcome of the relationship. This is the final point from Genesis. The author after providing the underlying assumptions about marriage then offers a definition. He writes, "For this reason a man will leave his father and mother and be united to his wife, and they will become one flesh" (Genesis 2:24). There are three pieces in that definition.

"First there is **leaving** the family of origin. A son or daughter belongs to the parents until they give the child permission to create a new family unit. So important is the family unit that one of the Ten Commandments was dedicated to its preservation, "Honor your father and mother." When honoring occurs and when parents provide an environment of love and trust this leaving might be painful but it will never be hurtful like it was for you when you were married.

"The second part is being **united**. This refers to the vows that a couple speaks. The only glue that holds a husband and wife together until death is their commitment to each other.

The husband's faith in his wife's faithfulness and her faith in his faithfulness are what enable their life together. That's why they are called vows. Those promises are best said in public so that those who witness a couple's intention can help them fulfill their intention.

"The third part is **becoming one flesh**. This is sexual intimacy, intercourse. This grows out of an intimacy already long established in the relationship. God has reserved intercourse for the marriage bed. It is to be shared only between a husband and wife and only after leaving and a public commitment have taken place. It is perhaps the only private act that will belong exclusively to that couple. The sexual act is primarily an act for creating life. When sperm and egg unite and a child is born that child is one hundred per cent the father and one hundred percent the mother. Their child is two who has become one. Their commitment to each other carries over into their commitment to raise their one flesh.

"When sex happens outside of this commitment and life is created what happens to that life? The odds are very good that it will not be as loved and cared for as fully as it would have been in a marriage of commitment.

"Simply, in God's design marriage is a whole man and a whole woman who can stand on their own but who trust that God has chosen to give them to each other. Once they realize that, they secure the permission and blessing from their families and commit the rest of their lives to discovering and serving each other and possibly the next generation.

"That's the basics of what I believe that marriage is. Others believe that it is something different. That doesn't mean I'm right and they're wrong or vice-versa. But now you know most of where I'm coming from. It's up to you if you still think I'm the marryin' kind."

"I'm not quite sure what kind you are yet, Coop." Beth laughed. "I'll tell you one thing; you are giving me a lot to think about. I didn't know that there was so much that I didn't know."

"Yeah, the longer I live the more I realize how much I don't know. But I do know this. I really enjoy you and your company." Beth smiled and lay back on her chair. I lay back in mine too but with both eyes focused on her.

Seventy-five

Beth was searching frantically through her pack and not coming up with what she needed to come up with. "I must have left my lip screen and sun glasses back in the room. Will you excuse me while I go back and get them?"

"Why don't I get them for you?"

"No, I need to walk. You stay here and hold our places. I won't be long. Is there anything you need?"

"No, just time with you." She smiled, stood up and replaced her cover garment over her suit and headed back to the room.

She wasn't gone long when Lou came strolling up. "Where's Beth?" There was a bit of uneasiness in his voice.

"She just went back to the room. She forgot a couple of things."

"By herself?"

"Yeah, why?"

"Let's go, now!" He started running toward my room and I ran after him. I didn't even pause to put on my sandals or shirt.

As we flew down the corridor of my stateroom Lou called back. "Do you have your room key?"

I reached into my swim trunks and removed it just in time to slip it in the door lock and push it open. There on the bed was someone on top of Beth, choking her. I didn't hesitate a millesecond but lowered my shoulder and mustering all my strength and anger rushed the offender with the intent of driving the perpetrator off of Beth and into a state of unconsciousness.

I'm sure that I got within inches of my goal. Unfortunately before I reached my prey, it sprung up and somehow redirected my energy and sent me crashing into the furniture and walls. I wanted to bounce back up and try again but my body said, "No way!" Lou was hot on my tail and with the same objective. But quick as lightening the invader, who I now recognized as Svetlana, whipped out a steak knife and forced Lou to halt his attack. She waved, jabbed and threatened with that knife as they danced around the room. Gradually she worked her way to the door, opened it and exited before slamming it behind her.

Lou put his hand on the door as if he intended to pursue the woman, but he stopped, having decided that the well being of Beth and me were his higher priority.

He hurried back towards us looking first in my direction. I mouthed that I was okay and told him to check on Beth. As he evaluated her I struggled to my feet. I knew that it was going to be another day on pain pills. "How is Beth?"

Lou looked up. "It's a good thing we got here when we did. I think it would be wise to have someone from the medical staff come up and check you both over." I nodded in agreement.

Lou went over to the house phone. I knelt down on the floor by the bed next to Beth's head and began stroking her hair. She opened her eyes and gave me a weak smile. "You're safe now," I assured her. "The doctor's on his way."

In the background I heard Lou first talk with medical personnel, then with his partner Mike Andrews and finally with Sashi. He asked the security man if he could somehow track Svetlana's escape route through the video cameras. Sometime during his calls he had switched from the room phone to his own communication device. He closed it and walked over to us. The doctor should be here in a few minutes. Sashi is going to see if he can track Svetlana's whereabouts and I have Andrews attempting to secure Genette and Susana.

That got my attention. "Are you worried about them too?"

"Let's just say I'd rather be safe than sorry at this point."

Beth tried to sit up at the mention of her niece. I helped her successfully complete the painful ordeal. She wavered slightly and then finally gained her balance. Her voice was raspy as she spoke. "Why would Svetlana want to hurt Genette and Susana?"

Lou was working his jaw and lips. "Let's wait and talk about that after the doc checks you over?"

Seventy-six

Medical gave us an all clear. Nothing appeared to be broken or damaged. Ibuprofen should handle our discomfort. There would be some ugly bruising on both of us. Normal clothes would cover mine. Beth would need a scarf or turtlenecks if she wanted to hide her primary injuries.

After the doctor left, Lou debriefed Beth. It was apparent that Svetlana had been watching us on the serenity deck for awhile. She had followed Beth when she went to the room. The Russian had grabbed her outside the room and forced Beth inside. She drug her over to the bed and threw her down. She then got on top of her, pinning Beth's arms with her knees and wrapping her hands around Beth's neck. Before she began applying enough pressure to kill her Svetlana had informed her that this was payback for what the Gambolini's did to Alexi and that they would know it. That's when we busted in.

"When you came looking for us, how did you know that Beth's life was in danger?" I asked Lou.

Lou went through the events leading up to our mad dash to rescue Beth. Lorenza had been unsuccessful in getting Emilio to admit anything about his overnight hiatus. He said he had run into an old friend from his high school days and the two of them had talked and drank well into the night before he fell asleep in his friend's room.

As agreed, Lorenza contacted Lou and Lou came calling. It didn't take long before Emilio began singing a different tune. Evidence like photographs, dates, places and eye witnesses are pretty condemning. In addition they encourage singing. Emilio admitted rendezvousing with Svetlana several times during the last three months. He said that he didn't know that she was going to be on this cruise and that he was surprised to learn that she was on the ship. He claimed that when he contacted her she was surprised too.

Emilio also said that Frankie had assigned him to seek out and get friendly with Svetlana. Frankie wanted him to find out what the Russians were up to in their territory back home.

Lorenza's response to Emilio's revelation went something like, "Frankie is a bigger (*fill in the blank*) than even I have given him credit for being. There is no way Emilio could pull something like that off. What was he thinking?"

It didn't take rocket scientists to figure out the rest. Even though Emilio swore on his mother's grave that he had told her nothing, Svetlana had certainly played him like a Stradivarius.

She no doubt learned from him that Alexi had killed the wrong woman and that Beth was the one tied closest to the family and that if she needed more marks, Beth's niece and great niece were also on the ship. She probably even got him to implicate the Gambolini's in the Alexi hit although she wouldn't have needed any verification.

Lou finished his summation of the meeting, "When my confrontation with Emilio was over, he hung his head in shame. Lorenza went over to him. I thought at first he was going to slap him and chew him up and spit him out. Instead he stood in front of him, grabbed Emilio's face in both his hands and forced him to look him in his eyes. He said something to him in Italian. When he finished he kissed Emilio on both cheeks. My guess was he said something like, 'you big galoot, why didn't you come to me? Aren't we like brothers? I could have saved you from all this heartache. You stupid fool, don't you know I still love you.' After Lorenza was finished with Emilio he turned to me and said, 'If I was you, I'd locate Mary Elizabeth as quickly as you can.'"

Seventy-seven

Lou answered the knock on my stateroom door. It was Sashi who entered the room. He nodded at Lou then looked at Beth and me. "Good morning Mr. Meyerhoff and Ms. Malone. It is good to see you. I am sorry about your troubles today. I am thankful that your injuries are not serious."

I spoke for the two of us. "Good morning Sashi. It is good to see you too. Thank you for your concern."

He turned to Lou. "I have the information that you requested. We tracked Ms. Zabbarova until she disappeared through a door into the crew area of the ship. That is not good news."

"Why?"

"Two reasons. One is that we have very few cameras in the crew area. The ones we do have are for safety purposes or for observing secure or sensitive areas and in engineering. It is a violation of workers' privacy rights to be spying on them with cameras."

"What's the second reason?"

"There are many places to hide."

Lou considered what Sashi had said. "How easy will it be for her to get off of the ship without being detected?"

"This will not be an easy task. Her best way would be to jump overboard sometime during the darkness of the night and hope that she could either swim for a couple hundred kilometers or that some boat would see her and rescue her. I suppose she could wait until we were closer to shore and jump, but then it will be light and she would more than likely be noticed by someone and the authorities would certainly be contacted."

I offered my two cents. "If that's her best way off then I'm not seeing much hope of her getting off this ship at all."

"As I suggested, it will be very difficult. She could return to the passenger section of the ship, presume another guest's identity and attempt to slip through security. This would not be easy unless she already has someone singled out that has her looks and size.

"She could also try to sneak off through the crew egress. This also would be difficult unless she could again presume someone's identity. We know exactly who is on this ship and who is off this ship at all times. Anyone who tries to check out who never checked in will be caught. The only advantage she might have as part of the crew is that we don't screen our workers as closely as we do our passengers."

I offered another two cents. "Could she be smuggled out, like in an empty barrel or a half full carton of crushed cans or mixed in with the suitcases?"

"It is possible but she would need to have how do you say it, ah, accomplices. Perhaps she has already arranged this or has the power to arrange it now. It would be very risky especially since I am sure the FBI is going to search every container very carefully. Let me also add this. We are not very merciful to any worker who violates company policy. And aiding someone fleeing a crime would result in immediate termination."

I had only two cents left. "Could she stay hidden on the ship and then sneak off at some other port next week?"

"Again the same arguments apply. The major difference might be that in those foreign ports she would not have authorities looking for her."

Lou reentered the conversation. "It sounds to me like she is trapped. What we don't know is if she realizes how trapped she is. We have to do two things. One is we must protect Beth, Genette and Susana from another potential attempt on their lives. Second, we must prepare for her to make her escape from this ship. She's been trained to survive and her first instinct will be to survive. That's good news for Beth and the others. Her mission to eliminate them is secondary. She can always finish that next week, next month, even next year, but she has to live to fight another day so getting off the ship will be her primary focus."

Seventy-eight

"You don't need us any more do you Lou?" I raised this question as I sensed the strategy now being discussed by Sashi and Lou was a waste of time for Beth and me. We could be spending that time together in the still beautiful Caribbean outdoors.

"No. You can go. However Beth will be shadowed by a security guard until we get this situation with Svetlana resolved."

"I understand."

Sashi opened his communications device and ordered up a guard. "Your escort will be here in a couple of minutes."

Beth gathered up her things while I put on a fresh t-shirt. I opened the door and we waited in the doorway for our guardian angel.

We went first to check the status of the stuff that we had left several hours earlier on the serenity deck. It was still there. I decided that I needed to get something to eat. Beth passed on lunch and instead stretched out on the lounge chair. Our angel disappeared to a carefully chosen observation perch.

My last cruise lunch would be a cheeseburger with lettuce, tomato, fresh onion, mustard and sautéed mushrooms along with a side of potato salad and a glass of lemonade. I brought a second glass for Beth. Dessert would come a little later.

As I ate I eyed the hot tub. Near the end of my delightful meal I asked Beth if she wanted to jump in the tub since it was open. She agreed.

The water was warmer than the air. The jets pounding on my sore body felt good. I reached over and found her hand and grabbed it while turning my head to look at her. She clenched my hand and looked at me. I smiled at her and she returned a very weak one. A day that had begun with so much promise quickly was spoiled by someone's obsession to get even, by someone's hunger to control another someone's destiny.

"I'm so sorry that this had to happen to you. I shouldn't have let you go to the room alone."

"You couldn't have anticipated her doing this to me. I just thank God you got there when you did or I'd . . . be dead." Beth broke into tears and heavy sobs as she wrapped her arms around me.

I let her empty herself of her emotions before I spoke. "I thank God that you're alive too. You're safe Beth and that evil, greedy, nasty woman is going to get caught."

"I hope so. I certainly hope so. I hope she burns in hell."

Seventy-nine

Beth let me bring her some soft serve after we finished in the hot tub and returned to our deck chairs. I could feel its healing powers working with every bite. I finished my bowl, set it on the deck, leaned back in my chair and closed my eyes hoping for a short nap.

"Hey, Cooper are you asleep?" It was Lou Bender. Who else?

"And if I was asleep, would it matter?" I didn't bother opening my eyes as I answered him, but did offer a slight smile.

"Of course, I would never interfere with your alone time or your happiness either for that matter."

"What's up?" This time I did open them and turned to face him.

"I just came from Lorenza's room. I was there updating them on the situation and still trying to fit all the pieces of this case together when guess who called?"

"The Jolly Green Giant?"

"You're close. She ain't jolly and she ain't green but she's big."

"Svetlana?"

"In person."

"She called you?"

"No. She called Emilio. Fortunately I had just talked to him about this very possibility. Am I brilliant or what? I told him that she might feel trapped and that she might turn to him as her only friend on this ship for help. If she did he needed to keep playing the game. He needed to do whatever she asked and he couldn't let on that he was wise to what she was doing to him. Lorenza promised him that if he did this he would personally find him a nice Italian woman who could not only cook but could yank his chain better than two Svetlana's at once. That seemed to get his attention and cooperation."

"What did she want from him?"

"She needed something from her room and she wants him to get it and bring it to her. Apparently she's afraid to come out into the passenger area and can't trust anyone in the crew to get the stuff she needs."

"What does she need?"

"It's probably an alternative identity packet or maybe a kit for altering an identity or emergency cash. I hope it's not a weapon. She must think that she'll be able to sneak off this ship somehow."

"So how's it going down?"

"She told Emilio some convincing story about being victimized at the casino and how these guys she beat out of a lot of money are watching her room so she can't go back there. She needs somebody she trusts to collect this packet. Emilio played the gullible lover role like he really was a gullible lover. Lorenza was even impressed. Once Emilio gets the stuff he is going to contact her and they'll arrange a meet."

"How long before this unfolds?"

"I would think within the hour."

"Then what, do you try to nab her when they meet?"

"I doubt that she'll come in person. She'll probably send a runner. Hopefully we'll be able to ID whoever it is and get the info we need. If we get real lucky a camera might pick up her hiding place."

Eighty

B efore Lou stood up to leave, he gave me a two way phone. "I'll call you when it's time for Emilio to pass along the package." He provided the details of where I should go and how to get there. He gave me a badge that would insure my safe passage to the observation room. He apologized that the invitation didn't include Beth. His excuse was that the room wasn't large enough. We both could see that it was a bogus reason but neither of us raised an objection.

As he turned to leave, Beth called out. "Is there any word on Genette and Susana?"

"Oh, I'm glad you asked. Susana is fine. She was with the ship's child care staff. She told us where her mother had spent the night and we found her safe and sound in the protecting arms of some old geezer. We checked him out. He's a twice divorced, currently single, retired real estate tycoon living in West Palm Beach. He isn't anyone for us to worry about. We explained the reason for interrupting their effort at enhancing inter-generational relations, but that did nothing to quell the woman's temper. She might not be able to do much better in finding a potential mate and provider, but he sure could." Lou chuckled. "Be assured that we will be shadowing both girls all day." He walked purposefully away.

I turned to Beth, "That's good news."

"Yes. I'm glad they're okay. I still wish there was something I could do to help poor Susana. That is no life for a little girl."

"I agree. If I understood Lou correctly she stayed by herself last night and had to get herself up, dressed, fed and to her youth activities all on her own."

"And she's only ten years old!"

"Sad to say, she's probably used to doing it."

Beth sighed and shook her head. "You're probably right."

"Changing the subject back to you for a moment, I'm been thinking about this meeting between Svetlana and Emilio. Unless she is using it somehow to mislead the authorities that she knows are watching her, then I would assume that you are not in any danger from her."

"I just want her caught and put away forever."

"I do too."

Beth sat back in her lounge chair. I continued to watch her. "Can I get you something? Tea, lemonade, a sandwich, a chocolate chip cookie?"

"No, thank you I'm fine. The ice cream is doing its magic."

"How about some sun screen on your back?"

"Now that's an offer I can't refuse." And for the next several moments nothing else in the world mattered one bit.

Eighty-one

Fortunately the call came from Lou after I had finished slathering Beth. I put on my sandals and shirt and excused myself.

"Be careful," she called out after me.

As Lou predicted, I didn't have any trouble using the badge that he had given me to negotiate the hallways that led to the room where the team was set up. He informed me that Emilio had been wired for sound. Unfortunately something was interfering with the video wireless feed.

"You can do that too?" I asked incredulously. "You can put an undetectable wireless camera on a person? I thought they only did that in the movies."

"The movies get most of their ideas from us." Lou quipped.

"There's Emilio now," Sashi reported as his hulking figure showed up on the video monitor. "Our cameras will follow him to his rendezvous point at the entrance to the crew area."

"Do you guys read me?" Emilio paused before speaking again. "Okay, got that."

"What was that about?" I asked.

Lou responded without looking away from the screen. "Verbal communication is only one way. We talk to him through a tiny vibrator attached to his back. One buzz is "yes," two buzzes is "no" and a continuous buzz is "get the hell out of there."

Emilio continued his careful movement through the hallways and stairwells until he arrived at the appointed door. He knocked and it opened a crack. "I'm here to see Suzie."

"Give me the package," a voice but no face responded.

"No. I will only give it to her." Emilio was defiant and no one argued with a defiant Emilio.

"I will be right back."

Emilio stood motionless and calmly in front of the closed door. He was someone who was accustomed to waiting. I wasn't. Not this kind of waiting. Around me Sashi was working at trying to learn who it was that came to the door. Did anyone recognize the voice? Could we pull even a partial image from the video?

Finally the door cracked open again. "Suzie says to follow me." Emilio didn't hesitate.

"Give him a *yes*," Lou said, even though his command was too late.

Without a camera from the ship to inform us, we were now in the dark. Sashi told us where he thought they were based on his knowledge of the ship. We hoped that the two of them would enter an area where a camera could pick them up again. Emilio tried to keep us informed of their whereabouts. He asked questions like "Where are we going?" and "What is your name?" and "How is Svetlana?" but his guide never said a word in response.

Sashi handed Lou two pieces of paper that had been handed to him. "This one lists all the workers who are of Russian or similar nationality and are potential accomplices for Svetlana. The ones with a check mark are not presently scheduled to be working. This one lists those workers who indicate that they also speak Russian but who live in other countries."

Emilio and a woman in coveralls with a cap pulled down over her eyes appeared on the screen. They walked across the large open area of the ship's hold and then disappeared once again.

The wait continued.

Eighty-two

"I think we have a positive ID on the messenger," Sashi excitedly informed Lou. But before he could give him the details we heard the sound of a heavy door opening and closing. Then Emilio spoke.

"Svetlana, it is good to see you. Are you alright?"

"It is good to see you too, Emilio. Yes I am much better now that you are here. It is good to have a friend such as you. Were you able to bring what I asked you to get for me?"

"Yes of course."

"Did you have any trouble getting it?"

"No."

"Were you followed here?"

"I don't think so? Why? What is this all about?"

"Please can I have the package and then I will tell you."

"Of course." There was a pause and rustling of clothing.

"Thank you. My dear Emilio I must go away and will not be able to see you again, perhaps for a long time. "

"No, don't say that. I can help you. I can make whatever trouble you are in go away."

"My big, wonderful, teddy bear of an Emilio come close to me my love so that I might thank you for all your kindness." We heard more rustling of cloth and then a gasp.

"What have done, you bitch?"

"Die you big, ugly fool." Svetlana screamed. The sound of a struggle ensued. We could only imagine what was happening. Surely it involved a steak knife. The security team who had picked up Emilio had followed them to the incineration room. Lou instructed Sashi to tell them to enter the room and secure it. As he gave the order, we lost Emilio's feed.

"Sashi, get us down there as quick as you can. And somebody call a medical team." Lou ordered. I followed Lou and Sashi through a maze of hallway's and stairwells until we arrived at our destination.

Sashi addressed the security team still standing outside the door. "Why haven't you gone in?"

"The door has been secured somehow from the inside. Our keys do not work. Maintenance in on their way to cut it open."

"Is there any other way out of that room?" Lou asked.

"No, not unless you climb up the chimney and can overcome several thousand degrees." Sashi quipped.

The door was freed by the torch in a matter of minutes. Medical arrived as they finished. Sashi drew his pistol and entered the room. His team followed and then Lou. Less than fifteen seconds later Sashi popped his head out. "It's clear, send in medical." I followed. Emilio was sitting on the floor propped up against the wall next to the door. A pool of blood had collected beside him from a wound in his right side. His eyes were closed and he looked pale. He was breathing.

I looked around the room for Svetlana but she was nowhere to be found. I looked at Lou. "Where is the woman?"

He shrugged and looked at Sashi who gave a similar "I don't know gesture and look."

Eighty-three

I left the heat and smell of the incinerator and hurried to find Beth. She was right where I left her. She was now in a sitting position and writing on a tablet. It was good to see an empty plate on the deck beside her. She looked up when she heard me arrive. There was relief and anticipation on her face. "What happened? Did you get her?"

I related everything that happened including the mysterious disappearance of Svetlana.

"Where could she have gone?"

"Nobody knows. The only door in and out of the room was guarded. There were no hiding places except the incinerator itself and it was burning at a temperature that would spell death to anyone who ventured into it. Even if it were not operating no one could climb out of the chimney. The carbon dioxide fumes from the engine exhaust would also kill you. The only one that can possibly tell us what happened to her is Emilio."

"Is he going to be alright?"

"Yeah, he lost a lot of blood, but that big muscular and fat belly of his kept the blade from doing any serious internal damage. "

"Can we go see him?"

"Sure. I don't know if he's alert enough to receive visitors, but let's go."

Lorenza was pacing in the hallway outside the infirmary. "How is Emilio?" Beth asked as he looked up and acknowledged our presence.

"He's alive; thank God and the Blessed Virgin Mary."

"Have you talked with him at all?" Beth continued.

"Yes. But just for a brief moment. I am so proud of him." Lorenza was on the edge of tears. "Agent Bender is with him right now talking about what happened. I am anxious to find out."

"We all are," I said.

Beth and I went into the infirmary waiting area and sat down. We didn't have long to cool our heels before Lou and Sashi came out.

"How is he?" Beth asked Lou.

"He's one tough bird. The doc has given him some blood, stitched him up, put him on an antibiotic and has ordered bed rest."

"Can I go back and see him?" Beth wondered.

"The doc said no more visitors until later today."

"Did you learn anything about what happened after we lost audio?" I inquired of Lou.

"Yeah, let's go out in the hallway."

Lorenza turned and faced us as we exited the door of the infirmary. "Did you get to see Emilio?"

Lou spoke first. "Yes, he told us what happened in the incineration room before the doctor made us leave. He wants Emilio to rest."

"I don't care what the doctor says. I am going to sit by his bed until he is released from this hospital." Lorenza moved toward the infirmary door and grabbed the handle.

"Don't you want to hear what happened to Svetlana?"

Lorenza stopped momentarily. "Maybe, later, right now my place is with Emilio." Lorenza turned and headed toward into the infirmary while we stayed put in the hallway eager for Lou's report.

Lou told us that Emilio and Svetlana had struggled for a moment before Emilio got the best of her. He had been ready for her attack even though he was surprised at how quickly she produced the knife. He knew that she was up to something the moment he entered that room when he noticed how she lingered at the door after she closed it. Fortunately when she made her move to embrace him, he was gripping her upper arms just enough to slow and redirect the force of her knife thrust. He was able to wrestle the knife away from her and then he had the advantage. Her martial arts skills were no match for someone who at one time in his life was an amateur wrestling champion and who continued to work out and even wrestle on occasion.

"He also claimed that during their struggles she fell awkwardly against the conveyer feeding the furnace and broke her neck. He decided to load her onto the belt, then he pushed the forward button and fed her body into the fire."

"So she did disappear into thin air?" I offered sarcastically.

"And I got my prayer answered," Beth added. "She burned in hell."

Bon Voyage
Lust
Envy/Jealousy
Anger
Sloth
Gluttony
Greed
Pride
Debarkation

Eighty-four

Beth and I were still outside of the infirmary discussing what to do with the rest of our afternoon when a ship's officer appeared. "You are Mr. Meyerhoff and Ms. Malone?"

"Yes," I answered. His name tag said Aiden Pagglazio.

"Is Mr. Bender still here?"

"He just left with Sashi Squatchma one of your security people."

"Of course. The reason for my visit with you is to request your presence at the Captain's table for dinner this evening. He would very much like to show his appreciation to you for all that you have endured during this cruise and for your help in resolving the several misfortunes that have occurred during these days."

"Thank you very much. That is very kind of him." I looked at Beth and then back at the officer. It always gave me pause to laugh inwardly when people of importance condescend just enough to include people like me in their lives. In this case it was the Captain, the proud ruler of his ship, lowering himself by sending one of his up and coming minions to call upon the common man. This wannabe would do almost anything to please the chief, hoping to one day himself climb the ladder and achieve the same position of privilege. "May I consult with Ms. Malone for just a moment before I give you an answer?"

"Most certainly, I can give you my card and you can leave a message for me any time up until 5:00 p.m." Of course even generosity has its limits.

"I don't think that will be necessary. I can give you our decision right now." I indicated to Beth that I would prefer to decline. She agreed.

"Please extend to the Captain our most sincere thanks for his most gracious offer but include our deepest regrets that we will not be able to attend. I'm sure that he will understand that we prefer a quiet final evening alone after the trauma of the week and this last day."

The officer showed no emotion. "I will pass on your message. The Captain will be most disappointed but is also most understanding." The officer bowed slightly, turned and walked away. I hoped that my refusal didn't interrupt his climb or ruffle the feathers of any peacocks. No, I didn't care if they did. I didn't particularly like pomp and circumstance and wasn't comfortable with all that strutting, preening and posturing that tended to go on among certain classes or ranks of society.

Don't get me wrong. I believe in being polite and respectful to everyone regardless of their station in life. One should even be respectful to those who have an air of superiority about them. I take comfort in the proverb that affirms, "Pride goes before destruction and a haughty spirit before a fall" (Proverbs 16:18). The prideful will topple on their own. I don't need to push them.

There are some folks however who would never pass up the opportunity to hobnob with the so-called elites of society. They enjoy both elbow knocking and name dropping. They crave their fifteen minutes of fame. I'm not one of them. The people who impress me the most are the humble, steady, behind the scenes, unsung, even nameless heroes.

Eighty-five

We decided to sit by the pool for the brief period that we had before it was time to get ready for dinner. Beth was obviously relieved. She was as relaxed and at ease as I had ever seen her. "Could I interest you in sharing a strawberry margarita with me?" The offer came out of me so suddenly that I hadn't even bothered to ask if she liked them or not. Even worse I hadn't given a thought to whether or not that offer would be a betrayal of Amy or perhaps an attempt to relive my life with her.

Before I could work through much of the psychology inherent in that simple request, Beth said, "That would really taste good right now."

It wasn't long before we were taking turns sipping the icy delight. Beth pointed out a young family, two adults and two barely elementary age children, gathered not too far from us playing a game together. They were obviously a happy family. They were laughing and having a good time with each other. Before their game they had all been in the pool, jumping and splashing and laughing. "That is such a wonderful sight," she said.

"Yes., every family should be like that. They keep life simple. Mom loves dad and dad loves mom and mom and dad both love the kids."

I steered Beth's eyes in another direction, toward another family who seemed to be just the opposite. "Look over there at those two parents and two children. It's almost the same set up. But nothing is going on there. Instead of joy you can almost feel the tension from here. The kids have their backs to each other and the parents aren't talking. When one of them does talk to a child they use sharp looks and gestures. In that family things have gotten complicated. I suspect dad has put a bunch of other things ahead of mom and mom has put a bunch or other things ahead of dad and the kids don't have a clue where they fit in."

"How do you know so much about everything?"

"I don't. I tend to make stuff up on the fly."

"Come on. Don't give me that."

"No, I'm serious. Studies have shown that seventy-five per cent of what people know is made up on the spot as are, I might add, seventy-eight per cent of all statistics." I placed a sarcastic smile on my face.

Beth groaned as I knew she would. "Would you get serious for just a moment?"

"Okay. I guess I know what I know through a lifetime of observing people and studying human behavior. I tell you what. Let's learn something right now. Let's go ask them why they are behaving the way they do?" I started to get up.

Beth reached out and grabbed me in an effort to stop me. "You can't do that. You can't go up to strangers and ask them something like that. They'd think you were nuts or at best meddling, maybe even a pervert."

"You think so? I bet that first couple wouldn't care. People that keep life simple wouldn't mind me walking up to them and saying, 'I noticed how much fun you are having together as a family. It really warms my heart to see that.' They would probably thank me and even give me a reason if I asked them, 'Why.'

But if I went up to that other couple and said something even as innocent as 'I noticed that your kids have no one to play with and my kids are looking for some playmates,' they would probably make excuses and shut me out, no doubt because their life is already too complicated and they are afraid I will just compound it even more.

"It's just my opinion but I tend to trace part of that non-cooperative and isolationistic attitude to the political correctness movement. PC has made life complicated. It encourages people to be overly suspicious of others by assuming that behind every comment or every offer or even every word there is a hidden agenda meant to bring hurt or to offend. This is nothing more than one's pride trying to protect itself from having to deal with the real world.

"People shouldn't be so worried about what might hurt them as much they should be working to grow their own self-confidence. Loving and encouraging each other keeps life simple, grows confidence and keeps fear at bay."

"So you're advocating that we bring back the good old days?"

"No, just certain attitudes from days gone by. I wouldn't want to live without microwaves, cell phones, the Sham Wow and half a dozen varieties of M&M's. But enough talk. Isn't it about time to get ready for dinner?"

Eighty-six

Getting ready for dinner required some serious coordination if I was going to stay clear of Beth's charms. Showering and dressing in the same small space after today's ordeal was an invitation for emotions to go wild. The tension of the last twenty-four hours had trumped all but some minor, cursory affection between us; however with all that strain now mostly behind us, the pressure curtailing our sexual inhibitions and romantic inclinations was almost non-existent. For me that meant that I had to be on prime alert.

I escaped any personal contact with Beth other than assisting with doing up the zipper on her evening gown. The *Festival* was sponsoring one last formal night. We both wore the same attire that we had worn to the previous formal night which seemed like it took place in a previous decade.

Marta welcomed us as we entered the dining hall. I presented her with a generous gratuity in an envelope the ship had provided. On the cruise ships that I have traveled, tipping can be automatically charged to the guest's account. The tip is divided between the housekeeping and the wait staffs. The bartending team adds their tip to each drink served. Only the maitre d' is left out of the tipping arrangement. Obviously a guest can always give certain deserving staff more than the minimum amount suggested and workers certainly appreciate that. What they also appreciate is our comments. Any time we specifically praise a worker by singling him or her out, that compliment weighs heavily in any promotion that might be considered for the worker.

Nora and Randaldo met us as we approached our table. Randaldo handled Beth's chair while Nora unfolded and offered our napkins. "Enjoy your dinner," Nora said as they hurried to welcome other guests.

"Did I tell you how beautiful you looked tonight?"

"Yes you did. But thank you for telling me again."

I reached across the table and took her hands in mine. I looked at her and for a moment became lost in her features.

"Excuse me Mr. Meyerhoff and Ms. Malone, but I have a gift for you." I looked up. It was Marta. "Captain Finelli missed the pleasure of your company tonight but understood your reason for wanting to be alone. He has sent this wine for you to enjoy with his compliments."

Maybe he's not such a peacock after all. "Please thank the Captain for his generosity."

"Shall I have Nora serve this to you now?" I glanced at Beth and she nodded her approval.

"That would be fine. Thank you."

"And thank you sir for your generous gift."

"You're welcome. Before you go, could I ask you a couple of questions?"

"Of course."

"How long have you been working on cruise ships and serving as a maitre d'?"

"It has been twenty-one years now. I started as wait staff and worked my up. This is my first time, my first contract as a maitre d'. I had been an assistant maitre d' for eight years before this promotion. It takes a very long time and a lot of training and schooling and some bit of luck to be a maitre d'."

"You are very good at your job."

"Thank you very much. I enjoy this work."

"Do you have family back home in Austria?"

"Yah, I have a husband and two children."

"Isn't it hard to be away from them?" Beth asked.

"It is. I am gone many months at a time and then I am home many months at a time. My parents are very helpful to me. It has worked for me over the years. It is a hard life but a good life. With a little more experience as a maitre d' I can go back to Austria and perhaps get a good job in a hotel or restaurant. In the mean time, I work at this." She smiled and excused herself.

"I could never be away from my family that long?" Beth sighed.

"Nor I."

Eighty-seven

It is fascinating to watch a fine dinner being served. The staff takes pride in everything that they do. The table is immaculate. Every utensil is perfectly set in its place. There is a proper fork or spoon or knife for nearly every food. The serving of wine is also an art form. The displaying of the food on the plate is another art form. The service itself is an art.

There is a fine line between taking pride in what you do and being prideful. The men and woman who serve the *Festival's* guests take great pride in what they do. For most it appears to be more than a job. As they go about their work they demonstrate skill, enthusiasm, friendliness and confidence. I think that most people appreciate and are willing to applaud people who believe in themselves and in their abilities to not only do something well but to do it without fanfare.

You can usually tell when people lose pride in themselves. Their hygiene, their appearance, their property, their language and most everything about them and around them goes to pot. It's a tough climb out of the pit of lost pride but the rungs of that ladder normally are spelled h-u-m-i-l-i-t-y.

I also believe that most people don't like braggarts. People don't care for someone who makes every conversation about himself or herself. We don't like someone who walks into a room and demands that the attention be shifted in their direction. I'm not sure anyone really likes trash talking either. Nor do I think people like the person who says that it's not boasting as long as you can do it.

Prideful people come in all shapes and sizes and classes. Some of the proudest people I've met are stone poor. They need help but refuse to ask for it or worse refuse to accept it. They would rather go hungry or lose their home than accept a handout. Prideful people are often demanding people. They expect others to meet them on their terms. Prideful people are usually hard headed in that they don't like to change. For prideful people life is about three things – me, myself and I. Prideful people don't think about *we*. The prideful might think about other people but only when they're looking for someone specific to blame or for someone to use.

I remember when I was a kid and someone would point an index finger at another kid and there would always be one whiner who would say, "You shouldn't point your finger at someone else because there are three pointing right back at you!" Part of the reason for pointing was we were judging behavior. We didn't realize it at the time but we were looking for speck-like flaws in other kids behaviors while failing to see the log-like flaws in our own. This is what pride does to us. It first convinces a person that he is superior to others. In order to maintain that superiority he must either keep demonstrating superiority through lifting himself up by words and actions, or he has to maintain his status by knocking those around him down. A prideful person says, "I'm right and you're wrong. I'm good and you're bad. I'm smart and you're dumb. I'll rule and you'll serve. I'll decide and you'll listen, and so forth."

For prideful people, life is all about themselves.

The President of the United States was visiting a fourth grade class. The teacher asked him if he would like to lead the class in a discussion of the word "tragedy." So the President asked the class for an example of a tragedy. One boy stood up and said, "If my best friend is playing in the street and a car comes along and runs him over, that would be a tragedy." "No," said the President, "that would be an accident." A girl raised her hand and said, "If a school bus carrying fifty children drove off a cliff, killing everyone on board, that would be a tragedy." "I'm afraid not," the President said. "That's what we would call a Great Loss." The room went silent. The President searched the room and asked, "Isn't there someone here who can give me an example of a tragedy?" Finally, way in the back of the room, a boy offered, "If Air Force One, carrying you and your wife, was struck by a missile and blown to smithereens, that would be a tragedy." "That's right! And can you tell me WHY that would be a tragedy?" asked the President. "Well," he said, "because it wouldn't be an accident and it wouldn't be a Great Loss."

For prideful people, life is all about themselves.

Eighty-eight

"Beth, do you realize that we are well into our main course and Lou hasn't interrupted us yet?"

"Will wonders never cease."

"Believe it or not I sort of miss him butting in."

"No you don't."

"You're right. I don't."

"He's really a good guy. And he's good at his job."

"Yes he is. Speaking of jobs I don't remember you ever mentioning what you do. I know that you said you had your own business."

"I help manage people's assets."

"That's an unusual career, but certainly necessary. Would you be managing large people with small behinds or small people with small behinds?"

"What are you talking about?"

"You said that you manage *assettes*. An *assette* is the diminutive form of a coarse word for a person's derriere. An *assette* is a small behind, a small butt."

Beth let out a sigh and shook her head. "That's not even worth a comment."

"I know. It was bad even for me. But they can't all be gems."

Nora stopped by our table to ask if we needed anything. We invited her to stay for a little conversation about herself. She briefly told us her cruising history, her rise in rank to become a waiter and team leader among the wait staff. She started nearly thirty years ago. She said that the process has remained unchanged over the years. It begins with a year of schooling in the art of waiting tables. The next step is to be assigned to a ship where you answer room service for several months. Then you move up to serving the crew and finally are accepted as an assistant waiter. At each stage there are tests to pass and classes to take. She had been a full waiter for the last eight years.

She informed us that workers other than high ranking officers don't have a lot of choice in determining which ship they work on. "When my contract runs out and I return from my vacation I will catch on with whatever ship needs my services when my new contract begins."

Her children were grown and she showed us pictures of her two grandchildren. She said that she had one more contract after this one and then she was retiring. Her children needed her to help raise her grandchildren.

Randaldo's story was similar. He said that he was moving up on the list and hoped to become a full fledged waiter within a year or two.

I said to Beth after Randaldo left us, "Every time I'm on one of these cruises, I think about what job I would like to do on a cruise ship. How about you, have you entertained such thoughts?"

"Funny you should ask. Marta's and Nora's stories are intriguing. The idea of working for several months at a time and then having several months of vacation is somewhat appealing. I think going to exotic locations and interacting with such a variety of people, both passengers and crew, has a certain fascination about it. I'm not sure which job I would sign up for. How about you?"

"I agree with the allure that cruise life and travel to exotic places has, but I asked you first about job choice and I'm not letting you off the hook."

Beth smiled. "Okay, you win. I don't know which job I would do since all or most of them, at least to me, appear to be monotonous and tedious. The jobs are pretty much blue collar factory type assembly line jobs complete with twelve hour shifts. Not that I have anything against jobs like that, it's just that I'm wired a different way."

"I hear what you're saying. I'm wired the same way. I like variety in my work."

"Consider housekeeping," Beth continued. "I don't mind cleaning my house and I think that I do a good job of it, but those poor folks have to make up and clean the same block of rooms every day for months at a time. I can't imagine some of the messes they must walk in on. Yet they're always smiling and friendly whenever you encounter them.

"The maintenance people are the same way. They appear to have a well scripted routine of scrubbing decks, washing windows, painting, cleaning, picking up chairs, setting out chairs and a host of other routines that don't seem to vary at all."

I jumped in. "I could probably be a waiter. I know it's the same routine for every meal but at least the clientele changes every time the ship returns to its home port, and the interactions with people I think would keep a physically demanding job fresh."

"Yeah, I can see that. The same might be said of the bar staff, although mixing the same drinks over and over would get boring and considering the amount of walking they do makes my legs weary just thinking about it."

"What about working in the infirmary or with security?" I wondered.

"I guess with the proper training I could handle that, although I'm not real calm in emergency situations. I would like to try my hand or should I say legs at being a dancer. Those kids seem to have a lot of fun."

"You're right, although they do the same show for months at a time."

"That's no different than Broadway or off Broadway."

"Point taken. You also see the dancers working a lot of odd jobs. One was at my muster drill, another was manning the library, some were helping the cruise director and others were assisting the photographers."

"Speaking of photographers, that would be a job I would enjoy, again if I had the right training."

"You realize that they do more than take pictures. They print them, post them and sell them too. All of which would get old in a hurry. Although, I've been thinking that if I had a dime for every picture that the crew has taken on this cruise, I could retire to Costa Rica."

"What jobs does that leave?" Beth asked.

I thought for a moment before answering. "Duh, . . . the cooks and the ship's officers."

"I like to cook, but didn't Marta tell us that the cruise line sets the menu for a year at a time and the same meals rotate like every seven days?" I nodded as she continued. "That would get boring too I would think."

"The life of the ship's officers also seems rather mundane," I pointed out. "They appear to walk around in no big hurry looking impressive in their uniforms and creating the impression that everything is under control. I'm sure though there are times when they earn their money, when they must make decisions that affect the welfare of several thousand lives. I'm not sure that I'd want that kind of responsibility."

"So," Beth said, "What did we decide? What job would you pick?"

"No matter how much thought I put into this subject I always come back to the same conclusion. I'm doing what I'm doing because that's what I do the best and I'm glad that I've got what I do to do. Thank God other people like doing other jobs. That way everything gets done."

Beth added. "I like that answer. Things sure get done and done well on this ship. I was surprised to learn from Marta and Nora and Randaldo how much schooling and training the workers on this ship have had and continue to get. Do you know if that's true for all the jobs?"

"As far as I know it is. The Captain was telling us on our tour that he began studying at age thirteen at an academy designed for future ship captains. He continued his training in the Navy and then he enrolled in Captain's school. This school is apparently located in Italy which is why most of the Captains along with first officers and chief engineers are Italian. He said that way should there be an emergency the key persons on the ship could communicate in the same primary language."

"That's good to know."

Eighty-nine

Beth put in her order for Baked Alaska and I chose warm apple pie with a vanilla ice cream chaser.

"Bring me a cup of coffee please, black." It was the familiar voice of Lewis Bender. He swiped a chair from a nearby table and joined us.

"How was dinner with the Captain?" I was making conversation only.

"You should have been there. That man knows how to put on the feed bag."

"What's the latest with Emilio?" Beth asked.

"He's doing just fine. The doc still has him on liquids tonight. He wants to make sure that there's no internal bleeding or that his bowel wasn't nicked."

"Is Lorenza still with him?" I asked.

"Yeah, he hasn't left him except to relieve himself."

"What's going to happen to Emilio and Lorenza after we get to shore," I asked. "He did kill Svetlana after all and both of them were involved in the hit on Alexi."

"I'm still trying to work that out with my superiors. Here's how it's looking. The biggest problem we've got is that we don't have either body. It usually takes a body to convince a jury that there's been a crime."

"What happened to Alexi?" I inquired.

"Don't know for sure. The local officials or un-officials probably made him disappear. As I was saying, without a body and without witnesses it's a 'He says, She says' situation."

"Don't you have the phone records?"

"Yeah, but they are circumstantial and incomplete. We don't have the actual recordings and people can't be thrown in jail for making a phone call even if it is to a known hit man. A good lawyer would argue, 'wrong number.'"

"So you're saying everybody goes free."

Lou's jaw was working. "What I'm saying is that Alexi murdered Anne and he's been tried and executed for his crime so to speak. Svetlana, who attempted to kill two people, is also dead. She was killed by a man who thought that he was dying and who freely admitted to killing her in an act of self-defense. There is no convincing evidence to link Lorenza or Emilio with Alexi's death nor is there any convincing evidence to disprove Emilio's self-defense story. In fact we have recorded evidence that she did stick him with a knife first. Given all that, it is highly unlikely any charges will be forthcoming."

I guess that I was okay with that. I looked at Beth and she seemed okay with that too. Neither one of us really understood the fine points of the law. I wasn't personally overly concerned with such fine points as I was of the belief that sooner or later every man, woman and child was going to have an accounting before the Creator for how they lived their life anyway. That included even every careless word that was uttered.

I kind of liked Emilio and Lorenza but that didn't make them any less accountable. There are a lot of good, likeable people that still do some terrible things, create unnecessary havoc and bring a lot of hurt into people's lives.

Lou finished his coffee and looked at me. "Do you have some time later that we can talk privately?"

I looked longingly at Beth. She nodded ever so slightly. I turned back to Lou. "I suppose. Can you tell me what it's about?"

"Rachelle and me."

"Sure." I looked between Lou and Beth. "Is about thirty minutes from now good?" I received positive assurances from both.

As Lou was leaving, Marta introduced her wait staff and gave us one last opportunity to show our appreciation for their fine service. After a round of applause and some whooping and hollering, she keyed up the music and they sang "You're Leavin' Off Our Cruise Ship, Don't Know When You'll Be Back

Again; We're Sad To See You Go..." As we are prone to say in our part of the south, it was a hoot! For anyone needing a translation I think "hoot" means, good, clean, down home, but not necessarily Oscar quality fun.

Ninety

Before joining Lou in his room I walked with Beth in the gradually cooling evening air. I regretted making that appointment, but there was unfinished business with Lou that needed some finishing. She would meet me at Lou's room in about hour and we would take in a final stage show and perhaps go dancing.

She dropped me off at Lou's door on her way to tour the shops one last time and perhaps find and purchase another photographic still that captured one of our moments together.

Lou didn't waste any time getting down to business. He wanted to talk about how he could be a better husband. He said that he had read the *"Love Languages"* book through twice and wanted some other resources to read. I gave him a couple of suggestions that I could think of off the top of my head, copied down his email address and promised to send him a few more titles sometime after I arrived home.

"When have you had time to read?"

"I told you before that I feel alive. I have all kinds of energy and when I'm not working this case, I'm reading."

As I had done earlier in the day with Beth, I shared briefly with Lou the importance of origins. He agreed with my position that there is a link between what we believe about our origin and the choices that we make.

He had grown up in the Church. He had married a minister's daughter and was still attached to the Church. He admitted that he was mostly a member in name only. He was what church insiders referred to as a *C* and *E* member, meaning Christmas and Easter. He blamed mostly his work schedule for his back-sliding. He gave credit to Rachelle for being the one who taught their children the faith and who lived the faith herself. This description of himself and his situation put him solidly in the camp of a majority of churchly people.

Lou's early life in the Church had helped him develop a good work ethic and gave him some high moral standards. He believed in absolutes. He fought for those who were victims of injustice. He was also fairly humble unlike most of the government people that I observed through the media. They usually came off as quite pompous. Lou had confidence in himself and his abilities but he didn't make you feel inferior.

His years in the Church had also developed his conscience. He could be made to feel guilty fairly quickly when he realized that he had failed. This is one aspect of the Church's mission that it should be given very mixed grades for. While it has excelled at teaching people the place of guilt in their lives, it has gone too far in somehow also convincing them that they need to continue beating themselves up for years after they have repented and been declared forgiven.

Like so many people who claim to follow Jesus Christ, Lou was stuck in the guilts and in the shoulds. This is so ironic because freedom is the heart of Christianity's gift to the world.

Tommy was doing very badly in math. His parents had tried everything; flash cards, special learning centers, tutors, nothing worked. Finally in a last dish effort, they enrolled him in the local Catholic school. After the first day, Tommy came home with a serious look on his face. He didn't kiss his mother hello but went straight to his room and started studying. His mother was amazed. She called him down to dinner and the minute he was done, he returned to his studies. This went on day after day. One day Tommy brought home his report card. He quietly laid it on the table and went up to his room and hit the books. His mom looked at it and there was an A in math. She went to his room and said, "Son, what was it? What changed your attitude toward math?" Tommy looked at her and said, "Well, on the first day of school, when I saw that guy nailed to the plus sign, I knew they weren't fooling around."

Because Lou had the background that he did with the Church, I felt that there was no need to muddle around the edges of the subject with him and that it would be to both of our advantages to go directly to the Bible to guide our discussion. I had stopped by my stateroom and had picked up my pocket New Testament. I decided to start first with Ephesians, chapter five.

Ninety-one

"**B**e imitators of God as dearly loved children and live a life of love as Christ loved us and gave himself up for us" (Ephesians 5:1-2).

"Being a good husband begins with knowing the ways in which you are loved, knowing that the one who made you loved you enough to give up his most valuable possession, his son, for you. That is your motivation for everything you do. We have a choice in how we live. We can imitate our Creator or we can imitate whoever else we want or we can attempt to forge a brand new way to live that others may eventually want to imitate.

"If we choose to imitate our Creator then the path we follow is one of submission. 'Submit to one another' (5:21). The word submit or submission comes from the joining of two Latin words – *sub* which means 'under' and *mission* which means a 'task' or 'errand.' Our natural tendency is to want others to under-task us, or for someone like you to submit to someone like me. Now, when I try to force you down or make you submit how does that make you feel?"

"Like fighting back."

"Exactly. Consider any argument or dispute that you and Rachelle have ever had. Whenever you want your way and she wants a different way, the result is, a war. You say, 'submit' and she says, 'No, you submit' and you say, 'No, you submit' and so on and so forth."

"So how do I stop that?"

"You stop it by 'loving your wife as Christ loved the Church' (5:25)."

"And how do I do that?"

"Ask yourself, how did Christ love the Church? How did he love the people he was most committed too? Did he force or even ask them to humble themselves before him? Did he demand that they perform a series of rituals before he would consider helping them? Did he expect them to make personality changes before he would talk with them? Or did he humble himself and become like the very people and even lesser than the very people he chose to love so that he could lift them up?"

"He was sent under us," Lou answered with an enthusiasm that grew out of a moment of personal discovery. "He was sent to suffer and die for us."

"Yes, in order to present people like you and me and everyone else in this world 'holy and without stain or wrinkle or any other blemish' (5:26-27). So what does that say about how we as husbands are to behave?"

"We are sent under them in order to lift our wives up. We work to make them more beautiful. Our mission is to lift and support them. I guess that makes me a twenty-four hour bra." That was an image that I had never thought of before and probably wouldn't ever use in a sermon or children's talk, although both Lou's comment and the subsequent image did generate a chuckle.

"I hadn't thought of it those terms. But yes, your mission is to make her more beautiful today than she was yesterday. Her mission to you is essentially the same. She is to submit to you as her head in the same way that she submits to Christ who is the head of the Church."

"Yeah, but that's a little confusing. I am her head. Doesn't that mean I have authority over her? Isn't she supposed to listen to me? Don't the vows say love and obey?"

"The answer depends on how you understand what being the 'head' means. Some argue that it means authority and power. You are the man, that makes you the boss, you know best and she needs to stay in her place and be obedient. I happen to believe that people who interpret the text that way are misinterpreting it. The husband is the head of the wife as

Christ is the head of the Church. Christ is more like the head-waters of a stream. He is the source of life. As the head, he protects and provides and nourishes. He loves and guides. As head he does not force the body to do anything that is unloving or that will cause it harm, nor does he bring it harm."

"So," Lou offered, "When two people submit to each other they won't have any more problems."

"They will always have problems to work through. What they won't have will be any more wars. Wars will cease, because the goal of a husband and wife is to lift each other up in love and not to tear each other down."

"You've thrown that word love around quite a bit. Can we talk about what love is?" There was a knock on the door.

"It's probably Beth," I said looking at my watch. "I told her to come by in an hour."

Lou went to the door and let her in. "We're almost finished. You're welcome to join us if it's alright with Coop. We're having a really interesting discussion." I nodded my approval. It was a topic I had hoped to get to with Beth also.

Ninety-two

"For most people, love is the favorable emotional response we have when something is pleasing to one our senses. We say that we love everything from hot dogs, to ball games, to sunsets, to the sound of laughter, to the fragrance of a flower, to an automobile race, to money, to a good story, to a vacation we took, to an appealing member of the opposite sex and to most everything else under the sky. The depth or duration or intensity of that love feeling tends to vary with each person and his or her need for a particular pleasure.

"We love those things and events and persons that make us happy. We love those things that fulfill our desires and that light our fire or fill our tank. That kind of loving motivates people to get involved in all kinds of relationships and to accomplish all kinds of good, but it also has some serious draw backs. Can you guess what some of them are?"

Lou spoke first. "When your happiness is based on things that are temporary you will inevitably be disappointed. Sunsets end. You can lose your money. A career can go down the drain. A beautiful and kind woman can turn ugly and nasty." That last comment earned a glare from Beth, so I jumped in.

"Yeah, or a person can have wanderlust. He gets tired of last year's models and decides to move on to what he thinks is the latest and greatest in houses, cars, careers, other products, friends and women."

Beth spoke. "I think the number one drawback is when whom you love stops loving you back."

"What do you mean?"

"I fell in love with Tony because he was everything that I thought I wanted. He was everything wonderful. When I learned that he wasn't those things there was nothing left for me to love."

"So you're saying that when something or someone stops making you happy it's no longer worth loving?"

"I suppose."

"Do you feel that way about your children?"

"That's different."

"How is it different?"

"You always love your children."

"Even when they're not loveable? Even when they change and maybe stop loving you? Even when they don't particularly like or respect you or your rules? Even when they bring shame on you or run away and tell you that they never want to see you again?"

"Of course you still love them."

"Why?"

"Because you brought them into the world. They're your flesh and blood. They're your responsibility. They're your children. Why wouldn't you love them?" Beth had mounted her soapbox and had become quite animated and a little agitated.

"Hey, back off. I'm on your side. But now you're talking about a completely different kind of love. You're describing a love that doesn't respond to its environment, you're describing a love that takes charge of its environment. You're describing a love that doesn't seek to be made happy but rather seeks to make happy or better to bring goodness to another.

"You see, most folks understand love as an emotional response. The emphasis is primarily on how something or someone or some event in my life will affect *me* and my happiness. Consider instead understanding love as making deliberate choices that have in mind the best interest of the *we* and how those choices will affect the well being and happiness of a couple or the family or even the community.

"We talked earlier about two becoming one in marriage and about submitting to one another. In marriage and in the family the *me* must disappear and give way to the *we*. The prideful attitude must give way to humility. Pride is *me*-love and humility is *we*-love."

I opened my pocket New Testament to First Corinthians chapter thirteen. "If you've ever been to a wedding in a Christian Church you've probably heard words read from the famous love chapter. 'Love is patient, love is kind. It does not envy, it does not boast, it is not proud. It is not rude, it is not self-seeking, it is not easily angered, it keeps no record of wrongs. Love does not delight in evil but rejoices with the truth. It always protects, always trusts, always hopes, always perseveres. Love never fails.'

"That is describing *we*-love and the choices that are necessary for an individual to make in order to overcome the *me*-love. For example I, the *me,* wants to be impatient with you, but for love's sake and for us, the *we*, I choose to be patient. Or, I, the *me*, want to give a tongue lashing to you, but for love's sake and for us, the *we*, I choose to be kind. And so on and so forth. Do you follow me?"

Lou spoke. "Yes. It sounds easy but I know it's not. How do I do it?"

"It's already being done within you by the one who creates love."

Ninety-three

Beth and I missed the start of the live stage show so we looked instead for a lounge that had some music that suited our fancy. Talking with Beth was most enjoyable although the subject of love and marriage that I talk about all the time to couples was a surprisingly uncomfortable topic for me to talk about tonight. I needed something to distract or redirect my thoughts. Music works well for that. Dancing with Beth also works well but generates a whole new set of issues.

We were looking specifically for the big band sound again, but we were not having much luck finding it. I'd forgotten to bring with me the daily calendar of activities that the *Festival* provides. That would have simplified our search.

We poked into one club and noticed Genette. We both hesitated pushing any further into the room and instinctively started backing out of it. Our move was a moment too late. She spotted us, waved, hollered Beth's name and ran over to us. She was well on her way to an evening and night that she probably would not remember in the morning.

"Aunt Beth. I have been looking for you all day." Of course you have, I muttered to myself. "You have to help me. The people on this ship won't leave me alone. They keep after me about mother's funeral arrangements. I told them to send her to Bottacelli's. They keep asking me to sign stuff. Would you go and talk with them and get this straightened out?"

I could see the veins in Beth's neck and face begin to throb and felt the grip of her hand on mine tighten considerably. But instead of a vocal explosion I heard the sweet voice that I so enjoyed hearing. "Genette, I would love to help you, but I can't. The paper work must all be signed by you. I already checked with them. I'm sorry, but there is nothing that I can do. You may call me first thing in the morning and I will be happy to go with you and support you, but right now Coop and I need to spend this last night together." She smiled, turned and we walked away leaving a stunned and speechless Genette.

Beth walked in silence until we came to a quiet and isolated area. She stopped abruptly, turned to face me and wrapped both arms around me. I responded and held her close. "You did good. I'm really proud of you." I sensed that she was crying. "What's wrong?"

She pulled back and wiped her eyes. "Nothing, it's just that I wanted to tear into her. I wanted to remind her of how cruel she has been to me. I wanted to tell her what a hypocrite she was and ask her how she dare pretend I would ever do anything for her again. After all she's said and done to me! And then I heard this voice say, 'love is not rude, love is kind' and I chose to say what I said. And you know what, Coop, I feel better for it."

Of course you do. That's the way it works. I smiled an inward smile of satisfaction.

Ninety-four

We never did find a good dance band. We walked and talked and sat and talked. None of our talk seemed to have much substance to it. I suggested that we take this cruise again some time since we completely missed seeing three of the ports. Beth agreed that it would be a good idea. She suggested that we tour some of the plantations and gardens around Charleston and Savannah. I agreed to that idea. And so our talk randomly rambled.

All around us people laughed or peacefully strolled the decks or sat at tables playing cards and board games or paused for pictures or talked or ate or drank or danced or gambled or maybe struggled just like us.

There was a cloud of uncertainty that was hanging over our heads and neither one of us seemed to want to part the cloud. Finally Beth said, "I need to finish packing my suitcase and set it out in the hallway so I don't have to carry it off the ship tomorrow." We headed back to the room.

Debarkation was an ordered process on the *Festival*. Sometime about 8:00 a.m., the ship would tie up back in Miami. Local customs agents would come on board and inspect what they needed to inspect and secure the proper signatures. Once cleared by customs, passengers could begin leaving the ship.

The *Festival* allowed certain people of privilege the opportunity to disembark first. Neither of us was a person of privilege so we didn't listen to those instructions. I had met a gentleman on a previous cruise who was a person of privilege. His privilege was twofold. He was actually getting off the ship and then turning around and getting right back on it. He had just cruised to the Bahamas and he was going to cruise right back. While his personal items could remain in his room, he had to leave the ship and then re-board. Those were the rules. At least he got to be first off and then first on. He was also given privileged status because at the time he was just completing his forty-fourth cruise and had already booked several more including passage on a ship's maiden voyage.

Forty-four cruises seemed like an exorbitant amount of cruises for someone to take, but it didn't come close to another couple that was introduced at a captain's reception during a different cruise that I was on. They were marking their two hundred and sixteenth cruise! Those folks are either obsessive, crazy, in love with cruising or frugal. I remember reading that it is actually cheaper to live on cruise ships than in a nursing home.

After the privileged disembarked then those who were carrying their own luggage were permitted to leave the ship, ostensibly in the order that decks were called. However I was convinced that certain folks entered the line early either because they were hard of hearing or because they pretended that they were assigned to decks that they really weren't or because they enjoyed cutting in line or because they thought of themselves as people of privilege.

The last group off the ship and certainly the majority of the passengers were those who had the crew handle their luggage. This is a huge job. On the day of departure the luggage is all brought from the passenger check-in area by hand and loaded into large bins. Forklifts move the bins onto the ship. From there each bag is hand delivered to the correct room. This usually takes the crew until late in the evening of the first day to accomplish. Off loading the luggage follows a reverse procedure.

Guests who want the crew to handle their bags must have those bags outside their stateroom doors with proper tags by midnight. They will then find their bags ready to be picked up just before they proceed through customs. Smart passengers keep some hygiene items with them as well as sleepwear and clothing for the next day. Not so smart ones, well . . .

The ship also provides a service that includes transporting your bags to the airport if you have any money left following a week of drinking and gambling and shore excursions and buying souvenirs.

If everyone cooperates with the system, disembarking the ship can be expedited in two to three hours.

Ninety-five

As we started our walk away from my stateroom I turned to consider Beth's bag standing by the door. It seemed to look the way I felt, sad. We had decided or rather I had decided to indulge in one final bowl of soft serve. Beth agreed to accompany me. My plan was to eat it and then go back to the room and get some sleep. I had a nearly eleven hour drive the next day. I was already tired from a long day and a trying week and I was tired because I was sad. Weren't vacations supposed to revive a person? Sadness, not rainy days and Mondays, seemed to always make me tired.

"What's wrong Coop?"

I had trouble answering. I knew what was wrong, but I didn't know how to put words to the wrongness. "I know that tomorrow is going to be a hard day. I don't want to say good-bye to you. I don't want to see you go one way and me go another. I want to enjoy tonight but try as I might I can't shake the impending gloom of tomorrow. I'm sorry. I want to be upbeat and happy, but tonight you're stuck with downbeat and sad."

Beth smiled. "I haven't been very good company either."

"You've been wonderful company. Everything that I've come to know about you is wonderful. It's going to be so empty, so lonely after we say good-bye tomorrow. I don't want to face that."

"You make it sound like we'll never see each other again."

"That's the way it feels and those feelings are powerful. I haven't experienced them in quite a while. I keep telling myself that even though those feelings are real, they are not giving me the whole truth. I know that I will see you again. I know that I want to see you again and soon."

"And I want to see you too."

"Then how are we going to make that happen?"

"You come to me for a few days and I'll come to you for a few days. We've got phones, we've got web cams. Worse comes to worse we've got the U.S. mail." We both laughed. I could sense a break in the cloud.

Ninety-six

Beth came out of the bathroom wearing a very impressive full length nightgown instead of her pajamas from the night before. She noticed my notice. "I thought that since this was our last night that we would be spending together for a while I should leave you with a good memory of me." As if I didn't have enough good memories of her etched in multiple places in my mind.

"You know I really don't need this vision of you. I had hoped to get some sleep tonight in anticipation of a long drive home tomorrow. What I need is a Lucille Ball image of you, the one with her hair all done up in curlers wearing a tattered flannel house coat and her face covered in cold cream."

"That could be arranged. Anything to make you happy."

"Hey, I'm very happy. And I'm sure that even in curlers and cold cream you would still look beautiful. It's just that this whole arrangement makes me uncomfortable."

"I know. I'm sorry."

"Don't be sorry for being you. We'll make this work tonight. We don't have much other choice." I had tried to move into Beth's old room. It had been cleared as a crime scene, but some other situation that had developed on the ship had already gobbled it up. I considered moving in with Lou and Mike but they had added another agent during our last port of call and he was on their couch.

We each crawled into our respective beds and turned out our reading lights. I had difficulty focusing my prayers. Images of the past week and visions of tomorrow's good-bye and speculations about next week's and next month's possibilities were a constant interruption. "Are you still awake?" I asked quietly.

"Yes. Is something wrong?"

"No. I was wondering what you were thinking about?"

"Us."

"Me too."

"They're pretty good thoughts."

"Yeah, they're pretty good thoughts."

Ninety-seven

I was up at my usual time and was watching the *Festival's* approach to Miami. It looked like we would be docking early. There was a little more activity on the ship this morning than every other morning that I had been on my patrol. Some of it might have been people anxious to be finished with their vacation. Some folks, and I used to among them, are workaholics and can't relax for more than a brief time. Others I suspect were up because they were interested in securing a front position in the disembarking line.

Off in a distance leaning against the rail I spotted a familiar figure. He was watching the *Festival's* slow advance to its home base. He was one of those interesting characters that I had met on one of my early morning strolls. He was an early bird himself even though he was retired. Every morning of his adult life he got up and went running. His daily ritual was limited on the ship, although there was a jogging track that a fair number of people utilized.

Because of his age he spent about forty-five minutes in stretching exercises before his run and then a lesser time after he finished what was always at least five miles. He had recently qualified for, ran in and finished the Boston Marathon. In addition he was quite the hiker. He had climbed all the four-teens in Colorado, the mountains that were fourteen thousand feet or more. His next goal was to tackle the Appalachian Trail although not all in one year. I think it was also him who told me that he had done some triathlons where athletes swim, bike and run.

He turned toward me as he sensed my presence. I saw a glimmer of recognition in his eyes.

"Good morning," I said. "JR, isn't it?"

"Yes. Good to see you again, looks like our week of fun is about over."

"That it does."

He turned and presented a woman who was standing next to him. She was a full foot shorter than his six foot four inch frame. "I'd like you to meet my lovely wife, Steffie. I'm sorry but I've forgotten your name."

I extended my hand to her. "Cooper Meyerhoff, a pleasure to meet you." She returned the greeting in a warm, friendly way. "Are you a runner and hiker too?" I asked her.

"Yeah, I do some but I can't keep up with JR."

I turned to JR. "Did you get some runs in on any of our stops?"

He shared some of his adventures along the roads and paths and beaches of Key West, Cozumel, Belize and our other stops, but I got the impression that he preferred running in the good old US of A.

I didn't have great interest in watching the docking maneuver, so I said my good-byes to the couple, refreshed my coffee and went back to the room to rouse Beth. She was already up and dressed. I took a few minutes to shave and pack up the rest of my belongings while she completed her packing. We left our bags in the room and went for our last breakfast. This would be an eggs, sausage, French toast and Danish day for me. No Raisin Bran. I needed energy for the long drive.

As predictable as freezing rain in a North Carolina winter, Lou Bender interrupted our breakfast. "Do you mind if I sit down?"

"No, please join us." I waved him down.

He told us about his late night visit to the infirmary. He had gone to check on Emilio. "When I got there I found Lorenza still holding vigil. He told me that Emilio was doing well and that if his vitals were all good in the morning he would be released."

"That's great news." I said.

"There's more." Lou had our attention. "I told Lorenza that no charges would be filed against either him or Emilio in either the Cherenkov or Zabbarova deaths."

"How do you feel about that?" I asked.

"I can live with it. The worse of the evils are dead. In this case the Italians did us a favor. They did what we probably could never have done ourselves or would have taken us months or years to do. Sooner or later something or someone else will bring them down. I know justice might be blind or maybe sometimes she just turns a blind eye."

Neither Beth nor I said anything. I knew in my heart that somebody much higher up was able to and would sort all this out someday. My preference was that he wouldn't wait until the end of time to do it.

Lou continued. "After I informed Lorenza that he was off the hook he suddenly got very talkative. He apologized to me for not being completely honest with me and for not being as forthcoming as perhaps he should have been about the Gambolini and Malone connection."

Beth perked up. "What connection?"

Lou looked at me. "You may want to duct tape your girl friend to her chair with what I'm about to tell you."

Ninety-eight

"The one relationship that we all knew about was Tony and Beth. All along we figured that Anne was more than likely a case of mistaken identity. I don't think that you, Coop, or me, for that matter, bought that completely. I always suspected that Anne was tied to the family more than Lorenza was willing to admit."

"What are you saying, Lou?" Beth asked.

"This is what Lorenza told me last night. Please hear me out. This may not be easy for you Beth." Lou took a deep breath and let it out. "While you were married to Tony he had an affair with your sister."

"What?" Beth and I spoke simultaneously.

"You should also know that Tony is Genette's father."

Beth was in too much of a state of shock to speak.

"Lorenza was confident that the affair was instigated by Anne, although he didn't hide the fact that Tony was a first class womanizer. I'm sorry. He claims that he overheard Anne talking to a friend of hers on the telephone where she said that she was always envious of you especially when you were able to marry someone so of the world and so successful. Her plan was to take Tony away from you, but when he wouldn't consider divorce she decided just to destroy whatever happiness you might have and take what she could from the arrangement."

"I don't believe a word of this," Beth growled.

"I'm sorry. It's true. Tony and Anne continued their clandestine relationship until he was killed. He left a sizeable inheritance for her and Genette."

"But that's been ten years ago," I said. "Why would the Russians target Anne any more than they would Beth?"

"I'm coming to that." He looked at Beth. "You said before that Frankie never paid any attention to you."

"That's right."

"Did he make any moves on you shortly after Tony was killed?"

"There was one encounter, but I took it as him paying his respects."

"Lorenza said that after Tony was gone Frankie, wanted everything that Tony had and that included you. Momma Gambolini intervened and told him that if he ever so much as wore extra cologne around you she would not only see to an early meeting with his Maker, but that she would also visit him in his grave for eternity. Lorenza knew this because he and Emilio were to enforce the matriarch's wishes."

I exhaled. "So Frankie knew about Tony's affair with Beth's sister, Anne, and went after her instead?"

"Bingo. But it gets better or worse depending on your perspective."

"How could this get any worse?" Beth growled. "I knew that family was a bunch of egotistical jerks but I didn't know that they were crazy too!"

"Anne liked her arrangement with Tony and it seems that Frankie also made her an offer she couldn't refuse. Frankie however wasn't able to duplicate fathering a child with Anne through no fault of his own he instead bedded Genette and managed to bring Susana into the world."

Beth buried her face in her hands. I suspect that she didn't know whether to cry or scream. Lou's report answered many of my unanswered questions like where had their money come from and why didn't anyone know Susana's paternity and why Anne was the target. There were a few loose ends that still troubled me. "Did Lorenza say how the Russians found out that Anne was on the ship?"

"He blames himself for that one. He phoned in his daily report to Frankie which included a status report on Anne and Genette whom Frankie had greater interest in than Beth. We were correct in assuming that the Russians had the main line to the house tapped and that they gleaned enough information from that tap and from other phone calls to decide that this was an optimal time to send the Gambolini's a message."

"Did Frankie order me to be roughed up?"

"No, Lorenza and Emilio did that on their own."

"So my phone call to Frankie wasn't the reason for the change in attitude toward me?"

"No. In fact Frankie thought you were an arrogant SOB and wanted you squashed like a cockroach. Anne intervened on your behalf."

"So much for thinking that I had such great powers of persuasion."

"The real winners here are Genette and Susana at least financially. Anne had set things up herself for them and Genette continues to milk the same cow."

Beth continued to sit in silence trying to process everything Lou had just dumped on her. He continued. "There's one more piece. I don't want this repeated. The FBI has good evidence that Frankie set up his brother's death. The family all believes and should continue to believe I guess that Tony double crossed the wrong guy and was in the wrong place at the wrong time. The truth is that Frankie had his brother killed."

Bon Voyage
Lust
Envy/Jealousy
Anger
Sloth
Gluttony
Greed
Pride
Debarkation

Ninety-nine

The *Festival's* PA system announced that the ship had cleared customs. Debarkation would begin shortly. The protocols for exiting the ship had been repeated by my count five times. The voice encouraged all passengers to wait and not proceed to the gangway until their deck or zone was called. We were assured that if everyone followed instructions, debarkation would go smooth for all. Even though I was in a hurry to get off the ship and hit the road, there was not the same urgency to say good-bye to Beth. She would be among the last groups to leave the *Festival.* I intended to wait with her and then drive her to the airport.

We had also agreed to meet up outside with Emilio and Lorenza after we passed through customs. Lou also told us that he had a surprise for us and that we shouldn't leave the meeting area until we saw him.

Beth was still shaken by Lou's revelation earlier that morning. We had walked back to the room in silence to pick up our carry off items. I asked her a couple of times if she wanted to talk but she said that she didn't and then she added that she was fine.

In some ways she was a lot like me. One of those ways was that she liked to think things through herself before talking with someone else about them. When she was ready to talk she would open up.

One hundred

Much of my sadness and loneliness from the evening before returned as Beth and I sat more or less staring at each other while we waited for our zone to be called.

"I'm sorry for being such poor company Coop, but I can't believe that my sister and my husband and his brother would stoop so low."

I nodded my agreement and waited for her to continue. "Why did they do such a thing? Why was Anne so envious of me? She's the one who had everything going for her. Why did she want what I had too? Why couldn't Frankie or Tony for that matter be satisfied with what they had? And what did all that wanting more lead to? People are dead, there are children who don't have fathers, there is all this suspicion and deception and no one feels any remorse. Why Coop, why?"

"It's a question every generation has asked since Cain killed his brother Abel."

"Who are Cain and Abel?"

"They were the first children born to Adam and Eve. Cain the oldest became envious of what he believed was preferential treatment of his brother Abel by God and so he killed him."

"Oh, yeah, I remember that story now."

"That act and every hurtful, selfish and prideful act since that first act can be written off as the result of the presence of evil in our lives, but people don't like to keep things that simple. They want to know the specific evils along with the motivations behind man's inhumanity to man. Both religious and philosophic thinkers have debated the cause of vile human behavior for millennia. One strong and enduring tradition has been to classify and label these despicable acts of hurt and cruelty as deadly sins or deadly vices.

"Over the centuries there have been numerous attempts to list these detestable acts by a variety of different people, both people tied to the Church and people tied to the study of human behavior. Most of the lists include the evils of pride, envy, gluttony, lust, anger, greed and sloth. Each of them are at work to a greater or lesser degree in every one of us. The more power they are given, the more destructive they become. And unfortunately within your immediate family their power has been brutally unleashed."

"How are these deadly sins or evils overcome?"

"That's the other question great minds have debated. Historically they've come up with a list of seven corresponding virtues that people can put into practice to counter the deadly sins and the evil they work. Those virtues usually include committing oneself to practicing humility, kindness, abstinence, chastity, patience, generosity and diligence, by or trying to become a person who is dedicated to works of mercy like feeding the hungry, watering the thirsty, sheltering the homeless, clothing the naked, visiting the sick, caring for the prisoners and comforting the grieving. The idea is that if a person busies himself with good then evil won't have an opportunity to operate in his life. It's a good thought but I believe that conquering these evils requires more than a change in thinking, it requires a new heart."

"I need that new heart."

"Don't we all."

"How do I get it?"

"God creates it within a person when he or she is exposed to His grace. I believe you already have that new heart. I believe that He created that new heart in you when your parents brought you as an infant to be baptized, 'that washing of rebirth and renewal' (Titus 3:5). I also believe that throughout those childhood and teenage years that you spent in the Church and your school, God was working to shape your heart and now he's continuing the work anew even as we speak. He's never abandoned His commitment of love for you even though you decided along the way that you could do better without him. He's never stopped calling out to you to follow him to green pastures and still waters along a path of righteousness that is filled with his mercy and good things."

"Zones 24, 25 and 26 you may go to the gangway." I stood as I said, "That's us, finally."

We each got out our key cards, passports and customs declaration forms, assembled our personal items and carry offs, and took our place in line with fellow passengers who mostly seemed happy to be getting off the ship and heading home with stories to tell. I was happy too, not because I was getting off, but because I had the courage to share a bit of my faith with Beth and because I could see that my sharing was having an effect. It appeared to me that some wheels that hadn't turned for a long time in Beth's conscience were once again turning. God hadn't turned his back on her.

One hundred and one

The line leading to the gangway moved quickly. We handed our key cards to the security man who jammed them into the machine. He checked to make sure that the pictures on his screen that were somehow coded to the cards matched our real selves. When he was convinced, he returned our cards, nodded us on our way and reached for the card of the next guest in line.

We were pleased to see Sashi standing watch over the debarking procedure. We stopped long enough to give him a hug and thank him for his excellent service to us and friendship. We continued the long walk into the terminal and followed the signs and stream of humanity toward baggage claim and customs.

"Genette must have taken care of all the paper work for Anne's disposition," I said as we stood in line waiting for our customs agent. "She never did contact you for any more help, did she?"

"No. She didn't. I guess my show of kindness worked."

"Just remember to use that same technique every time I rub you the wrong way."

"I just wish that you would rub me in any way at all!"

We passed through Custom Agent Toby Simon's station with no issues. He seemed rather young and overly friendly to be someone who was the last line of defense in preventing terrorists from sneaking into our country illegally. But then the more I thought about it, how many bona fide terrorists would enter our country after enjoying a week long Caribbean cruise. The thought of some radical Osama type cell leader telling a young Jihadist to spend a week on a luxury cruise vacation before blowing up a bus and meeting his seventy-two virgins in paradise made me laugh to myself.

During my encounter with the agent I flashed back to the many times that I had crossed the border between New York and Canada at Niagara Falls as a boy riding in the back seat of the family car. I was scared to death of those agents. They still make me uncomfortable because I fear that they will charge me with doing something wrong even if I'm not doing anything wrong. It harkens back to being taught as a child that "ignorance of the law is no excuse." In retrospect I think that my fear of authority was probably ginned up by my father. He used the threat of having us kids thrown into some Canadian dungeon as a motive to get us to behave.

We had nothing to declare. Neither one of us had purchased any Cuban cigars which are illegal to bring into the US nor were we anywhere near our limit of duty free liquor. With our belongings in hand we wandered outside and looked for our rendezvous point.

"There's Lou," Beth said as she spotted him and pointed in his direction.

"I wonder what his surprise is."

"Maybe a Presidential order never to interrupt us at a meal again."

"Don't count on it."

Lou saw us and motioned us over to where he was standing. When we arrived he said, "Hey, I want you to meet someone." He turned to a lovely woman standing next to him. "These are the folks I was telling you about, Cooper Meyerhoff and Beth Malone." He put his arm around the woman. "This is Rachelle." We exchanged greetings with this bubbly mother of four. She wasn't anything like I pictured her, but then I'm not good at picturing what people look like.

Lou turned to me. "Rachelle agreed to meet me. She wanted to thank you personally for all you've done." All I've done? I had a couple of chats with Lou. But then the results of chats with people are never predictable. With some folks I have spent hours spread over weeks and months and even years and have never gotten through to them. And then there are others I never even knew heard me say something at a wedding or funeral or at a family gathering and years later tracked me down and told me how that one word or brief conversation changed the direction of their life. I long ago stopped trying to manipulate conversations to my ends. I long ago stopped losing sleep over wondering whether what I should have said or not said would have made a difference to someone's life.

Whatever it was that pushed the right button for Lou and Rachelle, I was thankful to have played a small and perhaps beginning role. They were still in the woods but at least they were on a path that could get them through the woods, provided they chose to hold on to each other and stay on the path, provided they chose to love each other.

One hundred and two

We spotted Genette and Susana and a porter moving toward a limousine. Beth and I excused ourselves for a moment, left our belongings and went quickly over to see them.

"I looked for you on the ship this morning to say good-bye," Beth said, "but I couldn't find you. I tried your room several times but there was no answer."

"I'm sorry Aunt Beth. I wasn't in my room and Susana spent the night with one of her new friends." Genette looked tired and worn down.

"Have you been able to finalize the funeral arrangements?"

"No." Genette looked down and then looked back up at Beth. "Do you think that you could come with me to the funeral home on Monday and help me take care of them? I don't think that I can do it alone." There were tears forming in her eyes.

"Sure. Call me later tonight or tomorrow afternoon and I'll see what arrangements I can make for getting away."

We all said our good-byes and exchanged hugs and watched the limo blend its ways into the rapidly diminishing crowd of exiting vehicles.

As we walked back to reunite with Lou and Rachelle, I detected a slight bounce in Beth's step and a fresh glow on her face.

"What's with you?" I asked.

"What do you mean?"

"You are glowing and walking like you're on the moon."

"I guess I can't believe the change in the way Genette is treating me."

"Believe it. It's happening. When you return good for evil, look out because most of the time you'll be pleased with the results, especially if you've reconciled yourself with whoever is against you. Once you make peace with another person you no longer are threatened by them but are free to be kind to them and free to serve their best interest. If they choose to continue harboring a mean streak, then you are free to walk away. You owe them nothing except to love them. The path to freedom is forgiveness. There is not a more impressive moment in history than that moment Jesus, in his dying breaths, looked at those who had unjustly condemned him, failed him, betrayed him, flogged him, mocked and nailed him to the cross and said, 'Father forgive, because they don't know what they are doing!' Once a person knows that he is forgiven and then grants that same forgiveness to another, he is as free as he will ever be in this life.

"I think that I've forgiven Genette."

Our conversation was interrupted when we approached Lou and Rachelle. As we continued our talk with them we learned that he was stationed in Miami and that Rachelle had parked at the office and had taken a cab over to the dock to meet him. They were going back to the office where he would drop off his report and then they were headed to watch their twins play ball. Both kids were involved in different tournaments today. "Unless there is a full scale terrorist invasion of Miami this weekend," Lou bragged, "I will be making every game I can. And even if there is an invasion, I won't know about it." He pulled out his cell phone and turned it *off*. Rachelle rolled her eyes.

I spotted two familiar figures also accompanied by a porter. It was Emilio and Lorenza. The big fella was moving as if he had never been hurt. The four of us waved them over to where we were standing.

"How are you feeling?" Beth was the first one to greet Emilio.

He sensed her caution to touch him and possibly hurt him so he reached out and hugged her with his bear like arms. "I'm good. I'm glad to be alive."

One hundred and three

We talked for a few minutes and Lorenza said that he would go get the car. Emilio stopped him. "That's my job. I'll get the car."

"You're in no shape to drive."

"I could outdrive you with both my arms broke. You haven't driven a car in years. I always drive and you know it. I'll get the car." Emilio walked away and called back over his shoulder. "You wouldn't even remember where it was parked." He walked some more and called again. "You wouldn't even know how to start it." He laughed and kept walking.

"I'd say Emilio is feeling like his old self," Lorenza chuckled.

During Emilio's departure no one had noticed that Sashi and Lou's partner Mike Andrews had walked up. Sashi was carrying a large case. Lou introduced Sashi to his wife. She already knew Andrews. Sashi handed Lou the case. "Here are the materials that we gathered over the course of your investigation. I know that you said you probably won't need them, but I would rather that you have them and dispose of them than me."

"Thanks Sashi. You were a godsend. You will never know how much we appreciated your cooperation and your skills. If you ever need a recommendation to advance your career in law enforcement or security please do not hesitate to contact me. We can use men like you in the FBI." He handed Sashi his card.

"Thank you for your kindness. I will keep your offer in mind." Sashi bowed slightly and walked back to his ship, readying himself for the next load of passengers and hopefully a less eventful cruise.

Lou handed off the case to Mike and then after rummaging through his briefcase handed him another thick folder. "When you get back to the office tell Kitty (Agent in Charge of the Miami office Katrina Dozzier) that I won't be in at all today or tomorrow. Give her this report along with the materials from Sashi. I doubt if she'll even be much interested in any of this since we've been over everything on the phone. If she has any questions you can handle it."

"Ok. See you Monday." Mike walked several steps and began hailing a cab.

"Maybe, maybe not," Lou quipped out loud but to no one in particular. The new Lou Bender wrapped an arm around Rachelle and she snuggled up to him. The way both he and

Rachelle were acting I figured that they were going to do a little warming up in the bullpen before they made it to their kid's first game. Whatever happened to resolve their differences I needed to bottle and sell or maybe I needed to just accept the truth that miracles still do happen with me sometimes in the middle. My growing smile was wiped off my face by an explosion and a resulting plume of smoke that billowed from the nearby parking garage.

One hundred and four

Instinctively the FBI men ordered those around them to ground. They unholstered their weapons, displayed their open badges onto their shirt pockets and began scanning the horizon looking for threats.

The crowd that remained outside the terminal became eerily still and quiet. There was no falling debris only a small cloud of smoke from near the top of the garage. People were staring at the cloud and murmuring to each other.

I saw Lorenza stand up. His face contorted in anger. He said something in Italian. From his look and tone and gestures and reference to the holy mother of God, my guess was that he just vowed to either kill somebody immediately or be nice to them and remove their external and internal organs one by one until they did die.

Lou must have assumed the same message. He turned to Lorenza. "Do you know what just happened?"

"That son of bitch Frankie has killed my Emilio." He trembled as he literally spit each word out.

"How do you know that for sure?" Lou asked.

"It's his style. He is pissed at us for letting one of his whores die." I clenched Beth tighter. I knew that she knew he was referring to Anne. His choice of words made me feel uncomfortable personally but also uncomfortable for Beth since I don't think that kind of language is appropriate in the presence of a lady or in the presence of anyone for that matter. Maybe I'm a prude and maybe certain words are deemed as only letting off steam, but then again maybe words like that are actually more hurtful than they need to be or the situation calls for.

Lou directed Andrews to get on the radio and pass that information along to the local authorities so that they could more quickly secure and control the area. I heard him tell them that the explosion was probably a small car bomb designed to take out a single person and was not a terrorist threat.

Lorenza was still staring at the spot in the garage. He was taking rapid, deep breaths as he muttered. "He will suffer his hell on earth for this."

"Leave it alone Lorenza. There's been enough death. Let the authorities handle it." Lou said.

Lorenza continued his stare. "No, Mr. FBI man, this is personal. Frankie Gambolini has crossed a line he should never have crossed."

I stood up. "Lorenza. Please. Lou is right. This cycle of vengeance and madness has got to stop."

Slowly he turned and faced us both. His breathing had calmed. The flush from his face had disappeared. Whatever had been working on his insides had gone away. "It will stop. The cycle of vengeance as you call it will stop, my friends, as soon as Frankie keeps his appointment with the devil." Lorenza then stared hard at Lou. It was as if he were trying to communicate something to him. After a moment both men gave a slight nod and Lorenza walked away.

Lou's eyes followed his departure even as he spoke. "He knows."

Beth's response showed her confusion. "He knows what?"

"He knows what really happened to Tony."

The light clicked on for me.

Lou turned slowly and looked at Beth. "Do you know how Tony, your husband, died?"

"If you mean the method of his death, no, I guess I don't know for sure. I always assumed that he was shot. I never saw the body. I can't say that I wanted to see it. All the family ever said was that he was badly mutilated."

"Tony was killed by a car bomb." Lou turned back to look for the departing Lorenza.

The light went on for Beth.

"Aren't you going to follow him?" I asked Lou.

"What for? Like he said, 'it's personal.' There's no way we can watch him twenty-four/seven. There's no way we can protect Frankie either. We could try to warn him but that won't do any good. He knows what he's set in motion but I'm sure that Frankie believes that he's untouchable. Lorenza will kill him and disappear or he will die trying."

"I don't envy your job one bit."

"Believe me, there are plenty of days I think about quitting and becoming a Wal-Mart greeter, but then I hear that some of them are treated worse than the victims I have to deal with."

Lou holstered his weapon and put his badge back in his pocket. "Mike, I'm leaving you in charge. Give the locals any help they need. There's no point in arguing jurisdiction. Chances are when they learn what you know about the victim they'll shuffle the case our way by their own volition." He put his arm around Rachelle. "Besides, I've got a ball game to get to." Lou grabbed his stuff and went off to hail a cab.

One hundred and five

With no one left to talk to, Beth and I walked to my car. Fortunately I was parked on the first level of the garage. Only the upper area where Emilio and his car had been destroyed was now closed. Most of the vehicles had already gone. People arriving for the departing cruise were the ones now facing delays.

The drive to the airport was uneventful. Traffic was light. Even though it was after noon and I would not be arriving home until close to mid-night as it was, I still decided to park and accompany Beth into the terminal.

She checked the larger of her bags, grabbed her boarding pass and we headed for security.

She had sixty minutes before her flight boarded. We watched the line and discovered that it was moving fairly quickly so Beth waited to join the screening process. We spent a good portion of the time reassuring each other that this last week was not a dream or a night mare for that matter. We reaffirmed our plans to get together and suddenly it was that time. One last good-bye embrace and Beth headed for the "passengers with tickets" only line.

She told me that I didn't have to wait any longer but that's like telling water not to be wet. I watched her place her personal items onto the conveyer belt for scanning and then move to the line waiting to pass through the metal detector. What I wouldn't give for a chance to be a TSA screener with an order to pat her down right now, I thought as I smiled outwardly and inwardly. My eyes continued to follow her as she completed the security ritual, then gather up her things and put her shoes back on. We waved one last time and she blew a kiss. Before she disappeared completely from view she looked back over her shoulder and smiled. I loved that look and smile.

I turned and began a slow and deliberate walk to my car. I checked to make sure my phone was turned on with good reception and plenty of battery life. She would be calling when she boarded and again when she landed and again when she arrived home. Being reminded of that enabled me to quicken my steps. I needed to get on the road and place myself in the sure hands of my GPS and her comforting voice.

Once I was on the open highway, I would call my kids. What would I tell them? How would they take the news? I was confident that they would be happy for me. How would I get them and Beth together? It was way too early for those thoughts. Keep it elementary, Coop. You've only just begun.

Thank you very much Karen and Richard Carpenter for putting that song in my head for the next twelve hours!

They were right; we had only just begun, but what a beginning. We had learned a lot about each other in a short time and there was so much more we needed to discover. I had drawn a couple of conclusions from even our brief time together. I knew that I wanted to continue unwrapping her and that I wanted her to continue unwrapping me. I still didn't know where our relationship would wind up but I liked the direction that it was headed. There was a comfortable familiarity about it, but there was also some intriguing mystery about it too.

I also liked the course that we were on. Although I was inwardly aching to be with her, to hold her and to talk to her, I was suddenly glad for this break. We had only been separated for a few moments yet I was already finding myself looking forward to some time to spend a part, some time to reflect, and some time to be objective about our relationship. After all, most of our time together had been spent under some duress and while trying situations encourage rapid bonding they rarely produce quality bonding. Someone up above was looking out for our overall well being. Of course he was.

I reached my car, unlocked the doors and tossed in my belongings. I took a longing look back at the airport, flashed a final smile of satisfaction, slid in behind the wheel, shut the door, fastened my seat belt, fired up the engine and punched "home" into the GPS. Within ten minutes I had paid my parking fee and found a clear lane on I-95 North.

Before I had finished setting the cruise control my cell phone rang. Beth was boarding her plane. Everything was on time.

One hundred and six

As I replayed in my mind and reflected upon some of our moments together, I was glad that I had shown restraint and had resisted the temptation to become sexually intimate with Beth. I was not happy with myself for those two nights that we spent together in the same room. In my mind at least, that situation could have spelled disaster and still could because it cracked open a door that should not have been cracked open. Such a cracking would now make it harder for us to resist similar situations down the road.

Temptation is already an enemy that is tough to defeat. No one needs a tempter using ammunition like, "Nothing bad happened the last time, what makes you think something bad will happen this time?"

It was only by the grace of God that we didn't put the obligation and power of sex into our relationship and it would be that same grace that would keep those forces from deceiving our future feelings and judgments as well, provided we kept our senses about us.

I was glad that we had prayed before she left to pass through security. Given her past conflicts with the Church and God, I feared asking her if she wanted me to pray. But I decided that if we were going to chart a good course together prayer would need to be an integral part. I sensed an initial hesitation in response to my request. Her "yes" though didn't surprise me. My prayer was a simple thank you to God for bringing us together and then for protecting us. I followed that by a request to open our eyes, ears and hearts to each other and to create in us a willingness to follow his path and trust his love for us.

The miles eased by rather quickly thanks to long telephone conversations with my kids and grandkids. They were both surprised by my news of a "girlfriend" and they were happy for me although they were decidedly more interested in all the other drama of my week. That may have been because of where I put the emphasis. I admit that I played up my heroic role as much as I played down the role of my new found flame.

No sooner had I put my phone down than Beth called. She had landed in Charleston. It had been a smooth and an uneventful flight. She would call again when she arrived at her home and had unpacked. Her voice sounded strong and alive. She said that she missed me. I told her that I also missed her.

That conversation renewed the string of thoughts that I was following before I took up the phone. I knew that I wanted to pursue this woman. I feared though that my reasons for doing so were because I was lonely and craved companionship. While those are not completely deficient reasons, they are selfish. So, I needed to make sure that they were not my main source of motivation. That's why I wanted to chart a course for us that was godly and virtuous, and also a course that we would travel with deliberate caution. I believed that Beth desired the same thing.

We had parted today with no regrets and more importantly with no obligations. We didn't owe each other anything. We would fall asleep tonight wishing that there weren't five hours of distance between us, but we would fall asleep knowing that our best days were yet ahead of us, provided we chose to make them our best days, provided we made decisions with the "we" in mind and not the "me" in mind, provided submission and love guided our decisions and not emotional self-fulfillment.

This was the course that I wanted to sail in the days, weeks, months and who knew for maybe a lifetime ahead, not just because I believe that it's God's prescription for a happy and even blessed life, but because I know that it works every time it's tried. With Beth willing to sail the same course, the next weeks and months could well lead to a lifetime of happiness and goodness together.

We would have to be on guard so that we didn't fall prey, as so many do, to the destructive guile and power emanating from the deadly sins of lust, envy, anger, sloth, gluttony, greed and pride. Should one or more of them rule the day, then our hoped for happily ever after dream cruise would quickly turn into a deadly cruise.

THE AUTHOR'S AFTER WORD

If this book was an enjoyable read for you and you are satisfied with your read and you are ready to move on to another book then I thank you for your time and I wish you blessings on your next reading adventure. There is no need for you to continue reading the paragraphs that follow. However, if you would like to explore further the ideas expressed in this book then I invite you to investigate those possibilities by reading the paragraphs that ensue.

First Purpose of Writing the Book

I had in mind several purposes for writing this book. One purpose was to tell a simple and hopefully engaging story that wasn't too far removed from reality.

Second Purpose of Writing the Book

A second more important purpose was to present through story a glimpse of human behavior and interaction. I wanted to shed light on the *why* behind people's inability or unwillingness to "just get along." In addition, I wanted to highlight the many casualties to this failure of the cooperative and caring human spirit. Finally, I wanted to offer possible solutions to living productively, purposefully and without regrets.

As I suggested in the prologue and story, many throughout history have labeled the evil that threatens and often destroys human life and relationships as the seven deadly sins or vices. I also pointed out that those destructive behaviors or attitudes are opposed by the relationship building and life preserving seven cardinal virtues. Both the deadly sins and the cardinal virtues are at work around us, in us and through us as well as through others. Both the sins and the virtues are vying to establish an upper hand in controlling the very soul of our being.

You might find it a worthwhile initiative to call together your friends, specifically your living room/family room/dining room level relationships, into a discussion group of *The Seventh Deadly Cruise*. It could simply be a surface level discussion about the book that focuses on cruise memories or horror stories, or you could take the next step and explore more deeply how the seven deadly sins and seven cardinal virtues have touched your own lives by using some of the scenes from the book as launching points to sharing personal stories. I have prepared discussion guidelines for a gathering of this type.

Go to www.seventhdeadlycruise.com for a free download of these materials.

Third Purpose of Writing the Book

A third purpose for writing was to introduce readers to another force that is at work in our lives, I am referring to a gracious power that I believe is an even more significant help to us than whatever expertise we can bring from our own repertoire of resources as we struggle to manage, much less influence the battle between vice and virtue.

I am referring to the love and mercy of God and specifically to the God who has revealed Himself throughout history in the Bible and most completely in His Son and our brother in the flesh Jesus Christ (see Hebrews 1:1-3).

Although I made my lead character a Christian clergyman, it was not my intent to have him preach a treatise on the Christian faith. I did however attempt through Cooper's dialogs and disposition to portray the advantage that Jesus Christ living in and through a person brings to our daily adventure on this planet.

I don't know if you as a reader know much or little or anything at all about living as a Christian. Because of that, I endeavored to present Copernicus Meyerhoff as a genuine, living, struggling Christian. My hope was that you would be intrigued by his life and as such would be curious to learn more about *what made him tick.*

I intentionally had Cooper interacting as a man of the faith with a broad spectrum of people during his week on the *Festival*, hoping that you, my readers, might relate with one or more of his contacts. Among his interactions were people who had abandoned Christianity and the Church either completely or partially, like Beth and Lou. There were also those who were confused about what it meant to be a Christian, like Emilio, Lorenza and the woman in the infirmary. And there were those whose religious background he knew nothing about because the subject of their faith was never raised, like Sashi and Marta.

Christians and Christianity are presented and understood in many different ways by people. I would offer that the Christian faith is well expressed in Jesus' words, "Come and follow me and I will make you fishers of men" (Matthew 4:19). And I would suggest that the Christian life is well expressed in the words of the first great Christian missionary, Paul, who wrote, "I have been crucified with Christ and I no longer live, but Christ who lives in me. The life I live in the body, I live by faith in the Son of God, who loved me and gave himself for me" (Galatians 2:20).

If you are already a Christian or if you want to discover more about the Christian faith and life, I would encourage you to use this book as the starting point for a small group study. I have prepared a guide for such a purpose. Go to <u>www.seventhdeadlycruise.com</u> for a free download.

If you want to supplement your own understanding of the Seven Deadly Sins and Cardinal Virtues and deepen the Christian perspective of them, then you might consider purchasing *The Seven Deadly Sins And How To Overcome Them* by Graham Tomlin. This is a less than two hundred page paperback written by a member of Oxford University's Faculty of Theology, but is done in a surprisingly simple and clear manner.

If you want to add a bit of fun and nostalgia to your group experience, I would suggest that you beg, borrow or purchase the DVD series *Gilligan's Island*. This is produced by Stephen Skelton of Entertainment Ministry. You will be watching excerpts from the reunion episode for the castaways. Each character is tied to one of the deadly sins, i.e. Gilligan is sloth, the Howells are greed and so forth. It's a hoot especially if you break out the coconuts, grass skirts and serve banana cream pie at your meetings.

I am also attaching a brief annotated bibliography of resources. These are designed to benefit either your further personal or group study of the Seven Deadly Sins, marriage relationships, parenting, personal emotional issues and the Christian faith in general.

Fourth Purpose of Writing the Book

A fourth purpose, albeit not the final purpose for my writing this story, was to reveal some of my own personal faith and life journey and struggle, although I must admit that most of my real journey lies well hidden in the fictional drama of the characters. I hope and pray that your journey of faith, love, joy and service might have been revealed, challenged, enriched and even pointed heavenward through your time spent sharing my story.

The peace of the Lord be with you always.

Annotated Bibliography

The following bibliography represents a brief sampling of resources that the reader might consider for further study on the topics introduced by *The Seventh Deadly Cruise*.

Seven Deadly Sins Resources

DeYoung, Rebecca. <u>Glittering Vices: A New Look At The Seven Deadly Sins and Their Remedies.</u> Grand Rapids: Baker Publishing Group, 2009. An in depth, scholarly, yet practical, historic and contemporary perspective of the deadly sins.

Skelton, Stephen. <u>Gilligan's Island & The Seven Deadly Sins</u> (Seven Lesson DVD Study). The Entertainment Ministry, 2007. Join the castaways in clips from the reunion episode as they each encounter, discover and deal with each one of the deadly sins. This resource is best utilized as a group study. Let your hair down. Make some macaroons and banana cream pie, break out the grass skirts and coconuts and cast off for a good time.

Schimmel, Solomon. The Seven Deadly Sins: Jewish, Christian, and Classical Reflections on Human Psychology. New York: Oxford University Press, 1997. The author conjectures that the seven deadly sins are the main causes of unhappiness and immorality in our lives and why psychologists must incorporate them to effectively address the emotional problems faced by modern men and women.

Tomlin, Graham. The Seven Deadly Sins and How To Overcome Them. Oxford: A Lion Book, 2007. A simple, yet scholarly, contemporary analysis and application of the deadly sins and how the Christian faith offers the resources to overcome their destructive power in our lives.

Personal Emotional Struggles Resources

Backus, William. Telling Yourself the Truth. Minneapolis: Bethany House Publishers, 1985. The first in a series of books based on the author's assumption that we do a lot of unhealthy thinking because much of what we believe about living is based on lies. He helps the reader identify his own misbeliefs and replace them with the truth.

Seamands, David A. <u>Healing for Damaged Emotions</u>. Colorado Springs: Cook Communications Ministries, 2002. Practical help for victims who struggle with perfectionism, depression, low self-worth and other personality issues that result from emotions that were damaged early in life.

Christian Faith and Living Resources

Keller, Phillip. <u>A Shepherd Looks At Psalm 23</u>. Grand Rapids: Zondervan, 1970. This is a most impressive and informative read about one of the Bible's most familiar and important passages. A shepherd in the Eastern tradition presents practical life insights into how God shepherds his people throughout their life journey.

Miller, Paul. <u>Love Walked Among Us: Learning To Love Like Jesus.</u> Colorado Springs: Navpress, 2001. Jesus loved everyone whom he encountered, treating each according to their need. Some were easy to love, others were hard to love. We too can love like Jesus.

Ortberg, John. <u>Love Beyond Reason.</u> Grand Rapids: Zondervan, 1998. Encounter the God who loves you and is intensely committed to your well being and to setting you free to live life joyfully and lovingly.

Veith, Gene Edward, Jr. <u>God At Work: Your Christian Vocation in All of Life.</u> Wheaton: Crossway Books, 2002. An excellent presentation of the many different vocations that a person is engaged in every day and the call his/her Christian faith places upon him/her in those roles.

Yancey, Philip. <u>What's So Amazing About Grace?</u> Grand Rapids: Zondervan, 1997. There are few topics more important to the world than God's grace. The author does an excellent job discussing, describing and displaying grace.

Marriage and Family Resources

Chapman, Gary. <u>The Five Love Languages: How To Express Heartfelt Commitment to Your Mate</u>. Chicago: Northfield Publishing, 2004. Learn how to love your spouse in the language that they best understand. Is it through quality time, words of affirmation, gifts, acts of service or physical touch?

Dobson, James. <u>The New Strong Willed Child.</u> Tyndale Publishing House, 2007. A must read for parents and teachers struggling to raise and teach children who are convinced they should be able to live by their own rules! It deals with sibling rivalry, ADHD, low self-esteem, and other important issues.

Narramore, Bruce. <u>Help! I'm A Parent.</u> Grand Rapids: Zondervan, 1995. Helps parents discipline and raise children. Topics including handling temper tantrums, sibling rivalries, single parenting, working mothers, spanking, the difference between punishment and discipline and a host of others.

From Dr. David Ludwig who developed the concept of "The power of *We.*" Check out the following two websites for his resources –
a) For a six session DVD based parenting series that focuses on emphasizing the **we** in family, go to www.parentingfamilies.org.
b) For a seven session video based study on building better marriages that turns the focus in your relationship from the **me** to the **we,** go to www.thinkwenotme.com.

Wright, H. Norman. Communication: Key to Your Marriage: A Practical Guide to Creating a Happy, Fulfilling Relationship. Gospel Light Publisher, 2000. An excellent resource that includes practical topics like rules for fighting fair, how to listen, how to handle anger, coping with conflict and the like.

With Appreciation

Special thanks to the unnamed thousands who contributed to this book. I am referring to those who have crossed my path over the decades and have taught me about faith and life. They would include family, teachers, neighbors, mentors, passing acquaintances, brothers in the ministry and too many parishioners to count.

Specifically, I am indebted to several people who critiqued and were hands on in the creation of this manuscript: Charlie and Marilyn Heinemann for wisdom, some editorial refinement and proofing; Dr. David Ludwig for counsel on character development and for opening up insights into my own soul; Ellen Lund for editorial expertise; Gaye Yount for the original seven deadly sin and cruise ship graphics; Mike Haley for setting up the web page; and finally my wife Martha and married daughters Laura, Emily and Rachel for critically reading and for believing in me and a dream that is at least a decade old.

LaVergne, TN USA
17 October 2010
201091LV00003B/2/P